LOST, HIDDEN, OR STOLEN

A RETRIEVAL INTERNATIONAL NOVEL

Liana Mills

RegM ... EnJoy!

Liana Mills

WRITING PARTNERS PRESS
PALM SPRINGS, CALIFORNIA

LOST, HIDDEN, OR STOLEN

A RETRIEVAL INTERNATIONAL NOVEL

Liana Mills

To Catherine

As always

Lost, Hidden, or Stolen

Bailey's Buddha

It was a quiet Thursday in West Hollywood. I walked back to my office after drinking a Mai Tai One On at Tiki Ti's. It's a little bar on the Sunset Strip, that crazy mile and a half stretch between Hollywood and Beverly Hills that's loaded with music and comedy clubs, gay bars, restaurants and popular hangouts like Tiki Ti's.

Tiki Ti's opened in the fifties and the older regulars say it hasn't changed in the past fifty years. There are only twelve seats at the bar and a few scattered tables in the postage stamp-sized lounge and it is so crowded any time of the day or night that it feels like a giant grope fest.

Pete Scanlon, the owner, invented the Mai Tai One On, a stiff rum drink in a tiki cup with a pineapple wedge, a slice of orange, and a paper umbrella. When Pete or his son, Mike, serves one, they hit the gong and everyone in the joint yells, *it's tiki time*, which makes conversation just a bit unusual. Gays, straights, tourists, locals—we're all there to pay tribute to the man who turned tiki into treasure.

My name is Rae Talley and I'm a private investigator. I don't sneak around watching cheating spouses. I don't try to solve murders before the police or help corporations root out embezzlers. My business is retrieval. I find things that have been lost, hidden, or stolen. That's all I do. It beats being a probation officer, which is what I did in Los Angeles before striking out at thirty-five with what was left of my small inheritance. That was six years ago. To be honest, I wasn't very good at keeping track of criminals, but I've always been damn good at finding things that go missing. In an oddball way, you could say I followed my bliss.

I finished writing my report on a case where someone wanted something found that I didn't find. I had tried talking the guy out of hiring me, but he wouldn't listen to reason, and it cost him three hundred dollars to finally decide to give up his search. I hope he sends me a check by return mail.

I stood at the window and stared out at an androgynously beautiful dark-haired woman. She was wearing a jade green shirt, probably silk, and beige linen trousers that hang just right on tall, slim-hipped women. I watched her disappear around the corner and then walked back to my desk with her image still in my mind.

Someone knocked on my door. I waited for whoever it was to knock again so I didn't appear too anxious, then called *come in* in my most professional voice. Standing before me was a skinny blond kid with big blue eyes.

"Hello, miss, and what can I do for you?"

She just stood there so I tried again. "Hi, my name is Rae. What's yours?"

"Bailey. My name is Bailey Reagan."

"Like the president?"

"Yes, but I'm not related."

"Bailey, please sit down." We sat there staring at one another, so I tried hostessing to break the ice. "Would you like some water, or a soda?"

"I'd like a cup of coffee if you have it."

Maybe she was older than she looked. What kid passes up a soda? I got up and poured two cups of coffee.

"Cream and sugar?" She nodded and I pulled out my last two snack cakes. I had a feeling we both needed a cream-filled chocolate cakelette. "I'm curious, Bailey, do you know what I do?"

No child had ever been a client. I once helped my cousin's daughter find a diary she'd misplaced, but that was pro bono and I only got a meatloaf dinner out of the deal.

Bailey took a sip of coffee and looked around my office. There wasn't much to see—I had my dad's desk and chair. My big bargains were the credenza I'd found in a thrift store for forty dollars and my client chair for ten. The print of a Paris street scene above the credenza was a gift from a friend. I keep my laptop, printer, and coffee machine on the credenza for streamlined functionality.

"I found your card in the street on Rodeo Drive. I took a cab here, of course, and I have it waiting downstairs."

Hmm, I thought. *She may turn out to be a lucrative client after all.*

"What were you doing on Rodeo Drive?"

"I was shopping, with Gabriella."

"Who's Gabriella?"

"She's my mother and we like to shop together on Rodeo Drive."

"How old are you, Bailey?"

"I just turned thirteen two weeks ago."

I didn't tell her she looked ten. Most women don't like to be told that until they get older.

"Your card says you find things that are missing. I'm missing something important and I think it's been stolen."

I was still trying to figure out how my card got to Rodeo Drive, or rather, more probably discarded on Rodeo Drive, since Bailey found it in the street. Usually the Beverly Hills types don't hire me to find whatever it is they lose. But now we were getting somewhere. Bailey Reagan, no relation to the president, age thirteen, just barely, shops on Rodeo Drive with a mother she calls Gabriella. She most probably lives in Beverly Hills, and most probably with some degree of wealth, and has something, perhaps an object, that may have been stolen.

"Have you talked to your mother about this and does she know you're attempting to hire me to find it? By the way, Bailey, what is it that's been stolen?"

Bailey opened her backpack and took five one hundred-dollar bills from her designer wallet and laid them on the desk.

"Here, Miss Talley."

"Please call me Rae." My eyes were riveted on Ben Franklin's eyes staring right at me.

"Miss Rae, my friend, Connor McNeil, he's fourteen, reads Raymond Chandler and likes *The Maltese Falcon* on the old movie channel. He said I have to give you a retainer right away or you won't think I'm serious. Here." She pushed the bills to my side of the desk.

Reluctantly, I pushed them back. "Let's talk about what's missing and if I can possibly find it, and we'll have to talk to your mother. You're not old enough to sign a contract, which may not even be necessary and, besides, where are you getting cash like this?"

"I have boxes full of them in my closet, you know, like birthday and Christmas money from relatives."

No, I didn't know. I used to get a quarter from the tooth fairy and Aunt Anne would give me a silver dollar for my birthday. Christmas was a doll when I was young and books when I got older.

Bailey took another sip of coffee and a bite of her cakelette. I did the same. We were reaching a dramatic moment here. It was entirely possible that Bailey's mother could become a client, and I had already seen the money.

Leveling a cold stare at me that would have served her well at a poker table, Bailey picked up the bills and fanned them out. "Isn't this enough? I can give you more retainer if you need it to take my case."

"Bailey, we don't even have a case. You need to tell me why you're here."

"I think it was Gabriella, you know, my mother, who stole my Buddha. I'm almost positive she did it. It was a birthday present from my father, who mostly lives in Monte Carlo. And, Miss Rae, I want my Buddha back."

Okay, back to the *now we're getting somewhere.* Bailey Reagan at age thirteen has boxes full of hundred dollar bills she gets as gifts. She's relying on her older friend, a detective story fan, to advise her. Now she's using hundred-dollar bills to tempt me and has even offered me more to take the case. She thinks her mother, Gabriella, stole her birthday gift, a Buddha from her father in Monte Carlo, which seems like a weird gift for a child, and she wants me to find it. And she hasn't confronted her mother, even though Bailey thinks she stole the Buddha. What really happened to Bailey's Buddha, who stole it and, if it has been stolen, why?

Bailey and I finished our coffee and cakelettes while she described the Buddha to me. I have to admit I was intrigued and, quite frankly, hungry enough to grab the five bills, an action which my thin line of ethics and the prospect of possibly losing my license stopped.

"Miss Rae, will you help me?"

"I will help you, Bailey, on contingency, sort of. Do you know what that means?" Bailey shook her head. "It means I won't charge you while I'm investigating on your behalf to informally gather information that may lead us to your Buddha. You will agree to tell your mother the Buddha is missing, but under no circumstances are you to accuse her of stealing it if you want my help. Tell your mother you came here and ask her to call me. If she agrees, I'll take the case and a retainer from her, not from you."

Quite frankly, I thought that would guarantee the end of my association with Bailey Reagan, even though I liked her and thought she was okay for a kid.

"Yes, sure, that probably is the best way to do it."

I watched the five hundred dollars disappear into the backpack.

Bailey held out her hand and I shook it. She smiled quite warmly at me, like we had become friends, and I got that very rare pang in my biological clock. Then she gave me her cell number and walked out. I went to the window and watched her climb into the cab from the Beverly Hills Cab Company.

This had turned out to be an interesting afternoon. I have a client who is not a client, with a case that is not a case, and a retainer sitting in a teen-age girl's designer wallet. Suddenly, I spied the same androgynously beautiful woman I had seen earlier look up at my window and drive away in a black Porsche Carrera. Out of habit I memorized the license plate number.

Then, it hit me in a flash. She was Gabriella, Bailey's mother. She knew Bailey had come here. What did all this have to do with the missing Buddha? Why would Gabriella direct her daughter to me if she, Gabriella, had stolen the Buddha? And what was so important about the Buddha except that it was a birthday gift from an absent father who Bailey loved but didn't see very often?

I was ready to close up shop and hit Tiki Ti's for another Mai Tai One On, which, you may or may not believe, actually helps me think things through on cases. I couldn't make heads or tails of Bailey Reagan's missing Buddha, even at Tiki Ti's, but two drinks later I was sure I wanted to take her case.

On Friday, I called my friend Rina at the division of motor vehicles to use Gabriella's license plate number to get her address in Beverly Hills. I found out that her last name is not Reagan, it's Sabatino.

I drove out to Beverly Hills to take a look at the Reagan/Sabatino homestead. It turned out to be a grand movie star-style estate in Beverly Park, completely hidden by trees and gates. What in the world did Gabriella Sabatino do to live like this? Now I understood how Bailey came by her boxes stuffed with hundred-dollar bills and was even more driven by curiosity to solve the case of the missing Buddha.

I went back to my office and started a file. The phone rang with such sex appeal that I instinctively knew it had to be Gabriella Sabatino. My heart lurched at the image of her in that jade green silk shirt and those beige linen trousers.

"Rae Talley, Private Investigations."

"Hallo, Ms. Talley. I understand my daughter, Bailey, has asked you to help her recover her missing Buddha?" Her voice was so provocatively Italian that I could have been speaking to Sophia Loren.

"Yes, but you already know that, Ms. Reagan, or should I call you Ms. Sabatino? I saw you walk by my building just minutes before Bailey arrived at my office and drive away after she left. What's this all about?"

"I would like you to take the case, Ms. Talley. Shall we meet at the Polo Lounge at four? You know, in The Beverly Hills Hotel."

I agreed, then realized that I'm usually dressed for Tiki Ti's on the wacky side of Sunset Boulevard, not the Polo Lounge on the upscale Beverly Hills end, and definitely not for someone like Gabriella Sabatino.

I went home to change for my meeting with Bailey's mother. After my shower, I dabbed on a powder-puff full of Chanel No. 5, my secret indulgence, slipped on my good black dress, applied fresh make-up, and fussed with my shoulder-length blond hair. I put on the gold earrings my mother left me and twirled around in front of the mirror—not bad at all when I make an effort.

Gabriella Sabatino looked like she belonged at the Polo Lounge. I didn't, and was glad to see she was seated away from the area full of beautiful people. She stood up, shook my hand, gestured for me to sit down, and wiggled fingers at the waiter. She was drinking a martini, so I ordered the same. I laid my card down next to her drink. God, she was amazingly beautiful, beyond beautiful up close. I put business aside for a moment and fantasized that this was our first date, the best of the no-baggage coupling rituals. We were about to toast to our good fortune of finding one another in this complex city.

She picked up my card and stared at it.

"Two thousand dollars in advance, Ms. Talley, for following my instructions, no questions asked. And before you ask the question, what I am asking you to do is perfectly legal, at least from our end."

"Did you take Bailey's birthday Buddha?" I was not ready to use the word *steal*. She did just offer me a couple of thousand dollars to find it.

Gabriella raised her eyes and looked directly into mine. I thought I was going to pass out.

"Yes, I did." She speared the olive out of the martini, smiled for the first time, and popped it into her mouth. "I like women who are direct. I chose you to help Bailey because I knew you would not take her money, and that you would help us. You see, Ms. Talley, may I call you Rae? I've already had you investigated. Call me Gabriella."

I was so disarmed I didn't know what to say. I fished out my own olive and popped it into my mouth. We both took sips of our martinis.

"Oh, taste these little fishy things, Rae, they're delicious."

"I'll take the case." I swallowed a little fishy thing whole.

Gabriella took a leather checkbook out of her very expensive-looking bag and wrote a check. I slipped it into my three-year-old purse without even looking at it. Then we raised our glasses and clinked in celebration.

I know your next question. Did I solve the case of the missing Buddha? Did Bailey Reagan get her Buddha back? Yes—and no. Because of the delicate nature of the case, Gabriella and I worked together and successfully found and returned a Buddha to Bailey.

It turns out that Gabriella and Bailey are heiresses to the gigantic Sabatino fortune, which accounts for their Beverly Hills lifestyle. Phil Reagan is Bailey's father from a brief marriage to Gabriella. She knows her ex-husband buys stolen art and artifacts for private collectors, so she only allows him limited contact with Bailey. He sends her birthday and Christmas gifts and talks to her on the phone. This year he obtained an ancient Buddha, stolen from a museum, and sent it to Bailey as a birthday gift, probably to avoid being incriminated in the theft.

When Gabriella's suspicions were confirmed, that the Buddha had been stolen, she had a sculptor friend create an exact reproduction. Her idea was to let Bailey think her Buddha had been stolen, hire me to find it, and return with the reproduction. Then the original would be returned to the museum.

Did we pull it off? You bet we did. I managed to find Bailey's Buddha in Conner's garage, the reproduction looking exactly like the real one. He told Bailey it was a practical joke to see if a real-life detective, not a movie gumshoe, could solve the case of her missing Buddha. Conner knows how important Bailey's father is to her and agreed never to tell her the real story. Bailey forgave Conner and apologized to her mother for thinking she took the Buddha, which, in fact, she actually did. The original was anonymously returned to the museum though a third party in Australia without implicating Gabriella or Bailey. Thanks to Gabriella's quick thinking it all worked out fine. Smart woman, that one, for someone so androgynously beautiful.

Gabriella and I did have that no-baggage first date I fantasized about, and my fantasy dulled in comparison to the real thing. We had dinner at Giuseppe's on the Pacific Coast Highway in Malibu. I had never eaten a sixty-five-dollar pizza or sat at a table in a room full of movie stars. Johnny Del Russo sent a bottle of red wine, waved at Gabriella, and leered at me.

"*Grazie mille*, Johnny," Gabriella said to him, then turned to me. "It's a Masseto merlot made by Tenuta dell'Ornellaia near the village of Bolgheri on the Tuscan Coast. It's a great bottle of wine. My uncle, Timo, has a vineyard there. The estate is *bellissimo*."

Gabriella invited me back to her villa, as she called it, for an espresso and homemade cannoli. We had another one for breakfast and eventually finished the whole box. Gabriella thought it was hilarious, *spassosissimo*, that I am a sugar addict and can't get enough of her cannoli.

A year later I moved from Studio City to Beverly Hills, and my office from Sunset Boulevard to Wilshire Boulevard. Gabriella hangs around my office making lattes with hearts in the foam. I think it's *spassosissimo* that she wants to be a private investigator, like me.

Bailey gave us her blessing. She still calls her mother Gabriella, but now she calls me Mom.

Fighting for Her Life

Lauren Boyce sat slumped in my client chair with her head in her hands, looking every inch the victim she thought she was.

"I'm fighting for my life, Rae. Without Harry, I'm nothing."

Gabriella rolled her eyes, mouthing the word *bullshit* from the sofa behind Lauren.

Usually I see clients alone, but Gabriella and Lauren have been friends since they were in boarding school together in Switzerland. So, of course, I said yes to her and I'm glad I did. Gabriella said Lauren has always been a drama queen but, to tell the truth, I've never seen one up close.

First of all, Lauren Boyce is so thin she makes Cher look plus sized. I don't think there's a place on her face that hasn't been botoxed, filled-in, micro-abraded, plucked, or volumized.

Despite all the crying, hair-tossing, and chest-heaving, I had yet to find out what Lauren wanted recovered. Frankly, I don't know what to do with women like Lauren, although Gabriella has had tons of experience in that department. I tried to help Lauren narrow it down.

"Lauren, what do you mean that you're fighting for your life? Has Harry threatened you in any way? That would be a matter for the police."

"Oh, no." Lauren looked up briefly, mascara running down her face in black rivulets. One false eyelash had become loosened from the tears. "No, I just mean that Harry has left me, and I don't know what to do."

"I'd like to help you, Lauren, truly I would, but I don't do divorce investigations. Usually divorce lawyers have their own investigators." I felt momentary relief. Maybe I wouldn't have to be in close proximity to this ding-dong after all.

"I don't want a divorce lawyer. Harry just walked out on me and I haven't seen or heard from him in two whole days. I only bought a couple of cute horses and Harry was really, really mad. He said he's had enough of my reckless spending, and if I don't stop, he'll go broke. Rae, I love him so much and now I don't even know where he is."

Lauren uncovered her eyes and turned around to Gabriella, who I could sense was trying hard not to laugh at the hanging eyelash. Her self-control was admirable. I wasn't ready to laugh, I was getting pissed that I was wasting my valuable time on someone, friend or not, who clearly was not a potential client.

Gabriella came to Lauren and put a hand on her shaking shoulder and gave me a look that said *be patient with my migliore amica, darling*. There was a promise of such wonderful things to come later.

I took a deep breath and responded in my most soothing voice. "I understand."

"Rae does understand, Lauren, just tell her what's missing."

"Oh, Gabriella." Lauren grabbed Gabriella's hand and held it to her breast, doing the most perfect shudder I've ever seen. "I knew you'd understand and thank you for being here to support me."

Understand what? That she's fighting for her life? I don't think so. That her husband walked out in a hissy fit and has been gone for all of two days? He wouldn't even be considered a missing person, let alone someone who is on his way somewhere for a quickie divorce. All I needed to know was, had Lauren lost something and could I help find it?

"Lauren, I told you I don't do divorce investigations. Is something of yours missing besides your husband?" I asked, a slight edge to my voice.

Before Lauren could answer, Gabriella came back with a pot of tea and my favorite cookies from Belgium, obviously in the hope that a hot beverage and a couple of cookies would calm me down.

"I told you, Lauren, we only do retrieval," she said.

Ah—*we?* My business is not a *we*. Granted Gabriella Sabatino is the love of my life *and we* are a *we*, thank you, God. But her business is being an heiress and my business is finding things that are missing, like I did when she hired me to find Bailey's Buddha.

"I had nothing left of my inheritance, nothing, when Harry rescued me. I blew through the money, about two million, which granted isn't a great deal of money but, you know, would have been enough to get by on if I hadn't been so reckless with it." Lauren sounded like an eight-year-old child who had spent her allowance.

I thought, *not a great deal of money? Two million dollars?* My father died when I was twelve. My mother received ten thousand from a life insurance policy and she bought the house in Studio City I grew up in and still own. We got by on Dad's social security and Mom's paycheck from her job as a secretary at Universal Studios. These heiresses—they just don't know how most people live.

I saw Gabriella frown and my spine stiffened. Her money, with a capital *M*, was an issue we were working through. I was still trying to wrap my head around someone blowing two million dollars and having to be rescued by a husband with real money.

"Tell her, Lauren, you have to be honest with Rae if you want our help." Gabriella handed me another cookie.

Lauren lowered her voice to a whisper, even though there was no one else in the office. "My secret family jewelry is missing. I don't remember if I hid it somewhere else. Sometimes I move the box from place to place because I'm afraid Harry or someone will find it. Maybe Harry took it to push me over the edge."

With the hanging eyelash and too many blond extensions, Lauren already looked like she was over the edge. Gabriella didn't seem to be overly concerned so I figured she'd seen Lauren like this before.

"My grandfather mined diamonds and precious gems in Africa. When he returned a wealthy man, he took some of the best stones to Tiffany's and had them designed into exquisite jewelry pieces for my grandmother. They passed on to my mother and then to me after she died. They are unique and very, very valuable, my mother told me. I've always kept them hidden and never wore them. I didn't think Harry even knew I had them, and that I wasn't really totally broke when I married him."

I shot Gabriella a look. Did she know about the jewelry? She shrugged and held her hands out in a news-to-me gesture. Did I believe her? Would Gabriella lie to protect her oldest friend, whom she clearly loved? It didn't matter right now. I trusted Gabriella to know that Lauren was in trouble and that she was hearing the real reason at the same time I was.

This was serious business. I wasn't retrieving someone's lost briefcase at LAX or a beloved Cocker Spaniel named Maxie. That was Sunset Boulevard, and this is Beverly Hills. I knew sooner or later I'd run up against a case that would scare the shit out of me. I just didn't expect it to be this fast or this big.

"I'll take the case."

After Lauren left, Gabriella and I picked Bailey up at home and the three of us went out for dinner.

"Gabriella, did you know?"

"No."

"Know what, Mom?" asked Bailey.

We both ignored her.

"Do you think he really left her?"

"No."

"Who left who, who are you talking about, Gabriella?" Bailey clearly didn't like being left out of the loop.

"Do you think I can do it?" I sounded pathetic.

"Do what?" Bailey asked impatiently. "Do what?"

"Correction, Gabriella. Do you think *we* can do it?" There, it was finally out in the open after avoiding the subject for a year.

Gabriella smiled. "Just shop talk, Bailey, you know private investigators can't talk about their cases. Confidentially, you know."

"You're not a private investigator, Gabriella, just Mom."

"She's my associate on this case, Bailey, and she has to zip it just like I do."

And that was that. On the ride from home to La Cienega, and without any formal agreement, the *I* finally became the *we* of my retrieval business.

The next morning, I asked Gabriella if she knew how to get in touch with Harry. She called Lauren to find out if he had returned home and he hadn't. I drafted a contract and Gabriella asked Lauren to meet us at the Polo Lounge that afternoon.

"Of course, I know how to contact Harry." It took Gabriella exactly one telephone call to find him. No doubt about it, this androgynously beautiful woman is a keeper.

"Hallo, Harry? I need to talk to you. Where the hell are you? Oh, good, not too far away. Rae and I are meeting Lauren this afternoon. What? No, I can't discuss it on the phone, and Rae, you know Rae, my lover, my partner, is involved."

My heart pounded against my ribs. Rae Talley and Gabriella Sabatino, lovers and partners. I liked the sound of that being told to Harry Boyce.

"Yes, that would be great. I know they'll enjoy it. We'll be there tomorrow around lunch time. *Ciao.*"

"Harry's hiding out at his beach house in Santa Barbara. He said to bring Bailey so we can all enjoy a few days away. He'll stay on his boat and we can have the house."

Damn, it was fun living with an heiress. No one ever invited me to stay at their beach house while I interrogated them. And Harry doesn't even know that for the first time we, that is Gabriella, found a missing person.

Santa Barbara is lovely at any time of the year. We had lunch on Harry's deck overlooking the Pacific Ocean. Gabriella and Bailey went shopping on State Street while Harry and I lingered with coffee. I have to be honest, I was prepared to dislike the drama queen's other half, picturing him at least twenty-five years older than Lauren and showing off his trophy wife at the current cost of owning one.

I couldn't have been more wrong. Harry was an attractive man around fifty with an understated look and a soft voice. I did a mental head scratch. If the saying opposites attract is true, Lauren and Harry are the perfect example. It just goes to show there is no logic to love.

"So, have you left Lauren, like, for good?" I casually took a sip of coffee.

"No, of course not. Lauren and I had a rip-roaring argument about money, her spending it like a drunken sailor when I had asked her to cut back for a while. I just needed to get away, that's all."

"But you didn't tell her where you were going. According to her you just stormed out three days ago."

"No, I didn't tell her, because she would have just followed me here, and then we would have been fighting in Santa Barbara instead of Bel-Air. Look, Lauren's a big girl and can manage on her own for a few days while I cool off. And, by the way, Rae, don't buy that little-girl-lost crap. Lauren's a pretty smart woman. We don't need a private detective in the middle of our marriage, we need a marriage counselor who understands what goes wrong with couples with money. And don't get the wrong idea—I love her like crazy."

I poured myself another cup of coffee, gestured to Harry and poured one for him. I took a deep breath. "Harry, Lauren told me about her missing jewelry. That's why Gabriella and I are here. Did you take it?"

I stood still with the pot in my hand. Harry's hand stopped on the creamer. The air got thick between us. Neither of us moved or said anything. My intention to catch him off-guard worked.

Harry put the creamer down on the table and looked at me. I put the pot back on the warming tray and looked at him.

"Yes, I did."

I sat down at the table and waited, scarcely breathing. Harry picked up a linen napkin and started twisting the edges between his fingers.

"I wanted to have a special ring made for Lauren for our tenth anniversary. The jeweler asked me for her ring size. I didn't know, and I couldn't ask her, so he suggested I bring in one of her rings."

"While she was at the gym working with her trainer, I went into the closet where she keeps her jewelry boxes. I wasn't snooping, but there were so many cases I got fascinated and started looking in them. Wrapped in velvet and hidden at the back of the shelf in a plain cardboard box were fifteen of the most spectacular pieces of jewelry, certainly not anything I'd ever seen her wear. Believe me, I wouldn't have forgotten them. I took a ring for size and the hidden pieces to the jeweler."

Harry's ears were beet red and he got busy with his coffee. "I had them appraised."

I said nothing and he continued.

"I was shocked, Rae. Lauren told me she was nearly broke when we met. The pieces should have been worth a small fortune, but all those beautiful gems in the incredible platinum settings were fake."

"Fake?" I was not expecting that. "They were fake?"

"Rae, I knew right then exactly what had happened. The reason Lauren only inherited two million dollars was because her father had gambled away the family fortune, but he couldn't touch her trust fund. Instead he removed the valuable gems from her mother's jewelry and had them replaced with good imitations. Lauren assumed they were real because they had been, and has kept them hidden all these years, even from me."

Men can be such sneaky bastards, I thought, but found myself thinking that of Lauren's father, not Harry.

"I took the pieces back to Tiffany's and had the fakes replaced with new, good quality gems. It cost me a lot of money, but I didn't want Lauren to know what her late father had done. She has protected his reputation to this day."

Harry looked out at the ocean. "Later that day, the very day I picked up the jewelry and the ring, I got news that an economic downturn had temporarily impacted my business. Then Lauren and I had that awful fight and I drove away forgetting that I still had her jewelry in the trunk of my car."

"Where is it now?"

"Still in my trunk."

I had, technically, recovered the jewelry. The hard part of closing this case would be Lauren.

Gabriella and Bailey got back from shopping laden with bags. Gabriella bought me a red bikini and a stupid sarong wrap which I vowed never to wear, ever. Bailey bought me a snorkel and said we could go look for stuff on the bottom of the ocean. That's my girl. Sometimes Gabriella just doesn't understand me. Bikini, no— snorkel, yes.

For the next couple of days, Bailey and I went snorkeling for treasure. Gabriella found an exclusive spa with hot rocks and an Asian woman who would walk on her back.

When we got back to the office, I sent Lauren and Harry an invoice. A week later there was a check and a note. Harry had gone home to the woman he loved and confessed all. Lauren told us that she kept a spectacular diamond and emerald necklace, a diamond bracelet, and a pair of diamond and emerald earrings, which she and Harry insured, and she promised to wear. The rest she sold, along with the horses, to help Harry's business.

Gabriella insisted that we take a proper vacation after such an exhausting case. Bailey was on a field trip to the Grand Canyon with her class. We zipped down to St. Barts in the French West Indies. And, so what if I'm in the red bikini with the sarong wrap skirt... so what!

Lost, Hidden, or Stolen

Clementine's Secret

"That was Clementine on the phone, Gabriella. She's in Los Angeles and wants to see me."

"Your Clementine, the Clementine in Ventura from *Clementine's Secret*?" Gabriella looked distraught. She went into the bathroom and slammed the door.

After a few minutes, I knocked on the door.

"Gabriella, what's going on?"

"Go away, Rae—just leave me alone."

I don't like being told to go away by the love of my life, especially since I hadn't done anything wrong, so I gave the flimsy bathroom door one good smash with my boot and kicked it open. It was absolutely a Fellini moment.

Gabriella's eyes were red, and she was washing her face. "It wasn't locked, Rae."

Gabriella ignored me for the rest of the afternoon and busied herself setting up interviews for an administrative assistant we had agreed to hire because of our increasing business.

"Let's go somewhere and talk, Gabriella. Polo Lounge okay with you?"

She nodded.

Gabriella sat grim-faced staring out at the Wilshire Boulevard cityscape, and I sat tight-lipped staring at the back of the cab driver's head.

We went to our usual booth at the back of the room, the Siberia of the Polo Lounge, but a good place for quiet conversation. I ordered a dirty martini and Gabriella ordered scotch on the rocks. Now I knew it was serious. She started eating handfuls of pretzels and ordered four appetizers. I went into intervention mode.

Gabriella took a sip of scotch, then made a face. "I can't drink this, I'll get sick." She motioned to the waiter. "I'll have a dirty martini and bring a pot of Darjeeling tea with the food."

By now Gabriella's food and drink choices were getting me confused, and worried. Why all the drama?

When we had gotten serious, Gabriella and I confessed all, right up to the day we met. I told her that Clementine and I had worked together in the probation department when I transferred to Ventura. Clementine had been my only serious lover and I had expected it to last a lifetime. Clementine's father owned a boat named *Over the Rainbow,* which was a joke in itself, given that his daughter was a lesbian who had turned it into her secret love nest. When Mr. Van Alt died, Clementine changed the name of the boat to *Clementine's Secret*. We spent most weekends on that boat until we separated.

Gabriella had been amused by my story and told me she hadn't understood, until now, about falling in love and living happily ever after with the woman of your dreams. She, on the other hand, had one brief marriage, numerous lovers, live-in partners, steamy affairs with straight, married women, one trans-sexual dancer from Sweden, and many, many one-night stands, Italian jet-set style, of course. She told me she loved her *la dolce vita* lifestyle. Her philosophy had been *here today, gone tomorrow,* until she fell in love with me.

I banished impatience from my choices and went with sympathetic, which I figured would work better with Gabriella's strange behavior. "So, what's going on with you? This isn't like you at all." *Sympathetic but to the point,* I thought.

Gabriella busied herself with the prawns. I waited for her to answer me, which she didn't.

"Clementine wants to see me tomorrow at Tiki Ti's. She says she needs me to find her boat. *Clementine's Secret* is gone, and the harbor police can't find her. I meant it, Gabriella, when I said it was finished the day we broke up. But *Clementine's Secret,* I can't turn my back on her, and to find her I'll have to take Clementine on as a client."

"*We*, my darling, *we* decide who to take on as clients."

"No, Gabriella, I have to do this alone, and I have to go to Ventura without you. Do you trust me?"

It was at that moment that jealousy took possession of Gabriella. She muttered a few swear words in Italian, the same ones we use in English, and took a too large gulp of her martini. "The hell you will! She wants you back. What about me? One phone call from her and you're ready to abandon me for a Mai Tai One On at Tiki Ti's and go off to Ventura. Just like that!"

We cabbed back to the office to pick up our cars. This time I stared out at the Wilshire Boulevard cityscape and Gabriella stared straight ahead at the back of the cab driver's head. To say I was pissed off was putting it mildly. I had a case to work, just like any other case, except it wasn't just like any other case. My one and only ex-lover was back in my life. Did Clementine really want me to find *Clementine's Secret* or did she just want me back? Was I ready to meet Clementine at Tiki Ti's and go off to Ventura —just like that? Maybe the relationship wasn't finished, not as long as we had *Clementine's Secret* between us.

The next morning Gabriella was still sleeping when I left for the office. We had not spoken since the night before at the Polo Lounge. I left her a note cut out in the shape of a heart and wrote *If this is a test, we both better get A's. Trust me, my darling. I'm leaving a little something for you at the office. All my love. Rae.*

At noon, I drove to Tiki Ti's to meet Clementine. We hugged in that strained way that ex-lovers do, managing to touch one another while sending the message that it means nothing, and then we both ordered coffee. I had packed a bag and was ready to go to Ventura if this was a real case. I was ready to go back to the office if it wasn't.

I hadn't seen Clementine in three years, not since I moved back to Studio City. All I felt was curiosity and, I must admit, I was a little nervous until Clementine told me she had married a nurse and they have a three-year-old adopted daughter.

"Anne and Chloe are my life, Rae. I'm sorry it wasn't us, but we made the right decision."

"I'm in a relationship, too. Her name is Gabriella and we work together in my business. We have a daughter, Bailey, her daughter by a previous marriage. I know you and I made the right decision, Clementine."

I didn't tell her that Gabriella and Bailey are wealthy heiresses who will inherit gazillions one day, or that I live on an estate in Beverly Hills. No need. I told Clementine all that was important to me—Gabriella and Bailey.

"I share *Clementine's Secret* with Anne, Rae, but she knows it will always be yours and mine, and she's all right with that. *Clementine's Secret* is gone, vanished, and I don't know what to do. Anne is the one who suggested I call you."

I felt the tension leave my body and told Clementine I would go to Ventura today. We hugged, and this time there was warmth in it, like I get when I hug a friend.

When I got to Ventura, I took a long walk along the waterfront. I had forgotten how beautiful it is. The empty slip made my heart ache with memories of so much love on *Clementine's Secret*.

Gabriella called just as I pulled into Clementine's driveway. "Hallo, Rae. I'm on my way to Ojai. I booked a couple of days at The Pines for a body treatment with Margarite. Do you remember Margarite?"

I, indeed, did remember Margarite with the most incredible hands. Gabriella took me to The Pines, which she called Sappho Spa, not long after we met, for what she called a body treatment. Gabriella knows the owner, a woman she had bedded in her *la dolce vita* days. I was used to getting a massage now and then at a serene Japanese day spa in Encino. I was not prepared for the absolute decadence, however legal, at Sappho Spa. I liked it.

"Thank you for the lilacs, so *bellissimo, cara mia*. I have them in the car with the windows closed. Their glorious scent takes me back to my childhood in Milan. These deep purple ones are my favorite."

I smiled. Those lilacs had cost me plenty. *So worth it,* I thought.

"I'm sleeping alone in Clementine's guest room, Gabriella. Make sure you do the same in Ojai."

Gabriella laughed. "I'm just here to spend a few days with Margarite's magical hands on my body, that's all. Have fun finding your boat. *Ti amo.*"

Hmm, I thought, *that woman sure knows how to turn jealousy around.*

"Have fun yourself. See you on Monday. *I ti amo* you, too."

The harbor patrol had given Clementine a copy of their report. They concluded that the boat probably had been stolen and was not in the area anymore. I spent two days chasing leads. Not one person I talked to satisfactorily explained the complete disappearance of

Clementine's Secret and I suggested that Clementine file an insurance claim.

I called Gabriella and told her the case was closed. I did not find *Clementine's Secret*. Did she want me to join her at Sappho Spa?

"Margarite asked about you. I already booked you for a body treatment. We can plan our trip to Hawaii while we're here."

"How did you know I wouldn't go straight home?"

"A little birdie named Clementine told me," she said, then disconnected.

On Monday morning, I turned my attention to the interviews. Since posting the hire, Gabriella and I had read so many resumes our eyes felt permanently crossed. Gabriella screened half as many on the phone and settled on face-to-face interviews with the two best candidates. There was a third, but she wasn't from the resume pool. That interview was a favor for a friend of mine, a probation officer I had worked with in Los Angeles.

Gabriella had vetted all three for their administrative skills, so it was coming down to my basic requirement—the person we hired had to be a quick and persistent problem-solver and pass my no-fail test during the interview.

The first candidate, Emma Reese, was a nice enough young woman, if a little too conservatively dressed. Just as we were about to sit down, I went to the coffee machine and made noises that it was not working. I said I had to have coffee to start my day. Emma had a look between helpless and it's not my problem and, after chatting awhile, she was out the door. Test failed.

Maya Rojas, on the other hand, rose to the occasion. In her most efficient administrative assistant manner she offered to get me a coffee and came back in record time with a grande from Starbucks for me, but nothing for herself. I paid her for the coffee and told her I would let her know by Friday.

That night Gabriella, Bailey and I grabbed a pizza loaded with pepperoni and mushrooms, our favorite.

"Where were you, Mom, on a stake-out?"

"Bailey, we don't do stake-outs. I was on a case for a friend of mine in Ventura."

"What were you doing there?"

"Looking for a missing boat with secrets."

"Sounds like fun."

We watched Godzilla movies on the classic movie channel and all three of us fell asleep on the bed.

On Tuesday morning Gabriella came into the office while our third candidate was out on the problem-solving test. Gabriella gave me a smile and a kiss and ducked into her office.

"I'll see who you hire when she's behind that desk," she said and quickly closed the door.

Kibe Jackson arrived that morning at ten o'clock on the dot. She was a knock-out, looking a little like Halle Berry. She had light caramel-colored skin and hair to match. The first thing I noticed, she was wearing green suede open-toe shoes with pencil thin heels, which I've heard referred to as slut shoes. On Kibe they looked straight out of Vogue.

I checked out the shoes again. "Nice shoes."

She gave me a grin full of wickedness and briefly told me the story of her job search counselor's banishment of the green open-toe shoes and her order to buy a pair of conservative pumps for the interview.

"I decided to take my chances being me right from the jump. And green open-toe shoes, that's who I am."

Kibe, whose full name is Kathleen Isobel Barbara Elaine Jackson, said she had served time for assault and battery on her husband and his little whore when she found them together in her bed. Kibe said she be-bopped both of them with a wrought iron candlestick. They pressed charges, and she wound up in the slammer.

"I got an early release and now I'm on probation. I divorced that weasel. No children, thank God, and now I'm ready to get on with my life."

Good for her, I thought. I got up and went to the coffee pot.

"I'm getting myself a cup of coffee—how about you?"

Before Kibe could answer, I spoke again. "Looks like this old pot has finally quit and I need coffee to start my day."

Kibe stood up and headed for the door. "I'll get us some."

After some time, I was beginning to worry that she wasn't coming back. Gabriella stuck her head out of her office and I just shrugged. Maybe my problem-solving test wasn't as good as I thought it was.

Kibe returned out of breath with a new coffee pot topped by a big red bow and a can of dark Italian roast.

Gabriella came out of her office and just stared at Kibe.

"If I'm hired, I'll be glad to make us a pot of coffee." And there was that wicked grin again. That's how Kibe Jackson came into our lives, thank God.

"Are you upset you didn't find *Clementine's Secret?*" Gabriella asked, kissing my shoulder when we were in bed that night.

"No, not really," I answered, pushing her lips off my shoulder and flipping her onto her back, pinning her arms above her head.

Gabriella pretended to resist me. "So, is this case still unsolved?"

"Actually, it wasn't a real case. There was no contract, no fee, no report. I was just doing a friend a favor. I forgot to tell you that Clementine called earlier. She and Anne are buying a new boat and naming her *Little Chloe.*"

Gabriella pulled her arms down around my neck and kissed me.

I turned out the light.

Stealing in Style

I sat in my office and stared at the November cover of *L.A. Magazine* framed and hanging on the wall. It was us, Gabriella and me. The article was really about Gabriella, how and why an heiress with a fortune hooked up with me and got her license as a private investigator. And, of course, the article covered our personal life because lesbians are so in these days.

There was a good picture of Gabriella, Bailey, and me in our conference room and a spectacular picture of Kibe answering the phone in a leopard print dress that looked like it had been painted on her. She had on earrings the size of bracelets, something Kibe can pull off. The photographer couldn't take his eyes off her. Those pictures and the cover are hanging on the wall in our reception room.

In Los Angeles publicity is gold, and the story had gotten us a steady increase in business. Also, Gabriella immediately got two marriage proposals, one from a lawyer who said my being in their lives would not be a problem, and one from a well-known actress who suggested that Gabriella dump me. I got a bouquet of flowers from Tiki Ti's with a card that read, *Way to go, Rae, from your friends at Tiki Ti's, you know, the ones you don't visit anymore.*

The biggest winner of our instant celebrity was Kibe. She went on a date with this gorgeous guy named Jesus 'Wild Man' Smith, whom she strongly recommended we hire as our new receptionist and her assistant.

"Kibe, I'll be honest with you. I'll hire him on your recommendation if he fits in with us, but I don't want someone answering the phone, like, *Good morning, Jesus speaking*," I said, just kidding.

"It's pronounced Heysus, Rae, but he mostly goes by Wild Man," Kibe said, grinning.

"*Good morning, Wild Man Smith speaking*, and that's better, Kibe?"

"Will you interview him if we solve the name problem? He'll be invaluable since he knows every distributor of missing goods in Los Angeles. And not only is he reformed, he goes to church every Sunday."

A reformed fence, I thought, not believing our good luck. "Call him and set up an interview." We hired Jesus 'Wild Man' Smith on the spot.

This morning Jesus was watching Kibe walk by in black tights, a fitted black and turquoise beaded shirt, and a wide silver-studded belt that looked as dangerous as it was. I was amazed that Jesus could keep his eyes glued to Kibe's choice rear end and still answer the phone correctly.

"Good morning, Retrieval, Inc. This is J. Smith."

A while back we had decided to change the *Kibe speaking, how may I help you* or *how may I direct your call.* To tell the truth, it was really Kibe telling us with finality that she was not saying that shit. Gabriella and I also needed a business name when we incorporated. Rae Tally and Gabriella Sabatino, Private Investigations was too long and not specific enough. Kibe came up with Recovery, Inc. I said it sounded like we helped addicts.

"So, how about Retrieval, Inc.?" Kibe said. And Retrieval, Inc. we became.

"Hi, Gabriella. Yes, she's here," Jesus transferred the call to me.

Gabriella and I had decided to take Bailey to the BNP Parabas Open held every March at the Indian Wells Tennis Garden. Gabriella's friend, Marco Conte, invited us to stay at his home in La Quinta and they had gone ahead.

Bailey had been playing tennis with passion these days and she announced that she wants to become a professional tennis player. Much to our surprise her coach said it could happen. Up until then, Bailey had stated she wanted to join us in the family business after college. Sometimes heiresses to enormous fortunes can be so fickle. Or maybe it's just fourteen-year-olds.

"Hey, Gabriella, I'm about caught up and I'll be there before noon tomorrow. Is it sappy to tell you I miss you and Bailey already?"

"Rae, you need to come here right now. *Pronto*! Please, go home and pack your bag. Hurry!"

"What's wrong?" The urgency in her voice struck fear in me.

"Marco's been robbed and he's frantic. Bailey and I were in the store when it happened. I wanted her to look at diamond tennis bracelets and choose one for her birthday. Oh, the police are here. I have to get off the phone."

"Gabriella, I'll be there in a few hours."

I had been thinking if I got caught up early enough, I'd go to Tiki Ti's and catch up with my Sunset Boulevard friends. I had been feeling guilty since I got their card. I don't want to lose my friends just because I live in Beverly Hills and have been on the cover of *L.A. Magazine*. I would have to straighten that out when I got back.

I stopped at Ristretto, my favorite café in Palm Springs, for a quick coffee, then drove to Marco's jewelry store on El Paseo in Palm Desert.

I kissed Gabriella and followed her back to Marco's office. He had his head down and his dark hair fell over his face. I took his hand and he burst into tears. I must admit I'm not good with men who cry, so I just sat there patting his hand.

"Rae," Marco looked up at me with his chocolate brown, tear-stained eyes. "I don't know what I would have done if Gabriella and my darling Bailey hadn't been here." He looked up and gave them a weak smile as he raked his hair back from his face.

"This is a nightmare. I can't have this happen in my store. I'm insured, of course, but the publicity will be so bad for business."

Bailey went to the office and came back with four perfect cappuccinos and a plate of biscotti. "Uncle Marco, it'll be all right. Mom and Gabriella will find your bracelet." She looked at us. "Won't you?"

"Tell me exactly what happened, Marco." The store looked fine, no sign of a break-in or damage.

Marco gave a big, Italian sigh. "Gabriella and Bailey came to the store with me this morning. They were going to look at diamond tennis bracelets. My assistant, Layla, opened the store at ten o'clock, as usual, and she and Gino, my jeweler, were here when we arrived around eleven. About twenty minutes later this gorgeous, beautifully dressed woman walked in."

Marco took a bite of biscotti and wiped a few crumbs off his pants before he continued. "She had on one of those simple beige linen dresses that you know is designer and an absolutely gorgeous Hermès scarf. Her Ferragamo bag was to die for, and the shoes I'm pretty sure were Christian Louboutin, you know, soft green strappy heels."

Oh, jeez, I thought, *why do gay guys have to know every damned label on the planet? Next, he'll be speculating that she wears that fancy lingerie that Gabriella buys on Rodeo Drive—pearl something that doesn't show panty lines on your ass.*

I gave Gabriella a look that said, *do something.* I don't need to know from Ferragamo or strappy heels.

Gabriella smiled sweetly, which in Italian women is sexy as hell. I knew she was not going to interrupt Marco and she was going to enjoy making me listen to his prattling instead of giving me the facts. Don't get me wrong. I like Marco very much, I do. But as soon as I hear Gabriella or Marco mention Gucci, I make myself scarce.

"Her jewelry was expensive," he went on. "Pieces I would sell here. She had on an incredible David Webb bracelet. She looked like a wealthy woman, probably from the East Coast, New York, maybe, like right out of *Town and Country*. Someone who could do some serious shopping—like you, Gabriella. You can imagine how surprised I was when the police came and identified her as Dorothea Sinhurst, a well-known international jewel thief, and they detained her, right here in my store!"

"What?" That bit of news came right out of nowhere and now Marco had my full attention.

"She's a jewel thief, Rae. Apparently, this Dorothea is related to the Sinhurst billionaires. Her parents are on the lowest rung of the family's financial ladder because they squandered away a fortune. But Dorothea still has the Sinhurst name and learned how to act wealthy without having much money. She became a jewel thief to live a lifestyle that her truly wealthy relatives actually do. She's been in prison several times, but she continues to steal jewelry across the world. The police told us she's clever and gets away with it most of the time."

Gabriella finally came to my rescue. "Marco, tell Rae about the bracelet."

"This Dorothea Sinhurst made sure I knew she was from the Sinhurst family. She wanted to see diamond bracelets, but she was not interested in anything I had on display. When she told me her price range I went into the vault and brought out a tray of bracelets starting at a hundred thirty thousand. I knew she could afford it, she had on that magnificent David Webb."

Marco sighed again and his shoulders drooped.

"Show me where you were, Marco."

We walked out into the showroom and Marco went to a counter mid-way from the door to the back wall on the left side of the store.

"I was standing here, and she was seated across from me."

I turned to Gabriella. "And where were you and Bailey?"

They walked to a counter closer to Marco's office.

"We were here, Mom, and Layla was behind the counter showing us tennis bracelets. The bracelets that woman was trying on were amazing, weren't they, Gabriella?"

Gabriella just shrugged.

I looked at Gino. "And you were sitting here the whole time Dorothea Sinhurst was in the store?"

"Yes, except to wait on a customer who came in to pick up a repair, a broken clasp on her necklace. She and her daughter left the store while the other lady was still looking at bracelets."

"I was at the counter with Dorothea the whole time she was in the store. She liked one bracelet in particular and tried it on several times. It was a stunning diamond and sapphire bracelet priced at one hundred seventy thousand."

"In the meantime, Rae, another customer came in with a little girl who looked about seven. Her mother pointed the girl to a display of crystal animal earrings on the counter next to where Dorothea was trying on the bracelets. The little girl ran to the counter. Her mother followed and took a pair of crystal bears for her. Then she and the girl walked to the back of the store where Gino was sitting, paid for her repaired necklace and the earrings, and left the store."

"Dorothea told me she was interested in the bracelet she had tried on earlier and wanted to try it on again. When I looked in the tray, it was gone!" Marco started sniveling again.

Gabriella laid her hand on Marco's arm. "He was in a panic searching for the bracelet and finally, I called the police. Dorothea never left her seat at the counter. She stood up and made a show of looking for the bracelet. We were all in the showroom the whole time, except for the woman and her daughter, who were in the store for about fifteen minutes. They were already gone when Marco discovered that the bracelet was missing. The police did not find the bracelet on Dorothea. She said she did not take the bracelet and could prove that she had the money to purchase it if she had decided to buy it. The police let her leave but instructed her to stay in the area, and she agreed without protest."

I learned that the police had also contacted the repair customer, Christine Carson, in La Quinta and her story checked out. She and her daughter, Brittany, live in

Columbus, Ohio and they came for the tennis matches. She told the police that someone at La Quinta Resort recommended Marco's to repair the clasp on her necklace. Gino assured her that he could have it ready today. The concierge at the inn was questioned and said she did suggest Marco's or El Paseo Jewelry for the repair.

I drew the interior of the store in my notebook and marked where everyone was standing or sitting up to the time Marco discovered that the bracelet was missing.

"Is there film in your surveillance cameras?"

Marco told me the police took them. "I'm meeting with the detective assigned to the case tomorrow at ten. I'd like both of you to come with me. If the police come up empty, I want to hire you to find my bracelet."

Marco, Gabriella, and I met with Detective Mark Raley the following morning. He had the initial police report, which contained their investigation and interrogation of Dorothea Sinhurst and Christine Carson. There were interview notes and the results of the background checks on the two customers. Bailey and Brittany Carson were ruled out as suspects.

The surveillance video showed nothing significant except the movements of all the people in the store. The report noted thorough searches of the store, Dorothea, and her car, everyone else's car, including Gabriella's, and Christine Carson's rental car and her hotel room at La Quinta Resort.

Detective Raley said there was not enough evidence to arrest anyone or conclude how the bracelet had disappeared. The investigation would continue, and

Dorothea Sinhurst would be interrogated again as a person of interest.

Gabriella and I took the case. We learned from the police report that Dorothea was staying at Las Palmas Resort in Rancho Mirage. As much as we did not want to do physical surveillance, Gabriella and I agreed that Dorothea was the key to the missing bracelet and if she left the area, we would never find it. Dorothea hadn't seen me at the store, so I was able to watch her at close range.

While I was tailing the oh-so-freely-spending Dorothea in and out of stores on El Paseo, the very clever Gabriella learned that Dorothea had booked a flight from Los Angeles to Monte Carlo and was leaving in a few days. The police still had no charges against her. I followed Dorothea to the Los Angeles airport and watched her get on the plane. She had not met with anyone or gone anywhere out of the ordinary, so it looked like the end of the line for us. The bracelet remained missing. Perhaps the police would have better luck.

Gabriella stayed in La Quinta to support Marco, who was understandably depressed. Unknown to anyone, including me, Gabriella had called her ex-husband, Phil Reagan, in Monte Carlo and hired him as a consultant. No one knew that the shadowing of Dorothea was continuing across the Atlantic.

This case does not have a happy ending and certainly not the one we expected. I had asked to see the surveillance film again and it took me three tries before I figured out how the bracelet disappeared.

An envelope arrived at the office from Phil addressed to Gabriella. It contained pictures of Dorothea Sinhurst, Christine Carson, and an unidentified man sitting in the bar at the Royal Hotel in Monte Carlo. Phil had followed Dorothea from the airport to the hotel and he was able to get pictures of them together. Phil had found our jewel thieves. He had also enclosed an invoice and Gabriella wrote out a check for Phil right away.

Look at us, I thought, *we even have a consultant in Monte Carlo. I'll have to share that with my friends at Tiki Ti's.*

Gabriella and I drove back to Palm Desert and met with Detective Raley. The pictures clearly established the connection between Dorothea and Christine. The man turned out to be Carl Donahue, another notorious jewel thief.

The three naughty musketeers returned to Los Angeles on different planes at different times and each was arrested immediately upon clearing customs. What were they doing in Monte Carlo? Just having a little R&R and gambling after a job well done. Even thieves, I guess, need some down time after work and these three wanted to do it where they wouldn't be seen together.

Gabriella and I went to Marco's to let him know that we hadn't retrieved his bracelet.

"Please don't feel bad, my dear friends. It was a longshot and I appreciate you taking the case to try to help me. I've already met with the claims adjuster and submitted a claim for the loss. They have their own investigator and, of course, Detective Raley is still trying to make sense of it. Next time I'll be more careful with an elegant woman wearing David Webb."

"And Hermès," I added, proud that I had learned to pronounce it correctly, even though I was never going to have anything with that brand on my person—unless it was a gift from my Gabriella.

"Marco, Rae and I didn't say that we haven't found your bracelet, only that we haven't retrieved it yet. We're here to tell you we know where it is and how it got there. Let me tell you exactly what happened. How you, Dorothea Sinhurst, Christine Carson, and your new lover, Carl Donahue, pulled it off."

Marco stood quite still, and I saw his Adam's apple bob up and down as he tried to swallow.

Gabriella looked miserable and I continued. "I imagine Carl persuaded you to listen to a scheme that would make both of you some easy money with no risk to you as a well-respected El Paseo businessman. All you had to do is play your part as the owner of the jewelry store, which you are, so that wasn't much of a stretch. Carl planned it all down to the last detail, hiring Dorothea and Christine to join him for a cut of the take. For him and Dorothea it was the thrill of the heist. For you, Marco, it was greed and stupidity."

"I love him," cried Marco.

"Stop," Gabriella muttered and turned away.

They planned that Dorothea would be planted as the actual jewel thief she is, knowing that the police would spot her right away. Christine, on the other hand, really does live in Columbus, Ohio and has never even gotten a parking ticket. Dorothea recruited her and she jumped right in for the money.

The heist was executed as planned right down to the final detail. As Christine and the innocent Brittany passed by Dorothea to look at the crystal earrings on the counter, Dorothea, who was still holding the bracelet, quickly slipped it into Christine's pocket out of sight of the camera. Christine and Brittany were in and out of the store in fifteen minutes.

Outside, Christine passed the bracelet to Carl who gave it back to Marco after the police finished searching the store. He would collect a check for the full replacement value from the insurance company and then sell the precious gems in redesigned pieces.

Marco started crying and this time I did not pat his hand. Gabriella looked like her heart was breaking and I patted her hand instead. Detective Raley came into the store and told us that Carl had confessed and was turning state's evidence against Marco, Dorothea, and Christine. Sometimes there is no honor among thieves. I asked Detective Raley to have Marco open the vault. Just as Gabriella suspected, there was the bracelet, still intact.

Like I said, there is no happy ending to this story. Gabriella and I were quiet on the drive back to Beverly Hills.

Lost, Hidden, or Stolen

Trailers, Treasure, and Trash

Gabriella and I were amused and, I must admit, curious when Bailey and her best friend, Connor, made an appointment with Kibe to meet us at the office. They had been heads together in animated conversation for weeks during spring break.

Bailey and Connor showed up right on time. Bailey was carrying a large box and I saw the logo of their favorite donut shop. Connor had a bag from my favorite cafe. Bailey smiled at Kibe, clearly a co-conspirator, and already in the loop that excluded Gabriella and me. The unholy trio headed for the conference room and closed the door.

Gabriella came out of her office and we stood clueless in the reception room until Bailey poked her head out and invited us in. "Gabriella, Mom, please join us for a little treat."

The cups were brimming with exceptionally great-smelling coffee and Bailey took the lid off a cake plate piled high with donuts. Bailey and Connor exchanged glances as we sat down and lifted our cups to our lips.

"It's Kona, Ms. Talley, Ms. Sabatino, one hundred percent Kona coffee. Me and Bailey—"

"Connor," Bailey whispered, "it's Bailey and I, not me and Bailey." And she shot us a quick glance to see if Connor's linguistic faux pas could sink whatever it was they wanted. Connor reddened, took a deep breath, and started again.

"Bailey and I paid fifty-five dollars a pound for one hundred percent Kona from Hawaii. It's not that cheaper blended stuff."

Bailey and Connor watched us and waited. I quickly reached for the banana cream and Gabriella took a frosted old-fashioned. The coffee was like an aphrodisiac. We didn't know what the kids wanted but they definitely had our complete attention.

"We asked Kibe to stay. She's agreed to take notes and field calls from here. Is that okay with you, Gabriella, Mom?"

I looked at Kibe. She remained totally poker-faced, but with a gleam in her eyes as she busied herself with a donut selection. She definitely knew what was going on.

I had a mouthful of banana cream, so I just nodded. Gabriella pretended to be thinking about it. She took a deeply satisfying sip of the excellent coffee. "Proceed."

Connor pressed a few keys on his laptop and spoke in his deepest voice. "Bailey and I have a business proposition for you, a real business proposition."

Who are these two, the Beverly Hills dynamic duo gone entrepreneur? And what does this have to do with Gabriella and me, and Kibe?

I looked at Bailey. It was only three years ago that she, that skinny, just barely thirteen-year-old, sat in my office on Sunset Boulevard flashing hundred-dollar bills at me to find her birthday Buddha. Not only did I find Bailey's Buddha, I found my true love, Gabriella, God bless her, and got myself a wonderful daughter in the bargain.

Connor went on bravely. "We, Bailey and I, have a great idea, and we know it'll be a lot of fun for all of us and, the best part is, it'll pay for itself and maybe make some profit."

"Which, of course, we will donate to charity," added Bailey quickly.

Gabriella and I looked at one another. We knew hedging when it stared us in the face. There was more, we realized, as Connor glanced at Bailey and his eyes shifted back at his screen.

"It does require a monetary investment, but don't worry, Ms. Sabatino, Ms. Talley. Bailey's prepared to do that with her own money."

And, in the aftermath of telling us absolutely nothing about their idea, Connor finished. "Your investment will be your time and expertise, not any money."

All we learned so far is that the business proposition consisted of something that will be fun for all of us, require an investment that Bailey is prepared to handle with her own money, cover expenses, possibly make a profit, absolutely involve a time and expertise commitment from Gabriella and me, and without coming right out and saying so, the venture will also include Kibe in some way.

Gabriella and I were trying to look serious, and not doing a very good job at it as we made a dent in the donuts and coffee. Bailey caught our look and shot us an *oh, moms* stare. "We've put a lot of thought into this and it's a good opportunity."

Bailey was trying not to mention that the money they spent for the coffee and the donuts may have been a total waste if we didn't say *yes* to their scheme. "Seriously, we really mean it, don't we, Connor?"
Connor took a glazed donut and looked at Bailey with total admiration, which may turn into love if it hasn't already.

"Mom, Gabriella, you know my best friends from school, Sasha, Hadley, and Brooke, and Connor's best friend, Braxton."

I got distracted with the Braxton thing. What happened to good, old-fashioned names like John? I poured myself another cup of coffee. Braxton! Why would anyone name their baby after false labor pains?

Kibe got a call and stepped out of the conference room. I was distracted when she returned. Kibe looked mighty fetching in an orange, purple, and black print jersey wrap dress and her four-inch platform stilettos in purple suede. It had been our lucky day to get her, however unconventional she looks. Too bad a lot of those corporate tightasses didn't look past the wrapper. Corporate's loss was our gain. We can't even imagine running our ever-increasing business without Kibe. She can be sneaky, though, like setting up this meeting without a word to us until the last minute.

"Okay, so here it is." Bailey took a deep breath and actually stood up to give her presentation.

Finally, I thought, and Gabriella looked relieved.

"Connor and I, and Sasha, Hadley, Brooke, and Braxton would like you, if you want to, and we are absolutely crossing our fingers that you do. We want you to do a two-week summer camp-like thing with us, like workshops, to teach us how to be junior investigators so we can retrieve stuff, like stolen out of lockers and things. Of course, our cases would be pro bono. We would never charge our clients, who will actually be our friends or schoolmates. As junior investigators, though, we would like to consult with you now and then if we run into a problem, if that's okay with you. That's it."

"So," Gabriella said. "You want us to spend two weeks somewhere with the six of you doing workshops to teach you how to investigate lost, missing, or stolen items and retrieve them. Is that it?"

"Yes, that's exactly it, Gabriella. All you have to do is create the workshops and teach. Like I said, we have it all worked out, don't we, Connor?" He just nodded his head up and down and grunted.

Gabriella looked at me. I sat stunned and said nothing. "And where and when would we be doing these workshops?"

Bailey continued. "You know Sasha, Hadley, Brooke, and Braxton. They're great kids, and they're all interested in what you do, not boring things like their parents. Sasha's grandmother, Mrs. Shaloff, broke her hip and she won't be spending summers in Malibu anymore."

"It's true." Connor held up his hand as if he was testifying in court. "Her grandmother and her parents own two mobile homes side-by-side in an exclusive park in Malibu."

"Trailers in Malibu? No way," I said, then added that I had lived in Los Angeles all my life and never heard of that.

"It's hidden in the Malibu Hills off the Pacific Coast Highway, Ms. Talley, and you'd drive right past the road if you didn't know it was there."

"I think I did hear—" Gabriella said.

Then Bailey interrupted her, which we would discuss later. "It's called The Malibu Colony Estates, and it's really fancy, interior decorated, with swimming pools and decks and all. It's a secret get-away, mostly for movie people. You met Mr. Shaloff, Gabriella. He's a screen writer and won an Academy Award."

Yes, I thought, *one of the boring parents of the future junior investigators.*

"And they want to sell but they have to get approval from all the owners, and the homes can never be listed publicly or with realtors. They had to sign something agreeing to that," Bailey said with a smile that rested her case.

I glanced over at Gabriella. It could be fun spending two weeks with the kids teaching them some easy tricks of the trade, and the idea of owning a small getaway in Malibu was intriguing. Oh, no—I was starting to think like Gabriella. I reached for my third donut and she gave me a warning look.

Conner saw the dawn of my interest. "We've really worked it out. If you agree...."

"Whoa! Slow down a minute." Gabriella noticed my glazed-over look. "Rae and I have a meeting with a potential client soon. Call the future junior investigators and let's meet here at five. You can lay out the rest of it for us."

Our potential client, Lefty Collins, had inherited his great-grandfather's gold watch and chain worth more than six thousand dollars, which had once been featured on *Antiques Roadshow*. He and his wife recently divorced, and Lefty is pretty sure his ex-wife took the watch with her when she left. He said he kept it in his underwear drawer and it was not insured. It had just disappeared, and he wanted us to find it. Another day in the exciting life of retrieval experts.

Laughter floated out of the conference room when we got back to the office. Remnants of pizza, salad, and soft drinks were in the middle of the table. The kids were in deep discussion about retrieval methodology when Gabriella and I walked into the room.

Connor jumped up and started to clear the table. Everyone's mouth snapped shut at the same time. I managed to grab a leftover piece of pizza out of one of the boxes before it vanished.

Bailey came in with eight cappuccinos on a tray. I watched her walk across the room like I was seeing her for the first time. She was about five-foot seven, almost as tall as Gabriella, with soft dark blond hair, contacts instead of glasses, and a nice, little shape for sixteen. Sixteen! I glanced around the table. Connor and Braxton, at seventeen, were still gangly in their six-foot frames, but Sasha, Hadley, and Brooke—oh, my God, they looked like Bailey! I hadn't noticed how much they had grown. Gabriella was smiling at Bailey as she took her coffee. All she saw was her baby.

The next day Gabriella had news about Lefty Collins' grandfather's gold watch. "I found Lefty's ex-wife, Rae. They were both in community college when they met and married. She, Pauline, dropped out of school to work so Lefty could go on to become a landscape architect. He promised to pay her back. She got stuck in a dead-end job and Lefty divorced her as soon as he got his degree and started his business."

"He didn't tell us that. He made it sound like she was the baddie."

"Pauline is in nursing school now. She said she doesn't know what happened to the watch."

"Case closed unsolved?" I asked.

"Case definitely closed unsolved. We'll consider the retainer as *paid in full.*"

So, Gabriella and I didn't spend a romantic getaway at L'Auberge in Napa tasting wine and doing you know what. Instead we were approved by the Malibu Estates Colony and bought the Shaloff's two mobile homes. Well, Gabriella was approved. I was merely accepted.

Off we went with a workshop curriculum, six teenagers, and Kibe to our new getaway digs in Malibu. Lest you have a picture in your mind of two aluminum-sided structures resembling big rigs with windows, on a rectangle of concrete, let me wave in a new image with my magic wand. The two mobile homes combined give us thirty-two hundred square feet of hanging-out space. They sit on a twenty-one thousand seven hundred eighty square foot lot, that's a half-acre overlooking the Pacific Ocean.

Just to give you an example of what it costs to live in Malibu, even in a trailer, Gabriella and I could have bought four investment houses in, say, Fresno for the same price. We're satisfied with this investment, though. It has made Bailey very happy.

Developing a curriculum for the workshop wasn't as easy as Gabriella and I thought it was going to be. It was like being an experienced cook who throws in a pinch of this and a handful of that, and then has to translate that into a recipe. We were finally able to write down the basic techniques of retrieval: research, interviewing, gathering evidence, problem-solving, and closing the case. We also passed on a few of our standard practices: professionalism and ethics. We made sure they understood that we are only as good as our last case and our success hinges on our reputation. That will apply to them, too.

We ended the workshops every day at two. The rest of the day was spent sunbathing, swimming, and grilling. Worn out, the kids hit the bed pretty early every night. Leaving Kibe in charge, we headed straight for the very beautiful Malibu Beach Inn. Maybe it wasn't L'Auberge in Napa but the wine we had was spectacular and we still got to do you know what.

For the final test, which I'm proud to say everyone passed, the junior-investigators-in-training found three objects. Only Gabriella, Kibe, and I knew the story of what was missing, who took it, why, and where it was hidden. It was like a treasure hunt using the art and science of retrieval methods perfected by our company. The kids had until the next day to recover the missing items. Kibe contributed her first pair of slut shoes. Mine was an old briefcase full of Spy magazines. Gabriella hid a three-carat diamond ring she said an ex-lover gave her years ago. Oh, those heiresses!

Gabriella, Kibe, and I had a surprise graduation party for the kids. We gave each junior investigator a fancy certificate of completion. And that's how Retrieval, Inc. inherited the Junior Investigators—Bailey, Connor, Sasha, Brooke, Hadley—and Braxton.

Renzi Barcelona Comes Out

Gabriella and I were naked, playing Scrabble in Italian. I suck at languages and can barely order a chile relleno in my favorite Mexican restaurant, but armed with an English to Italian dictionary, I am actually learning a bit of Gabriella's native language. Gabriella was nursing a martini and I could tell she was waiting for this game to end. I'm not fun to play Scrabble with, not even in English.

My cell phone rang, and Gabriella looked relieved. It was Kibe. She and Jesus had strict orders never to disturb us at home on Scrabble day unless the reason was of epic proportions.

"Rae?"

"What?"

"Rae, she, she's on her way to your house—right now! She just left our office." Kibe sounded out of breath.

"Who's on her way here? What's going on, Kibe?"

"She said she'll only talk to you and Gabriella, and it has to be today, right now." Kibe made a croaking noise.

"Breathe, Kibe, breathe—damn it. Who have you let come here on our day off?"

"Renzi Barcelona!"

"Kibe—hello—are you there?" The line was so quiet I thought the call had dropped.

"She's coming, Rae. Jesus and I couldn't stop her. She knows where you and Gabriella live."

"Renzi Barcelona?"

"No, her manager, Leni Roth."

"Oh, for Chrissakes." I hung up.

Gabriella and I got dressed. The naked Scrabble mood was ruined.

Renzi Barcelona's manager turned out to be just barely five feet, muscular, and shaped like a Havana cigar. Her dark hair was just shy of a buzz cut. She looked more like a marine in basic training than one of Hollywood's most successful managers, and certainly not the one with the hottest actress in the world topping her enviable list of clients.

"Come in, Ms. Roth," Gabriella said to the top of Leni Roth's head, whose eyes were staring straight ahead at Gabriella's perfect breasts. She followed the voice upward, then quickly flicked back down for another look before Gabriella stepped aside and broke the spell. The love of my life can do that to women.

Once seated in a large upholstered chair where her feet didn't quite touch the ground, Leni looked like Edith Ann in drag.

"Renzi has had something very important stolen and she needs it found right away to avoid an international scandal, and possibly ruin her career." She took a large gulp of scotch that I had prepared at her request.

"Renzi and I read the article about you in *Los Angeles Magazine*, nice picture on the cover, by the way. Renzi feels, and I strongly agree, that you two are right for the job."

"What job?" I grabbed a handful of salted cashews.

Leni eyed the bowl and Gabriella moved them to the table next to Leni's chair.

"When she saw your picture on the cover, she told me 'If I ever lose something, I'm gonna hire those two cute lesbians to find it'. She needs you to start today. She wants you, and I agree, to make her case a priority. Money is no object."

It appeared not to enter Leni's mind that Gabriella and I needed to talk to Renzi Barcelona, herself, before deciding if we will take her case. Leni was used to negotiating contracts. To her it was never about *what* only *when* and *how much*. No one, it seems, ever says *no* to Renzi Barcelona. Leni Roth makes sure of that.

"Wait a minute, Ms. Roth...."

"Call me Leni."

Okay—Leni, where is Renzi Barcelona? With all due respects, she is the potential client, not you." Gabriella's voice was measured but I saw a vein pulsing in her neck.

Leni leaned forward and lowered her voice. "We think it's blackmail. We think it's been stolen to blackmail Renzi. She doesn't want to go to the police, and I strongly agree with her."

Gabriella and I looked at one another. How did this happen on our sacred, no-one-in-the-house-but-us day? The loser of naked Scrabble was supposed to be paying off right about now.

"What's been stolen? You can at least tell us that."

Leni ignored the question and looked around the room. "Who else lives here, Rae, if you don't mind me asking? Who is in the house right now?"

"I do mind you asking, Leni. I mind very much, and I'd like you to leave our house right now." Gabriella raised her voice firmly.

"Right now," I echoed. "Please tell Renzi Barcelona to find another investigator. We don't want her case. I'm sure she'll have no trouble finding someone else since she's Renzi Barcelona and money is no object. Only I'd advise her to make the contact herself and not let you botch it up a second time. Goodbye, Ms. Roth, I'll see you out."

Gabriella picked up Leni's empty glass and the mostly empty bowl of nuts and walked out of the room.

Leni just sat there staring straight ahead and started crying. I'm not good with people who cry.

"Ms. Roth...Leni?"

"Gabriella," I called. "Come back—right now."

We both stood there staring at that tough, ball-busting Hollywood agent that so many people feared. She looked about ten years old and she was crying, for God's sake. Honest to God, real weeping, and wiping her nose with the back of her hand to keep it from dripping.

"I'm sorry," she muttered, as she stood up and looked around for a way out.

The door banged. "I'm home early, Moms. Stacey's sick so tennis was cancelled," Bailey shouted.

"Okay," I shouted back. "We have a client here, Bailey. We're in the office and don't want to be disturbed."

"No problem."

Gabriella came back and closed the door. "Sit down, Leni. I'll make us some coffee. My daughter won't disturb us, and it's the housekeeper's day off."

"Renzi's in the SUV, on the floor, hiding under a blanket. I rented a Honda to come here so the paparazzi wouldn't spot her car or mine."

"In the car, on the floor, all this time, Renzi Barcelona?"

"She's probably sleeping. That's what she does when she's bored—or scared. That's why I asked who is in the house."

"Go get her and bring her in, right now. Wait—I'll go with you."

Everyone knows the Renzi Barcelona story. She was found abandoned in the Delores Mission Catholic Church in Los Angeles. She had a small gold cross hanging around her neck and a note pinned to her lavender blanket. *I am Catholic. My name is Renzi. Please find a good home for me.*

She was adopted by Rollo and Leanne Barcelona from Woodland Hills. Fourteen years later Renzi Barcelona played a bullied teen-aged girl with a stutter in her school play. In the audience was nineteen-year-old Leni Roth.

I looked at Leni's face as she helped Renzi out of the car. Her eyes had softened, and her face looked like mine does when I look at Gabriella. It's Leni. It's Renzi and Leni. I thought Gabriella and I were sort of the quintessential odd couple, or Lauren and Harry Boyce, for that matter. But Renzi Barcelona and Leni Roth?

Leni got Renzi settled on the office sofa and sat down next to her. Renzi laid her head on Leni's shoulder and took her hand. After introductions, Gabriella served coffee and freshly made *sfogliatelle*, a filled Italian pastry that can send my sugar addiction rehabilitation back to square one. Gabriella shot me a look and I put one on my plate with an innocent smile.

Renzi's voice was strained. "I told Leni we should not come here like this. Leni said it was all right, that your assistant called ahead, and you were expecting us. I fell asleep in the car. Thank you for letting Leni tell you my problem, our problem, really. Did she explain what happened? I'll answer any questions you have. Oh, thank you for taking the case. I told Leni we need you two to handle it."

"Drink your coffee first, Renzi. Do try the *sfogliatelle*. You, too, Leni. I made them this morning. Rae loves them."

I slowly munched on mine. I knew I wasn't getting a second one any time soon. Gabriella only made them because Bailey needed a dessert for her school potluck tomorrow.

"We're very interested in your case, Renzi. The only requirement is that you sign a contract and give us a retainer. You will be invoiced at our standard rate, none of this money is no object crap. Oh, and we have other cases that are just as important to our clients as yours is to you. Take it or leave it."

I looked at Leni and she actually smiled at me.

"Give us the background of why you think it was stolen."

Leni hadn't told us what had been stolen. We had kicked her out of the house before getting that information. I had to play it carefully to get the details from Renzi and not let her know her knight in shining armor totally screwed up.

"Renzi and I agree to your terms." Leni's voice was much softer than the voice she came in with.

Renzi told us that she and Leni had been friends since they met after the high school play, and that they have been secret lovers for twelve years. She said she dates men, mainly gay actors, who want a public cover.

"I had someone take a picture of Leni and me after the play, that was in two thousand two. I pasted it into a journal and named it *An Affair to Remember*. I didn't know then that *An Affair to Remember* was the title of an old movie. I've kept journals faithfully since that day. It's us, Leni and me—our friendship, our romance, our sex life, everything. There's pictures in it I wouldn't want anyone to see, ever."

"What makes you think the journals have been stolen?"

"Leni and I went to Africa for a month. I closed up the house and gave my housekeeper her vacation at the same time. I have a good security system and another security company that patrols the area."

"When we got back yesterday nothing in the house had been disturbed except that Renzi's bedroom had been tossed. Her journals were gone. Renzi and I had been talking seriously about coming out as a couple and announcing our engagement. Renzi is still apprehensive and wants to wait. I'm ready to get married now."

"So am I, Leni, so am I. I just want to hold off until the pressure of filming *Strangers at the Gate* is finished, that's all. Now I don't know what to do. I'm afraid everything about our intimate life will hit the internet, or be published in the smuts, or that I'm going to be blackmailed." Renzi crumpled back down on Leni's shoulder again.

"Where do—did—you keep your journals?"

"I have a wall safe behind a painting of me."

"Was it locked?"

"No—I never lock it. No one ever comes up to my bedroom except Leni and my housekeeper, Sofia. I trust them both with my life." Renzi patted Leni's hand.

"Didn't you think to lock your safe before you went away? Do you keep anything else in it?"

"'No, some of my jewelry is in a locked safe in another part of the house. Everything else is in a safe deposit box at my bank."

I was beginning to get a strange feeling that this was an inside job, but it just didn't make any sense. "Who else besides Leni and Sofia has access to your property, Renzi?"

"The landscapers and pool guy come frequently. They've been background checked and are only allowed on the premises when Sofia is there. They do not have the code to the gate. No one does except Leni, Sofia, and me. Occasionally repair people and others come in, but only by appointment. I don't have parties and keep my social life outside of my home. Very occasionally Leni and I have a few friends in for dinner. That's it."

"The first thing I want you to do is draw up a list of everyone who comes to your home, including your friends, with addresses and telephone numbers." Gabriella said. "Don't worry, they will not be contacted directly. Our resource operative, Jesus Smith, will come to your home tomorrow for the list. I want him to take pictures of your bedroom—you haven't touched anything since it was tossed, have you?"

"No. Renzi's staying with me until we get this sorted out." Leni looked pleased.

"Good." Gabriella left the room and returned with more coffee and a platter of fruit and cheese. This was turning into quite a party!

"Who was here today?" Bailey asked at dinner. "You don't ever see clients at home, and especially not on your everyone's gone and now we can play Scrabble day."

Gabriella and I exchanged looks. What does Bailey know about our playing Scrabble? Our little girl is growing up.

"We can't tell you. She was here incognito." I gave Bailey a *stop asking questions right now* look.

"Oh, so it's a *she*, is it? Someone famous, like famous enough to get your picture in *People* magazine?"

"We can't talk about it, Bailey. Stop pumping us." Gabriella gave Bailey a warning look.

"Okay, but it's not fair. I'm a junior investigator and have taken an oath of zipping it. Doesn't that entitle me to anything?"

"No!" Gabriella and I shouted in unison, and we finished our dinner in silence with our pouting daughter.

Later that night I slipped another *Sfogliatelle* out of the bag Gabriella had prepared for Bailey and ate it in the office while I thought about Renzi's journals. Sugar always helps clear my thinking and I didn't want to drive all the way to Tiki Ti's for a Mai Tai One On. I was becoming lazy in Beverly Hills.

The next day Jesus, Kibe, Gabriella and I met in the conference room to discuss the pictures Jesus took of Renzi's bedroom. It's a beautiful room, very serene and understated. Now clothes were tossed out of the closets, everything emptied from drawers, and the bedding was completely overturned.

Jesus had completed his report on everyone who had access to Renzi's home. By discreet inquiry, Jesus learned that not one of them had a motive for stealing the journals. No one had an axe to grind with Renzi. She was fair and generous with those who worked for her, and the few real friends who came to her home were fiercely loyal.

I stared at the picture of Renzi's bedroom on the screen. "Everyone, tell me what you see. Don't dismiss any detail as irrelevant. Kibe, keep notes on the key words we use."

The first word on the list was *staged*. We all studied the picture and agreed that the toss looked contrived. *Careful* was another word. Kibe noted that the painting of Renzi had been carefully placed with no damage to it, not thrown or even slashed, as some tossers do in their frenzy. There was no chaos to the disorganization in Renzi's room. The mattress and the bedding were thrown off the foundation but were clean. Sometimes tossers throw liquids, like perfume, or solvents on fabric, or worse. It was a mess, but one that could be cleaned up easily with no damage to anything.

"Why did someone go to the trouble of carefully contriving an undamaged mess in Renzi's bedroom?" The safe was in the usual place for wall safes, behind a painting, and it was open.

"I think I know why, Gabriella. Someone wanted the scene to look so dramatic that it pushes Renzi into action

"What action?" Kibe asked.

The phone rang. "It's Renzi Barcelona," Jesus said.

"Put her on speaker, Jesus. Hello, Renzi. What's up"

"It's blackmail, Rae, it's blackmail," Renzi screamed into the phone. "Blackmail. I knew it. They will suck me dry and run pictures of Leni and me all across the internet anyway."

"Where's Leni?"

"They want two hundred and fifty thousand to return the journals to me and another two hundred and fifty thousand to keep quiet and not sell stories and pictures to the smuts. I'm gonna pay it, but I'm gonna beat them at their own game and announce my engagement to Leni. It'll be the biggest wedding announcement since Ellen and Portia.

"Renzi, where's Leni?"

"I don't know. She's out making arrangements to pay the blackmailers and get my journals. We're getting off cheap for five hundred thousand to end this ugly mess."

That's the way Gabriella thinks, I mused. On the other hand, I couldn't raise that money if my life depended on it. I could have a gun pointed at my head and I'd have to cry *shoot!* Movie stars, heiresses—they just don't know how tough life can get without having much money when something goes wrong.

Gabriella left early for her weekly body treatment, as she calls it. Someone named Desiree has hands almost as magical as Margarite's at some day spa called Paris Nights. Hmmm.

I stopped at Gino's on Beverly for a couple of pizzas. We were dining *en famille* tonight and I was looking forward to dinner and a movie with Gabriella and Bailey.

The gray Honda was in the driveway. Gabriella met me at the door and motioned to the office. There was Leni in the Edith Ann chair with a bowl of cashews and a large scotch and soda.

"Hey, Rae, did Renzi call you? I was right, it is blackmail. Didn't take those bastards long to get in touch with us, did it? I got the money. Wanna come with me to the meeting place in Culver City? That way the find will be yours. Renzi says it's worth every penny, and I strongly agree."

Leni took a satisfied swig of scotch and popped a handful of cashews into her mouth.

"Why did you do it, Leni?" I asked quietly.

Leni choked trying to swallow the nuts. "What? I didn't do anything."

"You did it, Leni. Why?"

She remained silent for a moment.

"I got desperate. You don't know what it's like, waiting year after year for Renzi to marry me. You and Gabriella have a normal life. Why can't we?"

Because I'm not Renzi Barcelona, I thought.

"Where are you getting the money?"

"She's putting in two fifty and I'm putting in two fifty. I'll just slip hers back into her investment portfolio. She'll never know it's been returned. Mine comes out of my slush fund." Leni shot me a sly smile.

Out of her slush fund? I thought about my own slush fund, about twenty thousand dollars I have stashed away for emergencies or an occasional impulse purchase.

"How about we cut to the chase, Rae. You're sorta between a rock and a hard place here. I know you don't want to hurt Renzi, which telling her I'm the person blackmailing her will do."

"How did you get her bedroom tossed?"

"I did it before we left. I told her I had a little business to take care of and rushed to her house. Sofia was already gone, no problem. Look, Rae, how about you go to Culver City with me and find Renzi's journals in the rented mailbox. Then you won't be lying about retrieving them from the blackmailer. Okay? Is that a yes?"

"It's a yes, damn it, it's a yes," I said reluctantly. I got her another scotch and soda and two oatmeal raisin cookies for me.

The following March, Renzi Barcelona stood on the stage of the Dolby theatre in Hollywood and accepted the best actress Oscar for her performance in *Strangers at the Gate*. Her acceptance speech was a triumph.

"Winning this academy award is very special to me, but I want to share something even more special. I am getting married in June to the absolute love of my life since I was fourteen years old, my fiancée, Leni Roth."

Renzi blew a kiss to Leni in the audience and left the stage to a standing ovation.

Gabriella and I were propped up in bed watching it all unfold. "Hey, Gabriella," I said dipping a biscotti into my coffee. "How many lesbians clutching an Oscar come out on stage and announce their engagement to a standing ovation?"

"None, my darling. I would say that Leni is in so much more trouble with Renzi than you are with me, wouldn't you say?"

"Not on your hundred million-dollar-inheritance, I wouldn't. Not anywhere near close."

Gabriella bopped me on the head with her pillow. I took that to be a love tap.

Love is in the Air

It was an unusually beautiful day in Beverly Hills. An unexpected rain chased the smog somewhere else, or so it seemed, and the sky looked picture perfect. It's the weather that makes me hungry for sweets, and with Gabriella not around to stop me, I sent Jesus to the bakery on Wilshire Boulevard for a couple of strawberry cheesecakes. That, and the whipped cream-topped mochas should be able to hold me until Gabriella and Bailey got home from visiting family in Milan.

To be quite honest, I am happy to indulge myself in cheesecake and mochas without Gabriella giving me the evil eye. I am terribly lonely for the absolute love of my life and the amazing daughter I never imagined I would have, but, come on, it's great to be able to indulge in peace.

Most of the time I keep my sugar cravings somewhat under control. Although in times of dire stress, like sleeping alone for three weeks, reason goes right out the window and I can, with modest honesty, binge with the best.

I gave Kibe a warning look when Jesus came back with the goodies. "We are going to eat this and enjoy it right down to the last crumb, aren't we, Kibe?" She bobbed her head up and down.

"We are going to lick the whipped cream off our mochas without any comment, aren't we, Kibe?" The head bobbed up and down again.

"And we're not going to say a word to Gabriella about falling off the sugar wagon, are we, Kibe?"

Kibe's head didn't move. "That I'll have to think about, Rae."

"What?" A bit of strawberry topping dribbled out of my open mouth.

Kibe gave me one of her wicked grins. "Can me and Jesus take Friday off, then? We're going to apply for a marriage license."

Friday off—both of them—which will leave me in the office as receptionist and paperwork jockey for a day. Oh, hell yes. It was a small price to pay for the large wedge of cheesecake dripping with strawberries so I shoveled another piece in my mouth and nodded.

"Does your mother know, Jesus?" I asked, when I returned to planet Earth. They both said *yes* in unison. Good! Now, Roza Smith and I have a wedding to plan. I found myself humming "Love is in the Air".

Still under the influence of the sugar high and the *I'm so lonely, poor me* syndrome, I knocked off early and headed to the Sunset Strip and Tiki Ti's. On top of the strawberry cheesecake and the mocha, a Mai Tai One On or two and some chitchat with my friends should be enough to help me sleep alone for a few more nights.

I spotted Jay Cusak in the crowd and waved. Jay's an art restorer at the Getty museum and a damn good artist in his own right. I have a couple of his paintings hanging in my home in Studio City, the house I hold on to *just in case*. I don't know if it's because I'm afraid the Gabriella bubble will burst one day or it's just nostalgia for the home I grew up in. For whatever reason, despite the fact that I now live in an enormous villa in Beverly Hills, I still love it.

Jay saw me and waved. I grabbed a Mai Tai One On and screamed *it's tiki time* with the crowd as Pete's son, Mike, hit the gong.

I pushed my way to Jay, really glad to see him. "We haven't seen much of one another lately. It's been way too long."

"Hi, Rae—funny seeing you here today. I was actually gonna call you."

"Why?" I said. "You lose something?"

Jay took a gulp of something poured on ice. He wasn't a Mai Tai kind of guy, but he loves Tiki Ti's. I met him one night about eight years ago when I was a little tipsy. He was getting a jacket out of the trunk of his red Toyota, the same color as mine, and I actually drove away in it. Then I saw a pack of cigarettes in the cup holder and was sober enough to remember that I don't smoke. I came to a dead stop at the end of the parking lot. Jay caught up with me and we've been friends ever since.

"No, Rae, I found something that belongs to me. I'm pretty sure that the painting of Gallachio's *Two Women in a Skiff* hanging in the Getty is *my* Gallachio copy. It's signed by Gallachio, but I think someone forged his signature on the copy I did in art school twenty years ago. I gave it to one of my roommates when I moved to Los Angeles, but I swear I did not sign Gallachio's name or try to pass it off as an original."

"How can you tell it's your copy, Jay, especially since you haven't seen it in twenty years?"

Jay went to the bar to get us another drink. I was intrigued enough to want to hear the rest of his story.

"So, Jay, you didn't answer my question. How can you tell it's yours?"

"I painted my initials, JC, into the waves. You wouldn't see it, but I know where they are. Rae, my initials are there. I found them."

"Okay, so if it's your painting, just go to the director of the Getty and tell him or her you want it back. You don't need to hire me to retrieve it."

"I can't do that. If I prove the painting is mine, I'll be accused of forging Gallachio's signature and accused of art fraud."

"That's ridiculous, Jay. They'll know you're innocent when you reveal that the painting is a copy, your copy. You'll be a hero in the art world."

"Listen, Rae, Gallachio only painted a half-dozen pictures before he committed suicide at age twenty-eight in nineteen ninety-seven. His wife, Lila Emerson, permanently exhibited them in her art gallery in New York until her death a couple of years ago, and then they all disappeared into thin air. No one has seen a Gallachio since two thousand twelve so there was quite an explosion in the art world when *Two Women in a Skiff* resurfaced. It was authenticated without any doubt. The Getty bought it at auction for twenty million dollars when the owner, Laurence Motson, a hedge fund gazillionaire, produced a traceable bill of sale from Lila Emerson's heir, Tracy Emerson Ragsdale. She had inherited all six paintings. She sold *Two Women in a Skiff* to Motson, who then made a three-million-dollar profit selling it at auction to the Getty. I'm telling you, Rae, it may look totally above board, but somebody, somewhere, has the original because that's my copy hanging on the wall of the Getty. I want to hire you to get it back for me."

I told Jay I would discuss it with Gabriella and get back to him. It was absurd to think that Gabriella and I were going to attempt to remove a painting from the Getty museum and end up in prison for art theft. Actually, my answer was already no, but I didn't want to tell Jay just yet.

On the drive home, I thought about Jay and the problem he believed serious enough to hire us. Now the word *retrieve* is tricky, especially in the context Jay wants to use it. Ordinarily, when Gabriella and I retrieve something for a client that is lost, hidden, or stolen, we find it, not steal it, and return it to the rightful owner. A little-known definition of retrieve, though, is *to fetch to put right or rectify*, which in Jay's context means to steal what belongs to him and that justifies the theft.

While I wanted to help Jay, his request, it seemed to me, might lead us into dangerous waters. Although I understood his need, I really had to discuss it with Gabriella. And nothing we do could involve stealing a painting off the wall of the Getty. I was pretty definite about that, no matter what happened to Jay Cusak.

I was curious to see the twenty million-dollar copy that Jay said fooled experts so I drove out to the Getty. Without committing Retrieval, Inc. to the case and at no charge to Jay, I arranged to have him show me his initials on the painting. He and I stood very close to the painting as he guided my eyes into the waves below the skiff. I didn't see any initials. Finally, after four tries, Jay told me to look away, close my eyes, open them and look right at the spot. They were there! I saw them, so carefully blended into a wave that it was almost impossible to see them.

"Holy shit, Jay." I was stunned. "It really *is* your painting."

"Yup. I told you so. I don't care that the Getty got duped. That's my painting and I want it back without them knowing."

"Jay, don't you think they'll investigate when they see it missing off the wall. It is sure to lead to you and you'll be in deep doo-doo for not reporting the fraud. You've done nothing wrong—that is, until you want a picture stolen off the wall of the Getty, and you want me to steal it, which is against federal law no matter that it's your copy. It belongs to the Getty."

"Then you won't do it? Damn, Rae, I thought you could find the original and do a switcharoo." Jay gave me a sly grin.

"Find the original—and what? Steal it to hang back on the wall in place of yours? Are you crazy? We'll end up with three hots and a cot in a federal prison in Aliceville, Alabama."

"Don't you think they'll forgive us when they learn the truth, that the Getty will have the real twenty million-dollar Gallachio? If we're smart, though, they'll never have to know what we did."

"Wrong, Jay," I bellowed. "I'm not doing it, neither is Gabriella or anyone connected with Retrieval, Inc."

"I thought I'd be doing you a favor, giving you the job because you're a friend."

"Thanks, but no thanks. What I will do is have Kibe and Jesus, my resource operatives, gather some information on the provenance of the original leading up to the actual sale to the Getty. That's a gift from me to you, but it stops there. I won't do anything illegal, well, not as illegal as this."

I took some pictures of Jay's copy when the guard wasn't looking. He agreed to what I offered, but he was not happy about it. I, on the other hand, was ecstatic that I had not lost all sense of reason. Living in Alabama doing ten to twenty did not figure into my future, not by any stretch of the imagination.

It was lunchtime and I decided to grab a bite in the museum restaurant before heading back to the office.

"Rae, Rae Talley, is that you?"

I turned toward the voice. It was Janet Wilcox, an acquaintance of mine from the FBI in Washington. I had met her during one of my investigations.

"Janet, what are you doing here in Los Angeles? Oh, my God, I haven't seen you in ages."

She gestured to a chair and I sat down, always astonished when people pop up from my past.

We ordered lunch and got down to some serious catching up. We hadn't been friends, as such, but I liked her and could have become friends if we had lived closer to one another."

"I'm living here, in Silver Lake. I transferred from Washington two years ago. I'm married, Rae, and my wife, Ishigo Tanaka, was also an FBI agent. She and I moved to California and got legally married."

"Wow! The last time I saw you in Washington you were married to a man and had two kids."

"I still have the children, Kelly and Jon. They live with Ishigo and me during the school year. Greg is a college professor and he has them with him all summer and some holidays. It works for us. So, what are you doing now?"

I told Janet about Retrieval, Inc. and about Gabriella and Bailey, but downplayed the Italian heiress thing. I told her about some of my cases, and very briefly why I was at the Getty. I did not tell her that Jay wanted me to steal two paintings.

Janet laughed. "You're kidding. Wait 'till I tell you what Ishigo and I do now. I'm not much on serendipity, but if this isn't it, I don't know what is."

It turns out that Ishigo had been an agent with the art crime team of the FBI in Washington, and she received specialized training in art and cultural property crime cases. After Janet and Ishigo moved to Los Angeles, Janet took a job in the FBI Cyber Crimes Branch and Ishigo became a detective in the LAPD's Art Theft Division.

"Actually, the division is the only full-time unit of its kind in any city in the United States. Ishigo has handled some big national and international cases," Janet said proudly.

"Jay could definitely use your help, but I'll never be able to convince him to talk to an FBI agent and an LAPD art theft expert. No way!"

"Rae, Ishigo and I are independent now, like you and Gabriella."

"Where's your office?" I asked.

"In what was our guest room. We don't want to put out any money for an office right now. It's only been a couple of months and we want to make sure this will work out for us. Where's your office?"

"On Wilshire Boulevard."

"What are you near?"

"Robertson."

"In Beverly Hills?"

"It's a long story, Janet."

"I have plenty of time, Rae."

An hour later I phoned Jay and asked him to meet me in the museum restaurant. When he arrived, I told him I had an idea that could work for him. My idea was actually Janet Wilcox and Ishigo Tanaka. It didn't take long to convince Jay to meet with them and us at my office.

Gabriella and Bailey had been gone for three weeks and I wanted a week of *me* time with them. I thought we might run up to Vancouver and Victoria, British Columbia. It's one of the joys of being self-employed and, I suppose, one of the perks of living with Gabriella.

I booked a suite at the Wedgewood Hotel and Spa in Vancouver and two days at the Empress Hotel in Victoria. Gabriella and Bailey loved my surprise. We flew first class and everything. Okay, so I dipped into some of my emergency fund, but it was well worth it. Nothing is too good for the two loves of my life, especially seeing the delight on their faces when I got it absolutely right.

The following week Gabriella and I, Janet and Ishigo, and Kibe and Jesus met with Jay for a lunch meeting at our office. Gabriella had it catered, and I could tell Jay thought he had died and gone to heaven.

After all the information was shared and the last crumb of food was gone, Jay asked us to take his case. He had given up the idea of stealing and switching paintings, so Gabriella and I accepted and hired Janet and Ishigo as lead investigative consultants. The contract stipulated that Jay would give us a retainer of five hundred dollars for expenses. The balance would be paid in artwork. He had no idea that his retainer didn't even cover the Spago lunch.

Kibe worked the FBI and Interpol databases and found nothing involving any Gallachio paintings. Jesus made the rounds into the underbelly of art chicanery. Through his street contacts he learned that an art fraud ring was possibly operating out of Coldwater Canyon. It had just come on the LAPD Art Theft Division's radar. The owner of the Coldwater Canyon mansion in question turned out to be none other than the Gallachio/Emerson heiress, Lila Emerson Ragsdale, and her lover-in-possible-crime was Laurence Motson. Jesus happily passed that information on to Janet and Ishigo. A link to Jay's problem may have been found.

Roza Smith and I had a wedding to plan. She was in the office with Kibe and Jesus when Gabriella and I arrived the next morning.

"The *nino*s aren't making it easy for me. They have decided they want to get married at city hall in a few weeks with just a few of us in attendance." Roza frowned. "That is not what I want for my son and his precious Kibe. No!"

That didn't sit well with us either. I knew Bailey had her heart set on being a bridesmaid.

Kibe looked at Jesus, trying to muster up courage in the face of opposition. "We thought we'd stop in at city hall, do the deed, and be on our way to San Francisco for a weekend honeymoon. No muss, no fuss and back to work on Monday morning. We're both on the Cusak case, don't forget."

"Besides," chimed in Jesus, his arm around Kibe. "We've been living together, like married already, so what's the big deal?"

"There's another reason." Kibe had an edge to her voice. "My mother and two sisters live in Glendale. My relationship with them is in the toilet. I haven't seen them since I got out of jail. They didn't like Charlie because, because...."

"Because he's white," said Jesus. "And now she's marrying me."

"They didn't like Charlie because he was a drug dealer, Jesus, and, besides, you go to church."

"Exactly! That's why we should have a church wedding and a proper reception." Roza was smiling now.

"Invite them, Kibe," insisted Gabriella, my beloved fixer of everything. "They love you and this is the perfect way to repair your relationship. How about having the reception at the villa?"

"Really, Gabriella? Can I invite my old probation officer and a few friends I had before I moved to Beverly Hills?" Kibe looked at us questioningly.

"Of course. You and Jesus can invite anyone you want."

"We have a large family and a lot of friends. I have put money away for my Jesus' special day and will give it to you for the food."

"Wonderful, Roza." Gabriella shot me a conspiratorial look.

"And Jesus and I have saved, too. We can buy the champagne and the flowers." Kibe gave Roza a hug. "I'm the luckiest woman in the world."

"Good, all settled. Now back to work, you two. We have some criminals to catch and a painting to find."

Ishigo called and said she and Janet had some information. Gabriella and I met them at the Polo Lounge. We sat in the same booth Gabriella and I did that day we met to discuss Bailey's Buddha. Who knew how special this one booth would become? We always think of it as *ours* now.

"So," asked Janet. "When are you two gonna take the plunge?" Ishigo gave her a warning look, and Janet got busy with a drink selection.

"When I hit the lottery for the big one," I quipped.

Then I got the warning look from Gabriella, and that was as far as that question got.

After a moment of mental adjustment from marriage to business, Ishigo brought us up to date. "I met with Detective Barron about the Getty issue. He confirmed that the LAPD Art Theft Division does have significant leads on an art fraud ring, but nothing they can move on yet. He wants to meet with Jay. Do you think he can handle it?"

"Rae, can we convince him that his information may lead to the apprehension of the criminals, and get him off the hook at the same time?" Janet asked.

"It's worth a try."

"I have a plan that I think will work," Ishigo said.

After we agreed that Ishigo's simple plan was brilliant, the four of us had a lovely evening together without any more mention of marriage.

Plan Jay was implemented after Detective Barron interviewed Jay. He explained that he, Jay, was not a person of interest in a criminal investigation, but a very important material witness. Jay did not reveal that he had wanted us to steal his painting off the wall of the Getty. That would have been a stupid thing to do.

Kibe and Jesus looked petrified when we explained Plan Jay to them. "You want us to do *what*?"

"Go undercover at a party. It's not dangerous. Gabriella's friend, Maynard Houston, the art critic, will be with you the whole time. All you have to do is let Maynard take a picture of you at the party." I spoke in a calm, soothing voice as Kibe and Jesus clung to one another.

Gabriella came into the conference room with a batch of freshly baked chocolate chip cookies. Our two capable operatives dug into the cookies and we filled them in on the details.

On Saturday, the day of the party, Gabriella took Kibe and Jesus shopping on Rodeo Drive. A haircut by Adolfo, an expensive suit, shirt, and tie from Stefano Ricci, complete with a good knock-off Rolex and a tasteful wedding ring on his left hand turned Jesus 'Wild Man' Smith into Kibe's wealthy South American husband.

Hair and make-up at Adolfo's transformed Kibe into a more stunning version of herself. A dress from Gratus, shoes and a clutch from Ferragamo, and jewelry from Gabriella made Kibe look like a supermodel. Little did she know that the outfits, plus Jesus' wedding band, the watch, and one of Gabriella's diamond rings and bands were our wedding present to them. Maynard's beautiful niece and her handsome husband were ready to party.

I, on the other hand, had another issue to take care of that day. I had called Kibe's mother, Loray Jackson, to talk about Kibe's impending marriage. I was expecting to get a cold reception and, instead, got an invitation to lunch.

Loray is a handsome woman in her late forties. She had Kibe at seventeen, Rilla at eighteen, and Kylie at nineteen by, in her own words, a sexy saxophone-playing devil who abandoned them and moved to New York City.

"I was a roller-skating fanatic. All I wanted to do was dance, you know, like an ice skater, but the only work I could get was in the roller derby. I supported my three girls and made my living roller skating. That's all I ever wanted to do," she said. "My girls can roller skate real good, too, even Kibe."

I didn't know that about Kibe. But, then, I didn't even know she had a family close by. I always had gotten the impression that she was alone.

"I love Kibe, but I think she made some real bad choices, like marrying that loser, Charlie. Thank God she didn't have children by him. She has more potential than that. The girls and I never stopped talking to Kibe. We just drifted apart."

Loray was surprised to hear that Kibe and Jesus work for Gabriella and me at Retrieval, Inc., live in our guest house in Beverly Hills, and are planning to get married.

"Of course, the girls and I will come to the wedding. I have some money put away and I'd like to buy Kibe a beautiful wedding dress. I have my mother's veil and will be so proud if she wears it. I'll call her, Rae."

"What do you do now?" I couldn't imagine her still in the roller derby.

"My daughter, Rilla, owns the Midnight Magic Roller Rink here in Glendale and I work for her." Loray Jackson had the same wicked grin I saw on Kibe all the time.

Loray wrote down Roza Smith's phone number, and I left with a secret to share with Gabriella.

The night of Plan Jay, Maynard Houston took his spectacularly gorgeous niece and her polo-playing husband to Tracy Emerson Ragsdale's party. They met artists, gallery owners, and Laurence Motson.

On the walls were the six Gallachios. Maynard asked Tracy if he could take a picture of Kibe and Jesus with her and Laurence.

"Of course," Tracy said, with a delighted smile. Maynard positioned them to the side of the painting with a framed message. *The original of Two Women in a Skiff is in the Getty museum. This excellent copy is by an unknown artist.*

When the painting was confiscated, Gallachio's authentic signature was found hidden under a little paint. I think it's Tracy Emerson Ragsdale and Laurence Motson who will be doing time in Aliceville, Alabama.

Jay's copy of *Two Women in a* Skiff now hangs in our conference room, our fee for retrieving it off the wall of the Getty.

We offered Janet and Ishigo the opportunity to partner with us at Retrieval, Inc., and they accepted. Not only do we have an art and cultural property retrieval division, it's headed by former FBI agents. They'll never believe me at Tiki Ti's.

A month later Gabriella and I, Bailey and Connor, Roza Smith, Loray, Rilla, and Kylie Jackson, and a whole slew of family and friends watched Kibe Isobel Barbara Elaine Jackson and Jesus Ernesto Rodriguez Smith exchange vows of holy matrimony. Everyone was in gowns, tuxes, and on roller skates at the magnificently decorated Midnight Magic Roller Rink.

Unbeknownst to Kibe, Jesus, who had learned to skate on Venice Beach, took dance lessons from Kylie and claimed his bride for the first dance. The spotlight gracefully followed the couple around the floor as the band played "Love is in the Air".

Lost, Hidden, or Stolen

Mrs. Danzig's Slippers

Bailey walked into the living room with her hands over her ears and a shocked expression on her face. It's not that Gabriella and I never argue, but it is rare that we raise our voices.

"Gabriella," I shouted, exasperated by her persistence. "I do not want to go on a luxury cruise to Tahiti for a month. I don't want to go on a cruise at all."

"What's going on here?" demanded Bailey.

"Your mother wants...."

"Mom, I can hear you, both of you, stop yelling at one another."

I lowered my voice. "Your mother is redecorating again and wants us to go to Tahiti during the renovation."

"What's wrong with that? I thought it would be a fun family getaway. You'd think I was asking you to spend a month *all' inferno.*"

"Where's that, Gabriella? I do not want to go anywhere, not even to Italy."

"Mom, *all' inferno* means in hell."

Bailey and Gabriella laughed. I didn't.

"We can't stay here," Gabriella insisted in a lower voice. "The construction crew will be everywhere."

"I realize that, Gabriella, but I would like to do something that's not over the top for a change and doesn't cost a fortune. Why can't we do something simple, like camping?" My voice had lowered, too, but my *why* was tinged with *Why does whatever we do have to cost a lot of money?"*

Of course, there it was again. No matter how much we resolve the heiress thing, ignore it mostly, it always crops up in an argument.

Gabriella said nothing in response.

I turned to Bailey, accusingly. "Do you want to go on a cruise to Tahiti, too?" Then feeling guilty that I had pulled Bailey into our fight, I spoke in a normal voice. "What would you like to do, Bailey?"

"Right now, I'm contemplating running away from home." She left the room.

My phone rang and Gabriella used the opportunity to run after Bailey, probably to enlist her into the two-against-one tactic that passes for democracy in our family.

"Rae, hello, I've been robbed. Hello—can you hear me? Rae?"

I can hear you, Betty. Where are you?"

"I'm at home, tied to my kitchen chair."

"What did you say?"

"I'm tied up," she yelled again into the phone. "At home. That bitch tied me up, and her accomplice took all of James' stuff. She didn't even take the diamond off my finger or my Lladro collection. Come untie me, Rae."

"Call 911, Betty. They'll get there faster than I can from Beverly Hills."

"Rae, what about being tied to a chair do you not understand?"

"How did you call me?"

"The bitch said she would call one number for me. I gave her your number. Then she wiped her fingerprints off the phone, put the phone on the table, and walked right out the front door."

"Are you all right?"

"I'm as all right as I can be with a sphincter muscle working overtime. Please, Rae, call 911 and get here as fast as you can."

I put her on hold, then called 911 and directed them to Betty's address. "I called them, Betty. I'm leaving my cell phone on."

"Gabriella," I yelled as I ran into the hall. "Betty's just been robbed at home. The argument is over, let's go!"

Gabriella rushed in with Bailey right behind her.

"Betty? Are you okay?" I asked into my phone as we drove out the gate.

"The police just came in. The bitch was considerate enough to leave the door unlocked so they didn't have to bludgeon it to pieces."

"Who's on the phone, ma'am?" I heard Betty say 'a family member. She's on her way here from Beverly Hills'.

"Rae, I'm free. Here talk to—what's your name? Officer Stone. Talk to Officer Stone while I go to the bathroom. Oh, there's more people coming in."

I turned the corner onto Laurel Terrace Drive and my street looked like a scene right out of a television crime show.

Officer Stone came out and told us we could not come in until they were finished documenting the crime scene. I told him I was a licensed private investigator and Betty's niece. Neither the truth nor the lie got me in the house. Gabriella, Bailey, and I went to my house next door until Officer Stone let us know Betty was asking for us.

Betty sat on the sofa drinking coffee and eating a huge bear claw. She looked like she was enjoying the attention.

"Rae!" She gasped and fell into my arms.

I left Gabriella and Bailey in charge and headed for Jim's office to take a look. It was completely empty except for a few furniture pieces. The desk drawers were broken on the floor, the file cabinet drawers were yanked open, the lounge chair had been ripped to shreds, and the carpeting was torn up. The empty room looked strange with everything gone. Jim had been as much of a pack rat as Betty allowed.

James Danzig had been a tinkerer and an amateur inventor who spent a lot of time alone in his office. He worked at Northrop Grumman in Hawthorne as an aeronautical engineer. I would come home from school and head right to Betty's for cookies, milk, and crafts until my mother got home from work. Jim had at least an hour commute in traffic across Los Angeles to Studio City and I didn't see as much of him during the week.

Every weekend Jim would mow his lawn. He would wave to me and yell above the mower noise 'Hello, Rae. You're looking very pretty today', or a variation that always made me feel good. Jim wasn't much of a talker, which was good because Betty made up for both of them.

When I was twelve, Jim gave me a big, brand-new chemistry set because Betty told him I was interested in science. It wasn't even Christmas or my birthday. I think it was something he would have bought for his daughter or his son, but I may have been the only child he knew.

I checked out Betty's bedroom. Not one thing was out of place, or, it seemed, anywhere else in the house. This was no ordinary home invasion of an older widow. This robbery was connected to Jim in some way.

Detective Emilia Gonzales came up behind me. "Rae, what are you doing here?"

Emilia and I had been probation officers together in L.A. I left to become a private investigator. She became a detective in the industrial theft division of the LAPD.

"Hey, Emilia. Are you working this case? I didn't know you were with the burglary division."

"I'm not. I'm on an industrial espionage case with Northrop. James Danzig had a heart attack before we could interview him. A call came in that a Mrs. James Danzig had been attacked by burglars under suspicious circumstances. So, here I am. How do you know Mrs. Danzig?"

"I own the house next door. We've been neighbors since I was a kid. I'm the one who called 911."

Oh, so you're the niece?"

"In a figurative sort of way, you might say."

Emilia and I went back into the living room. Gabriella had made Betty comfortable on the sofa and was hovering around her. Bailey sat close holding her hand. I introduced Gabriella and Bailey to Emilia, and she shot me an approving look.

"Mrs. Danzig, I'm Detective Emilia Gonzales and this is my partner, Detective Joel Katz," she said, nodding at the short, bald man who had joined her. "I know this is a terrible shock, but I need to ask you some questions. I don't want to wait too long as memories fade quickly."

"I can in a minute. I need another trip to the bathroom. Nerves, you know, then I'm all yours."

"Rae, tell me what you know about James and Elizabeth Danzig." I gave her some background, right up until Betty returned with another cup of coffee.

"Mrs. Danzig," Gabriella said gently. "Don't you think you should not drink any more coffee until your stomach settles down?"

Betty smiled at Gabriella and turned to Emilia. "Fire away, I'm ready." She took a healthy gulp of coffee and finished off the bear claw.

"Start at the beginning, like a story, Mrs. Danzig."

"That bitch, she called me and said her name was Dr. Reine Findley and she was the new head of Jimmy's R and D project, that's research and development. She offered her condolences, said everyone on Jimmy's team really misses him, and she would do her best in his memory. She said she was calling because a couple of project files were missing. She asked if she could see if Jimmy had them on his computer. I said yes, of course, and invited her for tea. If I ever get my hands on that bitch for stealing my Jimmy's personal possessions. None of it belongs to Northrop, it was his own laptop and phone. He bought them. I was with him at Costco. I have receipts. I told Rae, didn't I, Rae? She didn't even take my diamond ring or anything valuable in the house, which, of course, I'm grateful for. Do I get Jimmy's stuff back when you catch her? I could use another cup of coffee."

I looked at Emilia and Detective Katz. "May I?"

They nodded.

"Betty let's start with the bitch's looks. How tall was she?"

"Oh, about your height, Rae, but thin—thinner than you, maybe a size six. She had dark hair, swept off her face in a bun, but not like a librarian bun, more like a loose bun, sort of messy, like models wear, but she wasn't as good-looking. And she had on a rose-colored suit that looks good on dark-haired women, and small diamond hoop earrings. And, oh yes, she had nice teeth but one in the front was slightly crooked. I remember thinking while we were having tea, thinking if she can afford diamond hoops, she must be able to afford to straighten that crooked tooth. It protruded a bit. But you know Europeans, not big on good teeth."

"What made you think she was European?" Emilia asked.

"She had a slight accent, not heavy. It sounded a little French to me."

"How could you tell it was French?"

"Her English was very good, educated, but she said *zat* for *that,* and I remembered from French movies that the French have a hard time with *th*, like in *that.*"

"What about her eye color, do you...?" asked Detective Katz when Betty stopped to take a breath. He was not fast enough.

"Oh, yes. Her eyes were brown. Very nicely made up, understated but effective. Her skin was quite light for a dark-haired woman, her hair had auburn highlights, as I recall. She wore a soft shade of lipstick, like a neutral."

"What about her hands?" I asked.

"What about them? I didn't see everything, Rae. After tea, she tied me up and I got distracted."

"Was she wearing any rings?"

"Yeah, now that I think about it. She used her left hand to call you and she had a wide gold band on her marriage finger."

"What about the man with her?" Emilia asked.

"I didn't see him at all, just heard him carrying things out the door."

"How do you know it was a man?"

"He asked her about something, and it was definitely a man's voice. Oh, I know what he asked, did she want him to take my Jimmy's model airplanes and she said yes."

Betty crumpled and put her head in her hands. "That collection was a lifetime of making authentic models. They are works of art. My Jimmy even named them, like pets. That guy, the bastard, took every last one."

As a kid, I was fascinated by Jim's model airplanes spread through the house. I felt like a knife had pierced my stomach. "Oh, no, Betty, not the collection."

We fell into one another's arms again. I think I was crying louder than Betty.

"We're done for now. You've been very helpful, Mrs. Danzig. We'll do everything we can to get your possessions back." Emilia motioned for Gabriella and me to follow her outside.

"I don't want Mrs. Danzig to stay here alone. The thieves may come back. Can she stay with you until we think it's safe for her to return?"

"Of course, Detective Gonzales, Rae and I will take good care of her," Gabriella said.

We went in and invited Betty to come home with us.

"I can't disrupt your lives, Gabriella. I'm all right, Rae. I can stay with my friend Marie."

"You won't disrupt us at all. We'd like you to stay with us. Won't you do that, Mrs. Danzig?" Gabriella asked.

"Mrs. Danzig, Mom told me once that you and she used to bake gingerbread men and even made a gingerbread house. I love gingerbread. Maybe we can make some while you're with us."

Betty took Bailey's arm and smiled. "Come help me with my suitcase, then we can get the gingerbread recipe and my pans, Bailey."

Betty had not visited me since I moved out of Studio City. I get together with her every couple of weeks for lunch and an afternoon of shopping. She knows I live somewhere in Beverly Hills with Gabriella and Bailey, but not exactly where.

Betty looked out the window as we drove in through the gates. "You gals sure were lucky to get a guest house to rent. They're hard to come by on these ritzy estates. I bet this sets you back a pretty penny."

I never told Betty that Gabriella is an heiress. She said she was glad I had *moved up* to have my office in Beverly Hills, and to share living space with Gabriella and Bailey. I probably should have prepared her for this, but what was I going to say on the ride from Studio City to Beverly Hills?

Bailey giggled. "No, Mrs. Danzig, this is *our* home. We rent the guest house to Kibe and Jesus. They work for Rae and Gabriella at Retrieval, Inc. They got married and now they live here."

Betty's eyes flew wide open. "Rae?"

"It's only a house, Betty, just with more bathrooms than we have in Studio City. You'll like having a bathroom in your own room instead of having to pad down the hall. Wait until you see the coffee maker."

"I could use a good cup of coffee, Rae."

A while later, Bailey came into the family room with lattes and sandwiches. "Mrs. Danzig's taking a nap. She had a latte and a sandwich. I feel so sorry for her. Isn't there anything you can do?"

"It's the LAPD's case, Bailey. We need to let Detectives Gonzales and Katz do their job without any interference from us. What happened is more involved than a simple home invasion. Our job is to keep Mrs. Danzig safe."

Gabriella's phone rang. "Hallo, Bill. What? I don't know. Let me talk to Rae about that," she said and hung up. "That was Bill Hendricks. He had a job fall through and wants to know if he can start on our job a week earlier than scheduled. Rae, we can still catch that cruise to Tahiti out of L.A.?"

"What about Mrs. Danzig?" Bailey asked. "Do we just take her home in a few days and sail off to Tahiti?"

"No," Gabriella and I said in unison.

"Then maybe we should spend our month in Studio City, at your house, Mom, where we can be of real help to Mrs. Danzig."

Emilia met with Gabriella and me at our office three days later. We sat in the conference room listening to her lay out a tale of high stakes corporate cat and mouse. Emilia told us that James Danzig had invented some sort of gizmo and Northrop wanted to buy it.

"We think a French company is trying to steal it, but we don't have enough evidence to prove it."

"Was James Danzig killed because of this?" I asked.

"No, Rae, there was no foul play. James Danzig died of a heart attack and Mrs. Danzig is an innocent victim. Northrop is going to pursue buying the gizmo from Mrs. Danzig, who is now its legal owner. We don't think the operatives are giving up yet. Can Mrs. Danzig still stay with you?"

"Betty wants to go home, Emilia. She says she doesn't want to be too far away from her Jimmy's spirit.

Gabriella and I are going to stay with her in my house next door for at least a month. Will that help?"

"That's perfect, Rae. Stay very low-key but report anything suspicious to me. I'll get you and Gabriella covered as consultants. Keep Mrs. Danzig away from her house at all times. Don't leave her, or anyone, alone in your house. I'm sorry to tell you that everything of Mr. Danzig's may already be discarded. Please don't tell Mrs. Danzig yet."

That's how Gabriella, Bailey, Betty and I ended up in my fourteen hundred square-foot house with three small bedrooms, one bathroom in the hall, a cramped two-car garage, and an inexpensive coffee machine. It's much better than camping.

Gabriella and I got settled in the master bedroom. It was actually smaller than Gabriella's walk-in closet at the villa, but the absolute love of my life just snuggled up in the double bed that night and purred to me. "Isn't this cozy, Rae?"

I thought about the years my wonderful parents spent loving one another in this room. "Yes, *cara mia*, it is."

The next morning, I found Gabriella in the kitchen staring at the coffee maker. A red-labeled can of coffee sat on the counter. The expensive bag of coffee she and Bailey had bought at Dean and DeLuca was nowhere in sight.

"It's good to the last sip," I said, quoting the famous saying on every can.

"I don't know how to make coffee in a machine like this. What do I do?" asked Gabriella.

"What do you do?" Betty bellowed from the hall. "Let me show you how to make the best cup of coffee in the world." She was in her yellow chenille bathrobe with a matching flowered scarf covering small rollers in her hair, and she was barefoot.

Gabriella and I stepped aside. Bailey came in from my old room, the closest to the kitchen.

"You see how easy it is, Gabriella. I don't know what you got at Dean whatshisname, but you can't beat my coffee at any price."

"Then your coffee it is, Mrs. Danzig," agreed Gabriella.

"You may call me Betty, Gabriella, now that we're living together. Where's Bailey? Oh, hi, Bailey, you can call me Aunt Betty. That's what Rae called me when she was your age. Rae, set the table, use the good—don't forget the tablecloth and the napkins. This is a special occasion. Bailey, get the bear claws and warm them in the micro, That's a good girl."

Betty poured the coffee into my mother's best china cups.

"Betty, do you remember my mom's special Sunday breakfast?" I asked, with a catch in my throat. "We had fluffy scrambled eggs, crisp bacon, fresh squeezed orange juice, and bagels and cream cheese from Jerry's Famous Deli. I'd like to do that next Sunday."

"Mom, that sounds great. May Gabriella and I do one after you?"

I looked at my family. Gabriella, Bailey, and I may be living in Beverly Hills, but this was home to me, and I still had Betty.

A week later, Emilia called and asked Gabriella and me to drop by her office. The news was not good. The operatives were gone without a trace. A box had been delivered to Betty in care of Detective Gonzales. The LAPD called in the FBI and the bomb squad before opening it. Inside were the broken parts of James Danzig's model airplanes. All the note said was, *Thank you for the tea."*

Bailey and Betty were making another batch of gingerbread cookies when I got home. The kitchen smelled like I remembered it so many years ago. Gabriella made coffee, slipping in her expensive brand from Dean and Deluca for the good to the last sip coffee.

"Hey, this coffee is pretty good," Betty admitted. "Almost as good as mine. It'll do in a pinch."

"Betty," I had a catch in my throat. "Betty, Gabriella and I saw Detective Gonzales this morning. A box came for you at the LAPD. I put it on the dining room table."

"Did they find the bitch? A box? Jimmy's stuff? Oh, Rae." She ran into the dining area.

The box was not large enough to hold all the things the thieves had hauled away. Betty stared at it. Gabriella and Bailey came in, and we just stood there quietly.

Betty started shaking and sat down in one of the dining chairs. "I'm scared," she said. "And my feet are cold."

"Bailey, please get Aunt Betty her slippers. She's barefoot and it's chilly in here."

"There's slippers in a box in my suitcase, Bailey." She looked up at us. "My Jimmy gave me a beautiful pair for my birthday, made with that Australian sheepskin. He died three days after my birthday, and I haven't even taken the slippers out of the box. I don't know why I brought them, maybe just to have Jimmy close."

Betty turned her attention back to the table. "Rae, this box has been opened. Why?"

"It was sent to the LAPD. They had to call in the FBI and the bomb squad to open it before releasing it to you."

Bailey came back with the slipper box. "Aunt Betty. They're beautiful."

Betty slipped her feet into the soft sheepskin with a deep sigh and opened the box on the table. She stared at the note.

Thank you for the tea, Betty read. "That bitch, Dr. Findley, may be a thief, but she understood me and my Jimmy."

I lifted the card out of the birthday slipper box and read it.

Happy Birthday, my darling Elizabeth, November 21. These slippers are just right for you and I hope they bring you much happiness in the future. With all my love, Jimmy.

"Aunt Betty, my friend, Connor, my boyfrie..." She shot a look at Gabriella and me. "He's good at this stuff," Bailey said. "He and our friends, Sasha, Hadley, Brooke, and Braxton can help restore the models. Honestly, we can do it for you."

I picked up the card again. "Betty, your birthday isn't November twenty first. Why did Jimmy write down the wrong date? He knows your birthday is May twelfth."

"I didn't even see the card, Rae. Jimmy wasn't feeling well on my birthday and I put the box in my closet. I just left it there after he died." She picked up the card and looked confused.

"Betty, can I take a closer look at your slippers?" Gabriella said. "Rae, do you have a screwdriver with a flat edge?"

Gabriella pried both rubber soles off the slippers. In a carved-out well in one was a key. In the other was a slip of paper. *MailBoxes USA. Number 1121. James Danzig, with access to Elizabeth Danzig.*

Gabriella had found what the thieves had been looking for.

"Jimmy was too smart for that bitch, wasn't he?" Betty's eyes were wet. She wasn't smiling. It was more like smirking. "Anyone wanna take a trip to MailBoxes USA with me?"

In mailbox eleven twenty-one, in a small box addressed to Mr. and Mrs. James Danzig, was a model of the gizmo, Jimmy's detailed notes, and a copy of the patent.

Gabriella, Bailey, and I spent Christmas Eve with Betty. She had put Christmas lights inside the restored model airplanes, and they hung in their usual places, twinkling. As a surprise, Betty made a gingerbread house for Bailey. The delight on Bailey's face made her look like a little kid. Gabriella and I gave Betty a gold custom-made pendant. It was a replica of the MailBoxes USA key with the number eleven twenty-one in small emeralds, Betty's real birthstone for May.

Gabriella came in with cups of eggnog and a plate of her Italian Christmas cookies. We stood by the Christmas tree and sang *Silent Night.*

Where's the Steinway?

"A grand piano just doesn't disappear, Gabriella."

"This one did, Rae. That was Judy Inkman calling. She and her husband just got back from Maui and her Steinway grand piano is gone."

"You mean Judy and Hank Inkman, our neighbors?" This was bad news.

"The very same."

"The Judy Inkman who seduced you years ago at The Beverly Hills Hotel while her husband was away on business in London."

"I wouldn't say she *seduced* me. It was pretty equal opportunity. We were both free at the same time in the same hot tub. It happens, *cara mia*."

Gabriella and I had no secrets from one another, although her history with women was far more colorful than mine. Hers included one-night stands with straight, married women. Mine never included one-night stands with anyone, straight or otherwise.

"Hank and Judy want us to come and take a look."

"Why?" I asked, with more than a little sarcasm in my voice. "What's to look at—an empty space in their living room, probably as big as an airplane hangar, where their Steinway used to stand? Don't you think they should be calling the police and their insurance company, not us? We should be asking ourselves why they aren't."

"Exactly! That's why we ought to hear what they have to say. It's an unusual burglary. Someone doesn't walk in and put a piano in a bag, like jewelry, and walk out. It's a lot of work, and why just the piano?"

"I don't care why, Gabriella, just call them and tell them we're not interested."

"Without even listening to what they have to say?"

"Yes."

Gabriella smiled and picked up the phone. "Judy, I just spoke to Rae. Of course, we'll help you and Hank find your Steinway. We'll be right there."

Bailey came in just as we were ready to leave. "Where are you going?"

"To Mr. and Mrs. Inkman's, next door."

"Zinni's house? Wait until you see it, Mom. It looks like Buckingham Palace, doesn't it, Gabriella? Zinni hates it. Mrs. Inkman is pretty weird."

"That's not all she is," I muttered under my breath.

Gabriella filled me in as we strolled toward the Beverly Hills version of a faux English manor house.

"You know that Hank's father is Henry J. Inkman, one of Los Angeles' top real estate moguls."

I didn't.

"And Hank is Henry J. Inkman, Jr., the Hollywood producer."

That I did know. I once had a client who worked for Inkman Productions.

Gabriella slowed down. We were almost at the imposing gates of the Inkman estate. "Here's the short version of The Hank and Judy Show. Hank was getting an MBA at Columbia. Judy, who was Judith Salk from San Francisco, was a Julliard graduate when she met Hank. He knocked Judy up, Mr. Salk knocked Hank down. Hank and Judy were married in Temple Emmanuel, and six months after that produced a beautiful baby girl named Zinni Hannah Inkman. After Hank graduated, Mr. and Mrs. Salk gave Judy and Hank this estate. Not to be outdone, Mr. and Mrs. Inkman gave Hank his very own production company. These days Judy plays at big celebrity fundraisers and Hank is frequently away on business."

"Like he was when you met Judy at The Beverly Hills Hotel. Does she swing both ways or were you just a one-off?"

The door to the house opened before Gabriella could answer, and we were ushered in by a woman wearing the crispest uniform I had ever seen.

"Mr. and Mrs. Inkman are expecting you. Please come through to the library." Her English accent was as crisp as her uniform.

The walk from our Italian villa to the Inkman's pile of bricks had transported us right to Merrie Olde England. I was having a hard time with reality. I expected to see Hank in a tweed hunting jacket and boots, with a brace of pheasants over his shoulder.

Judy came forward as soon as we were announced. "Millicent, prepare tea for us." She air-kissed Gabriella twice and hugged her just a minute too long.

"Rae, I don't know why it has taken this long for us to meet." I stared at Judy Inkman. She looked like a model in a Ralph Lauren ad.

"No idea," I said as I shook her hand with as few fingers as I could manage.

"Oh, here's Hank now." She took Gabriella's arm and moved closer to the door. I trailed behind as Hank materialized in the doorway in tennis whites. Behind him was a tall, blond, young woman, their daughter, Zinni, I presumed, and a pleasant looking young man a few inches shorter than the daughter.

"Oh, good, then, Zinni. You're home. Hello, Dave, dear. Hank, you know Gabriella. This is her friend, Rae, who's going to help Gabriella find my Steinway."

Gabriella laid her hand on my arm. With the final shred of social and business restraint I had left in me, I snatched it away and shook Hank's hand. He gave my hand a little squeeze, and his smiling eyes sent me the message I needed to stay.

Millicent, crisp as ever, served the tea with an assortment of scones, tea cakes, jam, lemon curd, and clotted cream. Maybe this wasn't going to be so bad.

Instead of talking about the missing piano, Judy spent teatime telling us how Zinni is the brightest light in the U.C.L.A. music department, and certainly headed for fame and fortune as a concert pianist. I'm sure Judy would have made Zinni play if the Steinway hadn't been stolen. Gabriella pretended to be interested. Zinni looked embarrassed and she and Dave left. I couldn't give a rat's ass and focused on a cranberry orange scone. Henry said nothing.

"Hank, we need details of the burglary from your perspective. Tell us what you know," I said.

His eyes changed in an instant to dark and tight. I got a glimpse of the power behind his laid-back demeanor.

"Millicent, our live-in housekeeper, also supervises the full-time day staff. We have a gardener, two house cleaners, and a cook. Everyone else, even the pool maintenance company, is on an appointment schedule."

"How did the thieves gain access to the house and leave with the piano?" Gabriella asked.

"Millicent has a routine schedule for shopping. While she's out of the house, Donna, the day cleaner who has been with us for eight years, answers the phone and any gate calls. Judy and I were away in Maui, Zinni and Dave were attending a music conference, and Millicent was off the estate, shopping. Donna answered the gate call and was told that the piano company was there to pick up the piano. She checked their ID's, let them in and signed the authorization to take the piano for repairs. It was that simple, Gabriella"

"It can't be that simple to move a grand piano," I said.

Hank picked up a photograph from the desk and handed it to Gabriella. "This is Judy's Steinway. It's a Model D concert grand. It's nine feet long, more than five feet wide, and weighs almost a thousand pounds." Gabriella handed the photograph to me without comment.

Hank continued. "Donna watched the three men disassemble the piano, tape every piece in plastic, and wrap them in blankets. The pieces were wheeled out on dollies and loaded into a van parked at the front door. The whole operation took about ten minutes. By the way, the uniforms, the van, and the work order had the company name prominently displayed, Beverly Hills Piano Movers—*you can trust us to do the job right*."

Gabriella stated the obvious. "I take it there is no Beverly Hills Piano Movers."

"You are absolutely right, Gabriella!" Judy looked amazed. "I tried to call them, and the number was fake."

Gabriella and I finally got to see where the Steinway grandly took center stage. The room itself looked like an artfully contrived period movie set.

Hank stared at the empty space and crossed his arms. "We don't want to call the police right now. Insurance will replace the piano if we don't get it back, so we're not even asking you to find it."

"That's what we do, Hank. If you don't want us to find the piano, why do you need us?" Gabriella asked.

"I want you to find out who planned this, and why. If you get a lead on where the piano might be, I want you to bring that information to me in confidence."

"I don't think Gabriella and I can help you, Hank."

Judy moved away from Gabriella and walked to Hank. He put his hand gently on her shoulder. She looked straight into my eyes. "Please find my piano."

"That was strange, don't you think it was strange?" I said, when we were walking home. "Judy acted as if she was making up for being socially remiss to neighbors by inviting us to tea, not hiring us to find her very expensive Steinway. Was it my imagination?"

"No," Gabriella agreed. "Hank made it very clear that he didn't expect us to find the piano, and Judy showed no emotion about it being gone. Not the usual way victims act when they've been robbed of something precious."

"There was that plaintive *please find my piano* at the end of our meeting."

"Yes, there was that."

"Judy is a very attractive woman."

"Yes, she is." Gabriella took my hand. "But, Rae, my life was filled with so many attractive women before I met you. What I really wanted was a beautiful woman to spend the rest of my life with, and I finally got one."

"Oh, Gabriella," I murmured, as she lifted my hand to her lips.

The next day Kibe faxed Hank Inkman a contract and we promptly received the signed contract and a retainer. With it was a note telling us that he and Judy were flying to Seattle to attend a wedding and would contact us when they got back.

Kibe, Jesus, Gabriella, and I met in the conference room the next day for a working lunch featuring Gabriella's fabulous Italian meatball sandwiches.

"There's something awfully wrong about this case. Let's put everything we know so far on the white board and see what jumps back at us. Kibe, you start."

"Mr. Inkman told me he bought his wife the Steinway Model D concert grand piano to replace Mrs. Inkman's Mason and Hamlin grand piano. That piano was a gift from her parents when she graduated from Julliard. He said he got great satisfaction seeing Mr. and Mrs. Salk's inferior piano, inferior to the Steinway grand, that is, relegated to an unused bedroom."

I was surprised. "I didn't get the feeling that Hank is a vindictive man who carries grudges."

Gabriella shot me a look. "Judy told me that Hank did not want to marry her, but their parents gave them no choice because Judy was pregnant. Mr. Salk believed that Hank ruined Judy's promising career. The Steinway saved their marriage."

"What's so special about the Model D?"

"Judy's Steinway is one hundred and forty-eight-thousand-dollar special."

"But Judy isn't a real concert pianist now. She plays at society fundraisers. Hank could have bought her a Steinway grand piano for half what he paid for the Model D and it would have been more expensive than the Mason and Hamlin. Why the Model D in particular?" I asked.

Kibe taped a picture of Judy's elegant walnut Steinway on the white board. "Because the Model D concert grand piano is used by famous concert pianists around the world and you have to have a really big space for it."

Jesus grinned. "We guys do it all the time. It's the age-old pissing contest to prove that mine is bigger and better than yours."

"It is a gorgeous piano." I thought about Judy's plea. *Please find my piano*. Oh my God! Was I beginning to feel sorry for Judy Inkman, that sorry piece of shit that seduced my Gabriella?" I swallowed and felt a piece of meatball stick in my throat as my chest tightened.

"Let's focus on how the perps got the Steinway out of the house and off the estate," Gabriella said.

I looked at the love of my life and smiled—giggled, actually–and Gabriella gave me a sharp look.

"Perps, Gabriella?"

Gabriella left the conference room and came back with a plate of pecan cookies. She placed the plate out of my reach and smiled—giggled, actually.

"Jesus, you're up. What have you found out about moving the piano.?" I eased out of my seat and made my way to the cookies. Gabriella followed me with her eyes. I took three cookies and returned to my seat without looking at her.

Kibe and Jesus were used to our games and I caught Kibe rolling her eyes.

"Jesus," I bellowed. "Come on, we haven't got all day here."

Jesus taped a surveillance camera picture on the white board. It showed one man at the speaker dressed in a dark blue one-piece uniform, a cap pulled low to his brow, and large aviator sunglasses. The other two men in the gray panel van were turned away from the camera. The lettering on the side of the van clearly said Beverly

Hills Piano Movers, and underneath it, *you can trust us to do the job right.* He also taped a copy of the work order signed by Donna. "I don't think the police would have found fingerprints. The thieves wore surgical gloves, so as not to damage the piano, they told Donna."

"I surveyed the piano moving companies in the Los Angeles area," Kibe added. "None show a record of picking up a piano at this location. I watched a YouTube video that showed how to disassemble a grand piano in about three minutes. The three thieves knew exactly what they were doing, right down to putting the hardware in the same type of plastic bag as in the video."

"So, what jumps out at us after looking at how the piano was stolen?" I asked.

Gabriella nodded. "It's an inside job, Rae, it has to be."

"That's why Hank and Judy don't want to go to the police or alert their insurance company, who will certainly send an investigator."

"They suspect Zinni, don't they? They think she may have orchestrated the plan. Why?" Kibe asked.

"That's what we're going to find out, kids, after Hank and Judy get back from Seattle," I said, easing the last cookie off the plate.

I made brunch on Saturday—French toast with bacon, fruit, and Mimosas. We spent an hour drinking coffee and speculating about the Inkman case, but we didn't say anything that could implicate Zinni in front of Bailey.

Sunday was another totally relaxing day. Bailey and Connor headed to the Santa Monica pier and Gabriella and I spent the day at the Getty Villa in Pacific Palisades. We especially enjoy it because it's inspired by a villa at Herculaneum and is dedicated to the arts and cultures of Rome and Greece.

Later, Bailey and Connor picked Betty up in Studio City and we all met at the guest house for Kibe's and Jesus' backyard barbeque. Loray brought chicken and ribs with her mother's secret sauce. Roza made zucchini and red pepper enchiladas with salsa. Betty and I contributed her mother's famous noodle salad and my mother's equally famous coleslaw from our own barbeque days. Gabriella made gnocchi with Italian sausages, a family favorite from her grandmother. Jesus wore a chef's hat and kept the coals hot for the chicken and ribs.

Stuffed and happy, we settled Betty into the guest room that was primarily hers already, and we called it a day.

Before heading to the office on Monday, Gabriella and I took Betty to The Griddle Café in Beverly Hills. Betty doesn't like most of the Beverly Hills restaurants. She says they're pretentious and too high-priced. She loves everything about The Griddle Café except they don't serve her favorite coffee. We drove her home and got to the office around eleven.

Suddenly we heard Kibe shouting. "You've got to be kidding! When?"

Gabriella and I came out of our offices and stood in-front of Kibe's desk. "Gabriella, Judy wants to talk to you."

"*Of course, she does,* I thought, and sauntered back to my office.

"Everybody to the conference room. I'm putting Judy on speaker phone."

"Gabriella, are you there?"

"We're all in the conference room, Judy."

"You know Hank and I went to Seattle for a wedding. My cousin, Amy, got married, it's her second time around. The food could have been better."

"Judy, forget Amy's wedding. Tell us about the piano." Gabriella shook her head and did a palms-out gesture.

"It's back."

"What's back?" I said into the silence.

"The Steinway, it's b-a-c-k, Rae, that what I'm trying to tell you. My piano is back in its place, like it never left here."

Now it was my turn to shout. "What?"

Kibe and Jesus looked confused.

"Did *you* get it back, Gabriella?"

"No, Judy, I didn't know anything about it. Hank said for us not to try to find the piano. We're still trying to find out who took it."

"While we were in Seattle, Millicent said a truck from Best Piano Movers showed up at the gate and said they had a piano to deliver," Judy said. "Millicent took the telephone number of Best Piano Movers, spoke to Sid Best, who said he was asked to pick up a piano from a warehouse in Pomona, deliver it to our address and set it up. Someone met their truck, gave them the address, paid them in cash, and left. Zinni was here and she told Millicent to let them in. My Steinway is home!"

"I guess the case is closed."

"No, Hank says Gabriella and you are still on retainer and he wants you to find out who did it and why."

"You have your Steinway back, isn't that enough?" I asked.

"No, not for Hank," she said and hung up.

Bailey came by the office later that day. "Hey, Mom, I ran into Zinni at The Beverly Center. She asked me to ask you if she can meet with you tomorrow at Charlie's Cafe, you know, on Sunset. Text her, here's the number, and don't tell Mrs. Inkman."

Gabriella and I looked at one another. Were we right about Zinni? Was she involved, and why would she only want to meet with me, and in Hollywood instead of Beverly Hills?

I texted.

Zinni, tomorrow at 4 at Charlie's Cafe. Rae.

She texted back.

I'll be there. Thanks, Zinni

I was two cappuccinos and an apple turnover down by the time Zinni arrived.

"Sorry, my hair appointment took longer than I thought it would."

I stared at Zinni. Was the caffeine in my cappuccino playing tricks with my eyes? Gone was the soft, blond hair. In its place was a magenta cluster of stiff spikes. She had on a black Pink Floyd tee shirt, a pair of ripped black skinny jeans, and pink Kibe-style boots that elevated her to a height of six feet. Enormous hoop earrings, black lipstick, and black nails completed the look. She looked oddly beautiful.

"Have your parents seen your new look yet?" I asked.

"No, Mom thinks I'm in San Diego at a student performance. Cool, huh?"

Zinni got a latte and I ordered another cappuccino against my better judgement. Something serious is going on with Zinni and, apparently, I am the only one she wants to confide in.

"I don't want to be a concert pianist, Rae. I want to be a rock singer, and Dave thinks I can become big. He wants me to break out of my mother's bullshit fantasy of molding me into a concert pianist."

Zinni put her head down on the table. "Dave did it— he had the Steinway stolen." She looked up at me. "I didn't know, honestly, I didn't. I may sort of hate my mother for trying to run my life, but I would never do that to her. That's the truth, Rae."

"Tell me the story. Start at the beginning."

"Dave will get his degree in business administration this year. He plans to go into entertainment management. We're saving money so we can go to New York, away from our parents, when I graduate. Then Dave will make me a star. That's our secret plan. No one knows about it, not anyone."

"Won't your new look give it away that you're not planning to become a concert pianist?"

Zinni ripped the magenta hair from her head, showing her blond hair under the wig cap. "It's a wig, Rae. By the time I get home, I'll look like Zinni, fucking, Hannah Inkman, the Beverly Hills good girl still doing what mommy tells her to do. That's why I wanted to meet you here, so you can see the *real* me." She fixed the wig back over her hair.

"Zinni, tell me why Dave stole the Steinway."

"I was home when the piano was delivered. Dave called after the movers left and said he wanted to see me right away. He didn't seem all that surprised that the stolen piano had come back. Rae, do you know what bearer bonds are?"

"Bearer bonds—I think the government issued bonds like that a long time ago. They had no registered owners. Whoever possessed them owned them."

I found the information online. "Yes, they were bonds issued by a corporation or a government a long time ago. No record was kept of the owners. It says all bearer bonds issued by the U.S. Treasury have matured. More than a hundred million dollars of bonds are still outstanding and redeemable."

"Dave's family inheritance comes from his grandfather. The estate is to be divided among his six children. Dave's grandfather has dementia, and one day he told Dave a story about some hidden bearer bonds that nobody knew about. Dave checked it out and, sure enough, there they were, nearly a million dollars in totally redeemable bonds. Dave stole them from his grandfather."

"You're sure about that? What does that have to do with the disappearance and reappearance of your mother's Steinway?"

"Dave said that his opportunistic windfall would let us go to New York in style, before I even graduate, and it will set him up in business. He said he did it for *us,* for *me,* so he could make me a big star."

"Do you believe him?"

"Yes, I do but, Rae, if I do it with him, then I'm a thief, too. I can't do that. That's why I'm talking to you. And, Rae, just for the record, I'm breaking up with that loser."

"Where are the bearer bonds now?"

"Hidden in the Steinway. Get this, Dave concocted this whole scheme to keep the bonds safe in my home until we're ready to go to New York. And he had no doubt at all that I would go along with it. Will you help me? I can pay you from some of my savings."

"I already have a retainer from your parents, and this is part of my investigation. Can we work on this together, quietly, just you and me?"

That night I tossed and turned. I didn't want to discuss it with Gabriella, not yet. I knew I should report everything to Judy and Hank. They are our clients but, dammit, Judy got her hundred and forty-eight-thousand-dollar piano back, Hank doesn't have to live with the knowledge that his daughter was involved in the theft, knowledge he would have suppressed anyway. Dave will never be implicated if Zinni doesn't testify against him, and she won't. She just wants him out of her life. Zinni will end up being the big loser. I woke up ready to help her.

Gabriella just shook her head when I told her the whole crazy story. "It's your call, Rae."

Zinni called to tell me she found the bearer bonds hidden in the piano. She returned them to Dave with a letter telling him never to contact her again or there would be consequences.

Once the bonds were out of the house, Gabriella and I mailed a report to Judy and Hank with a check for most of the retainer. We did not, after all, find out who stole the Steinway, Zinni did, and we let it go at that.

A couple of weeks later, Zinni showed up in answer to our search for an administrative assistant to replace Jesus, who is now our busy, full-time resource operative. She said she decided to take a break from U.C.L.A. To her delight, we not only hired her, we're letting her wear the magenta wig and the Pink Floyd tee shirt.

Lost, Hidden, or Stolen

Madness in Monte Carlo

Bailey came into the bedroom with three tuna fish sandwiches, three bowls of buttered popcorn and three coffee milkshakes for our monthly Sunday night supper and heist movie. It was Bailey's turn to choose the supper and the movie, which remains a well-guarded secret until it appears on the tray and on the screen. I agree that a sandwich, popcorn, and a milkshake is not exactly a nutritious meal, but a ritual is a ritual.

I was hostess last month and we watched *How to Steal a Million* with Audrey Hepburn and Peter O'Toole. I have always been madly in love with Audrey Hepburn. I served grilled pepper jack cheese and ham sandwiches with a Caesar salad. The month before that, Gabriella chose *The Thomas Crowne Affair* with Pierce Brosnan and Rene Russo. Gabriella has always been madly in lust with Rene Russo. Gabriella served eggplant lasagna with zucchini sticks. She serves the best suppers.

"You're gonna love this movie. Connor and I streamed it a few months ago. It's so funny, but heartwarming, too, even though they steal art out of a museum." Bailey hit play.

Gabriella and I had not seen *The Maiden Heist*. I had never even heard of it. It has a great cast, Christopher Walken, Morgan Freeman, William H. Macy, and Marcia Gay Harden. I settled down with my popcorn and milkshake. Gabriella and Bailey did the same, wrapped up in a blanket next to me on our queen bed.

The next day, Bailey and the junior investigators were sitting around our conference table after school. I had yet to find out why. We were waiting for Gabriella, who was out meeting with a disgruntled client. Gabriella is so much better handling someone with an exaggerated sense of entitlement. Our client, the owner of The Fancy Cat Boutique on Rodeo Drive, had asked Gabriella, with much indignation, why she had assigned Kibe to her case instead of taking it herself. If it was up to me, I'd have told the bitch to take a flying leap. If she wants us to find her missing cat with the stupid name of Divalicious, she cannot tell us who to assign to her case. That is, of course, why Gabriella deals with that aspect of the business.

Zinni came flying into the conference room and whispered to Kibe to come to the reception desk so I motioned for her to go. Then, Kibe waved at me to come to Zinni's desk.

"Rae, there's a phone call for Gabriella. It's Marina Reagan. She's crying and says it's urgent."

I looked at Bailey, drinking coffee and laughing with her friends. *Oh, no, not Phil*, I thought, and picked up the phone to speak with Bailey's stepmother.

"Marina, it's Rae, Gabriella's out of the office. What's wrong?"

"Oh, Rae," Marina sobbed so hard I could hardly understand her. "Oh, Rae, it's Phil."

Bailey came to the desk with her hands in *a what's going on* gesture.

"Bailey, I have to take this call. I'll be right back." I went to my office and closed the door.

Marina was still crying.

"Marina, please, tell me what's wrong."

"It's Phil." She started sobbing again.

"It's Phil, what? Stop crying and tell me, Marina."

"He's been arrested."

"He's not dead?"

"No, of course he's not dead. I didn't say he was dead. The police just arrested him and took him away in handcuffs."

Now that I knew Phil was alive, I waited patiently for Marina to stop bawling.

"Rae, you and Gabriella have to help us. This can't be happening. I'm just a week or so away from delivering Phil Jr."

I saw Gabriella come in and I waved her into my office.

"That woman is such a bitch, Rae," Gabriella said. "She didn't want Kibe on her case because—well, it doesn't really matter why."

"Gabriella...."

She went right on talking. "I told her Kibe is our best operative for finding missing animals, and she can take it or leave it."

"Gabriella, I have Marina on the phone."

"Oh, is she giving you an update on the *bambino*? Say hallo for me."

I punched the speaker button on the phone. Marina's sobbing filled the room. "Gabriella, Phil's been arrested."

Gabriella grabbed the phone and went off speaker. "Marina, what's going on?"

I went back to the conference room and told the kids that Gabriella and I have an emergency with a client.

"Mom, we can handle this case if Kibe agrees to be available to us."

"What's the problem?" I asked.

"It's about the American flag at school. Someone, we don't know who, lowered it to half-mast every day for a week. When we got to school today, the flag was, just, gone." Hadley waved her hand. "Poof!"

"Yuh, it just disappeared. We had a meeting and agreed that we should be the ones to investigate." Braxton said.

"We've solved two cases already involving theft at school. We think the missing flag is an important case.

"Do we get you, Kibe?" Bailey asked.

"You guys will sure be more fun to work with than that snobby cat lady," Kibe said.

Bailey, Connor, Sasha, Brooke, Hadley, and Braxton started their investigation at the white board as I headed out to talk to Gabriella. I didn't have the heart to tell Kibe she still had the cat lady.

Zinni buzzed into Gabriella's office and motioned for me to pick up. Gabriella was still on my phone talking to Marina.

"Who is it, Zinni?" I asked as I passed her desk.

"It's Mrs. Danzig. She said she's sorry to bother you at work."

Tuesday is my lunch and shopping day with Betty and I wondered what couldn't wait until tomorrow. I thought today was going to be a nice quiet day. I was wrong. I picked up the phone.

"Hi, Betty. What's up? I hope you're not cancelling our date for tomorrow."

"I am, Rae. I'm so tired."

"Didn't you get enough sleep?"

"It's not that. I'm just tired of everything, of life without Jimmy. I miss him so much. I'm just an old woman rattling around this house alone drinking coffee and I have to do something before I go bonkers."

"Listen, Betty, we don't have to go to lunch and shopping tomorrow. I'll pick up some chicken salad sandwiches, and we can stay in and talk, okay?"

"I'm thinking about selling the house, Rae, and moving into a senior facility, you know, like The Estates in Sherman Oaks. I'd like to take a look. Will you come with me?"

Not on your life, Betty, are you moving into one of those places, I thought. "Sure, Betty. I'll see you around eleven."

"Oh, and don't forget to buy extra pickles and a couple of bear claws."

Gabriella came into her office. She looked worried.

"I've got the information about Phil's arrest. Let's get out of here. The Polo Lounge all right with you?"

"I just got off the phone with Betty. I think a couple of martinis are just what we need."

Gabriella and I waved goodbye to the junior investigators, who were in deep discussion with Kibe.

Jesus came out of the elevator with a nice-looking guy whose arms were completely covered in tattoos.

"Hey, I was hoping to catch you in the office. Josh, these are my bosses that I was telling you about, Rae Talley and Gabriella Sabatino. This is my friend, Josh Pearlman."

Gabriella pressed the hold button on the elevator.

"Nice to meet you," I said. My eyes were glued to the artwork on Josh's arm as he shook my hand.

"We're on our way out, Jesus. Hallo, Josh."

"You're not gonna believe this. Josh is incredible. He helped me find Rex X's platinum records—all of them. His ex-wife sold them to a drug dealer who passes himself off as a music impresario. I couldn't have done it without him. He knows *people*."

"He knows *people*?" I asked.

"Yuh, he knows some of the biggies, like really well, and he's looking for a job."

Gabriella and I stepped out of the elevator.

An hour later the junior investigators were off to a place called Amar's for an exotic nosh of something that hardly looks like food. Kibe, Jesus, Zinni, and Josh were off to Tiki Ti's to celebrate. We had just hired Josh as Jesus' resource assistant. How could we not? He really does know *people.*

And us? Polo Lounge forgotten, we drove home and crawled into bed with a pot of green tea. We needed something to calm us down while we discussed Phil's arrest in Monte Carlo, Betty's impending sale of her home in Studio City, and another exciting day at Retrieval, Inc.

Gabriella's phone rang. It was Marina again. I took the opportunity to go to the bathroom. When I returned, Gabriella hit speaker.

"Marina, Rae's back. Tell her what you told me."

"Hi Rae, I'm so relieved. Our lawyer said he can get Phil released tomorrow on bail."

"Do you need bail money?"

"No, Gabriella already offered. We have enough. That's not why I'm calling. Phil swears on his about-to-be-born son's name that he did not have anything to do with the disappearance of a bust that was on loan from the Metropolitan Museum of Art. I believe him, Rae. Will you and Gabriella come to Monte Carlo to clear Phil's name? Please. We need you."

I rolled my eyes and shrugged my shoulders. "Marina, call Zinni at our office and have her set up a Skype meeting right away with Phil and his lawyer once Phil's been released."

Gabriella poured the tea and I produced a box of my expensive white chocolate cookies from my secret stash. Desperate times require desperate measures.

"Tell me what happened, Gabriella."

"Phil stopped his illegal art acquisitions on the day the window on Marina's pregnancy test said pregnant. He told her he screwed up with Bailey and me and he wasn't going to repeat that with her and Phil Jr. Marina said Phil has kept his word. A friend got him a job at the New National Museum of Monaco. It has something to do with coordinating the loan and shipment of art between museums. A bust of Queen Marie-Amelie by an important Monegasque sculptor, Francois-Joseph Bosio, completely disappeared after it arrived from the Metropolitan Museum of Art for a special exhibit."

"Why did they arrest Phil?"

"During the police inquiry, somebody mentioned Phil as a possible suspect because of his shadowy background. He was their only suspect, so they arrested him."

"What does Marina want us to do?"

"She suggested that you find out what happened to the bust of Queen Marie-Amelie and I help bring Phil Jr. into the world."

"That sounds reasonable." It sounded like sheer madness, but I kept that thought to myself.

I picked up the phone and called Ishigo. "Hey, Ishigo, I've got something right up your alley. Gabriella and I have an international incident involving the Metropolitan Museum of Art, the New National Museum of Monaco, and Gabriella's ex-husband, Phil

Reagan. Will you and Janet come to a Skype meeting we're having with Phil and his lawyer in our office? We can use your help on this one. Zinni will let you know when it's set up."

I turned back to Gabriella. "They'll meet us. That's taken care of."

"Good. Now, what's going on with Betty?"

A half-hour later, the tea was gone, and the cookies were mostly gone. Since we were already in bed, we turned off our cell phones and, in a manner of speaking, formally started our own investigation.

It rained on Tuesday and it was slow going into the San Fernando Valley. I stopped at Art's Deli on Ventura Boulevard for the chicken salad sandwiches on marble rye bread, two half-sour pickles, and four bear claws.

I had wanted to eat on the patio, but it was still raining. I would have been able to see into my yard from the patio table, just as I had done as a kid, happy to be home with Betty after school.

Betty had the kitchen table already set. "Mrs. Coleman, the resident counselor at The Estates is going to give us a tour at one. Let's eat. I'm starving."

It was quickly evident that Mrs. Coleman had led hundreds of tours in her fourteen years at The Estates. She pointed out every clean, shiny surface, every smile on the faces of happy residents, the retro cocktail lounge, and the movie theater with a popcorn machine.

"What! No bowling alley?" Betty asked.

Mrs. Coleman looked alarmed.

Betty looked pleased. "I'm kidding."

We went back to Mrs. Coleman's office to discuss the financials, Betty obviously unhappy with the brand of coffee she served. With great pride, Mrs. Coleman explained in minute detail how Betty could live independently in the cottages, transition to the assisted living building, with increasingly expensive levels of care, and die in skilled nursing without ever having to leave The Estates from the day she moved in.

"Very convenient," I said.

Betty practically dragged me out the door.

"What do you think, Betty?" I asked with a straight face when we were safely in the car.

"Don't be a smartass, Rae. Anytime I start feeling sorry for myself I'm gonna take another tour. I have a list of ten of them right here in the San Fernando Valley alone. Do we have time to go shopping?"

I thought about my mom on the drive home. She always said she didn't want to become a burden to me when she got old. I would give anything to have her here. Betty's not a burden. I love her and I love helping her. I had an idea that I wanted to run past Gabriella.

Gabriella and Zinni were sitting head to head in earnest conversation when I got to the office. I needed coffee and didn't stop to talk to them.

"Zinni," I asked when I returned. "Did you set up the conference for tomorrow morning?"

"Yes, Ishigo and Janet will be here at seven-thirty for the eight o'clock meeting with Mr. Reagan and his attorney. That's around four in the afternoon in Monte Carlo. Rae, what's the matter?"

Zinni's left arm was tattoo-sleeved from her shoulder to her wrist, an outline of beautiful shapes and swirls. I couldn't stop staring.

"Oh, my tattoo. I went to Josh's tattoo artist. He's incredible. Isn't it beautiful? Josh loves it. I'm getting some color done on Saturday."

"What did your mother say?"

"She's not talking to me."

That evening at dinner, Gabriella casually asked Bailey what she thought of Zinni's tattoo.

"Not my thing, Gabriella." She looked from Gabriella to me. "Why, are you worried that I'll do sleeves like Zinni?

"No," Gabriella and I said in unison. Of course, we were worried, or Gabriella wouldn't have even mentioned it.

"Listen, Moms, Zinni's a beautiful, talented girl and I think she'll be a big star one day. Me, I'm thinking about becoming a lawyer who helps poor people who can't afford one."

Bailey had gone through her private investigator phase. Then, she decided to become a pro tennis player, and now's she's thinking about becoming a pro bono lawyer.

"No tattoos?" Gabriella and I looked at one another.

"No tattoos. Wow. This ossobuco is delicious. Did you make it, Gabriella?"

"It's from *Il Tramezzino*. I'm not the only Italian in Beverly Hills."

The meeting with Phil and his attorney, Mr. Fenaldi, went well. Phil swore again on Phil Jr.'s name that he had nothing to do with the disappearance of the bust of Queen Marie-Amelie. His story rang true.

Ishigo and Janet, who impressed the hell out of Phil and Fenaldi, said they would start their investigation at the Metropolitan Museum of Art. Gabriella and I agreed to go to Monaco and discreetly poke around the National Museum of Monte Carlo.

Gabriella and I knew that Kibe and Jesus were ready for a challenge. Much to their surprise, we told them they would be in charge while we were gone. Kibe looked ecstatic, Jesus looked like he was going to pass out. We also called Jesus' mother, Roza, and hired her to look after the villa while we were away.

Bailey wanted to go with us. Gabriella said no and I backed her up. After much discussion, Bailey said she would invite Betty to stay with her. We promised Bailey that her father will not go to prison, and she will see him, Marina, and her new brother very soon.

Gabriella made the travel arrangements, the hotel arrangements, and we were packed and ready to go in less than a day. I never would have believed it. It took my mom and me two weeks to get ready to spend a week up in Big Bear. Gabriella says it's easy when you've lived *la dolce vita*.

"Why are we flying into Nice? Doesn't Monaco have its own airport?" I asked, taking a sip of quite nice dry Champagne. Gabriella wanted to spend a day in Manhattan and booked a suite at The Four Seasons. They sent a limousine to pick us up at JFK.

"It's the closest airport, just fourteen miles from Monte Carlo. Monaco is tiny, Rae, about five hundred acres, and more people live in Encino. My uncle Timo's vineyard in Tuscany is larger than the whole principality. There's an idea. We can visit Uncle Timo. Do you remember I mentioned him on our first date?"

I remembered it all right. I thought I had about as much chance of visiting the moon with Gabriella as her uncle's winery in Italy.

"Yes, of course I remember. It would be wonderful but, Gabriella, we're not on a pleasure trip. We're going to Monte Carlo to help Phil and Marina."

"Nothing says we can't go to Uncle Timo's if we find the bust and Marina has Phil Jr *rapidamente*. It's not always about work, Rae. Sometimes it's about *carpe opportunitatem*."

"*Carpe* what?"

"Seize the opportunity."

"And another thing, Gabriella, is Retrieval, Inc. paying for this suite and the one at the Hotel Metropole? We shouldn't be spending so much money."

"Of course not. Let's just say it's not an official case and I'm doing a favor for my ex just like you did for your ex. But I'm not willing to do it on a budget flight with seats ten inches wide and a bag of peanuts for lunch or stay in Monaco's version of a cheap motel. You'll love the pure luxury of Air France's first class, Rae."

Since this trip was now officially on Gabriella's dime, I ordered us filet mignon, garlicky potatoes, and baby asparagus from room service, and we sank down to our necks in our private hot tub. I was getting the hang of *la dolce vita* and felt almost ready for *carpe opportunitatem*.

Phil picked us up at the airport in Nice. I had seen him during our video meeting and thought he was a nice-looking man. I was not prepared for how unbelievably handsome he is in person, fit, tanned, well-dressed, and he has the most beautiful hair I have ever seen on a man. He and Gabriella looked like the perfect couple. I caught a glimpse of Gabriella and me in a mirror and smiled. They may look like a perfect couple but we, Gabriella and I, *are* the perfect couple.

After a good night's sleep on the cloud of a mattress at the Hotel Metropole, Gabriella and I spent the day with Phil and Marina. Gabriella and Marina got busy with preparations for bringing Phil Jr. home. Phil and I went to a local bar to meet Lorenzo Crovetto, the friend who got Phil his job at the museum.

After introductions and getting settled in with drinks, I asked some questions. "Mr. Crovetto, what do you do at the museum?"

"Call me Lorenzo, please. May I call you Rae?"

"Yes, of course."

"Rae, Phil and I have been friends since he came to Monte Carlo, a long time ago."

Lorenzo raised his glass, so I raised mine, then Phil did the same, and we clinked glasses. I'm not sure why.

"I'm the head of the department that arranges loans of art to and from museums, governments, institutions, corporations, and individuals for special exhibits."

"What about security?"

"My department coordinates with security to ensure maximum safety and protection while works of art are in transit."

"Lorenzo has a very important position, one that takes exceptional organizational and diplomatic skill. I was lucky. I wouldn't have gotten the job without Lorenzo's trust in me."

"Phil, there's no need to talk about that," Lorenzo said. "You are experienced and completely trustworthy. Now we must get you exonerated."

"I understand the bust was shipped from New York and arrived in Monte Carlo exactly as scheduled, no delays," I said.

Lorenzo laid some papers before me. "Here are the documents confirming that information."

Phil explained every step of the process. Nothing out of the ordinary jumped out at me.

"Was the bust examined when it was unpacked?"

Phil nodded. "That was my job. I was present when the bust was unpacked and examined to make sure it was not damaged. I was also present when our expert authenticated it to make sure it had not been switched in transit."

"We were all interviewed by the police and Interpol. Someone told them Phil was a known art thief, possibly working inside to steal the bust for a client collector. He was arrested and jailed. Just like that!"

No, I don't think so," I thought. We finished our drinks and parted.

The next day Marina, Phil, and Gabriella sat ready to leave at a moment's notice for the Princess Grace hospital. I took the opportunity to meet Lorenzo at the museum.

"Listen, Rae," Lorenzo whispered as I pinned the visitor badge on my chest. "I don't want anyone to know who you are or what you're doing here. You're my visiting American cousin and I'm showing you around the museum. Okay?"

It was an interesting tour. Lorenzo took me to lunch in the museum restaurant and we made pleasant conversation about America, which Lorenzo said he had visited several times. I came away with nothing useful.

There was a note on the hall table when I got back to the hotel.

Aunt Rae, We're off. Take a cab to Princess Grace hospital. XOXO, Zia Gabriella.

Three hours later I called Bailey to tell her that Philip Andrew Reagan Jr. was in the world and that I would send pictures.

"Mom, oh, Mom. thanks for calling. It's two in the morning here and I don't care." I could hear her yelling down the hall. "Aunt Betty, my baby brother is here."

They were talking to one another and had forgotten all about me. "Bailey, Bailey," I yelled. "Gabriella and I will call you later."

"Thanks, Rae," Betty shouted into the phone. "Come on, Bailey, let's have some coffee." She hung up.

Bailey called me back at nine that morning. "Mom, I just got off the phone with Dad and Marina. I heard little Phil cry. He sounds so cute. Thanks for texting the pictures. Oh, I can't wait until they get home. Dad says maybe in a month. Why maybe?"

"He can't leave Monaco while he's out on bail. We're trying to prove his innocence as quickly as possible."

"Mom, Dad didn't do it, did he? Tell me he won't go to prison."

"Bailey, I'm convinced your father is innocent. You know Ishigo and Janet will help us find out what's going on. By the way, how's the flag investigation going?"

Bailey snorted into the phone. "Principal Wolcott called me into her office. She ordered me and the other junior investigators to stop questioning students about the incident. She said it was a prank and that was the end of it."

"What did Kibe say?" I asked.

"Kibe told us to obey the principal's orders but to keep our eyes and ears open for evidence."

"That was good advice."

"The next day I found a note taped to my locker. *You lost the game. We won. JAXUS 1, Junior Investigators 0.*"

"What's JAXUS?"

"Don't know, don't care. We have better things to do than be manipulated by some stupid kids pulling a prank. Gotta run, Mom."

"Where are you going?" I asked.

"Aunt Betty and I are going to Chaumont for breakfast, then to The Altered Stitch."

"Why?"

"Mom, why do you think? Aunt Betty and I are knitting stuff for Phil Jr."

"You don't know how to knit."

"I do now."

Marina and Phil Jr. came home, and the next few days were a swirl of activity around the newborn baby. It was enough to help Phil Sr. forget his troubles and happily participate. I found it exhilarating and exhausting, especially since I had to fight *Zia* Gabriella to hold Phil Jr. and change his diaper.

I got a text from Ishigo.

I have a good lead from a reliable source. Janet is checking out FBI and Interpol data. I should have something for you in a few days.

Gabriella read the text. "Good. Phil and Marina need some alone time with the *bambino* and we're at a dead-end here. We're going to visit Uncle Timo."

"*Carpe opportunitatem?*" I asked.

"You learn fast, *cara mia.*"

It was a glorious drive from Monte Carlo to Bolgheri, Uncle Timo's village near Pisa. Phil had surprised Gabriella when he offered to loan us a car, and she gasped when he uncovered a nineteen sixty-three Lancia Flaminia and backed it out of the garage.

"Remember, Gabriella?"

Gabriella flushed beet red. "One never forgets special moments."

Gabriella and I stopped in Genoa for lunch. Gabriella had made reservations at Ristorante Zeffirino, one of her favorites.

I didn't understand one word exchanged in rapid Italian between Gabriella and the waiter. I heard her say *Tignanello*, and two crystal glasses appeared filled with the deepest ruby-red wine I had ever seen. We had lunch Italian-style—magnificent and leisurely.

I dozed off for about a half-hour in the Lancia as Gabriella headed along the Etruscan Coast to Bolgheri.

"Your phone dinged," Gabriella said. "I think you have a text."

I didn't want to be disturbed by electronics of any kind and I shut the phone off. We arrived at Uncle Timo's a couple of hours later. In the excitement of meeting Gabriella's wonderful family, more food, and even more *vino,* it was not difficult to ignore my phone.

Gabriella had neglected to tell me where we were staying in Bolgheri. I assumed it was with Uncle Timo. In my family, we just threw sleeping bags wherever there was space for them. After dinner, we drove to Bolgheri Castle. The only castle I had ever seen was in Disneyland. Now I was going to sleep in a stone cottage on the grounds of an Italian castle dating back to fifteen hundred. My life certainly has changed a bit since meeting Gabriella.

Uncle Timo and the family were waiting for us at Trattoria Aurelia for breakfast. I can't understand how people can eat and drink so much food and wine. I was bursting at the seams. I dozed off again in the car as Gabriella headed for Pisa to show me the leaning tower.

When we got back to Monte Carlo, Gabriella reluctantly parked the Lancia back in the garage.

"Where's Phil?" I asked Marina.

"He's at the police station," she answered. Phil, Jr. was asleep in her arms.

"What?" I bellowed.

"Shush, you'll wake him up. There's been developments while you and Gabriella were away. Didn't you get Ishigo's texts?"

"Developments? What developments?" I asked as I rooted around in my bag for my phone.

"Lorenzo Crovetto's been arrested."

"What?" I bellowed again.

Phil Jr. opened his eyes and made gurgling noises.

Gabriella came in and headed straight for Marina.

"Gabriella, Lorenzo Crovetto's been arrested." I took Phil Jr. into my arms.

"Phil's friend? What did he do?" Gabriella walked toward me, undaunted by my maneuvers.

"I don't know. I guess I better turn my phone on and read Ishigo's texts." With a sigh, I handed Phil Jr. to Gabriella.

The first text.

Ask Phil what he knows about Walter Green?

The second text.

Never mind. I called Phil myself. He says you and Gabriella have gone off to her uncle's vineyard for a few days. If you don't mind my saying so, that's not very professional, Rae, when you're working a case.

The third text.

Lorenzo Crovetto and Walter Green, his accomplice at the Metropolitan Museum of Art, set Phil up as the fall guy. Under U.S. Code 668—Theft of major artwork from a museum in the United States—Green is facing up to ten years in a federal prison. He confessed, implicated Mr. Crovetto, and is plea-bargaining for a lesser sentence. Sorry you and Gabriella missed it all.

Phil came in, took Phil Jr. from Gabriella's arms and pulled Marina into his. "It's all finished. Marina and I couldn't have done it without your help," I saw a tear on his lower eyelash.

Gabriella and I went out for a walk. It was sunset.

"I guess this was not the time for *la dolce vita*."

"Or *carpe opportunitatem*," Gabriella whispered.

"Gabriella, let's talk about Phil. Do you think he could be an asset to Retrieval, Inc., and should we make him an offer?"

"I know he and Marina want to return to California and, call me selfish, I know Bailey would love to have her brother nearby."

"And you?"

"Yes."

I squeezed Gabriella's hand and we walked back.

We were home two days later. I was propped up in bed holding Ishigo's report. Gabriella brought in a cocktail shaker of lemon martinis. Without a word, we read Ishigo's literary masterpiece of sleuthing, drained the cocktail shaker, kissed goodnight, got into our favorite sleep positions, and turned out the light.

The next day Kibe came into the office with a basket of four tiny multicolored fluffballs. "I found Divalicious hidden way behind boxes in back of the building's hot water heater. She's been nursing her kittens all this time."

"The cat lady must be awfully upset." Zinni had a gleam in her eye. "Doesn't she have a very expensive cat?"

"Upset doesn't begin to cover it. Divalicious, who is a purebred Snowshoe, took up with a mixed-breed tomcat and produced four unauthorized kittens."

"What's a Snowshoe?"

"It's commonly known as a grumpy cat. They're an intentional mix of Siamese and American White. Look at this bunch, they all have the Snowshoe white paws like their mother.

"Why are they here?" I asked.

"You said I was in charge, Rae. The cat lady doesn't want anyone to know what happened. She offered me the entire litter and I took them in lieu of the rest of the fee. Okay?" Kibe looked nervous and grabbed fluffball number one out of the basket for comfort. "I'd like to have this one."

Zinni picked up fluffball number two and asked if we could keep one at the office. I thought that was a good idea considering it was our fee.

Gabriella came in and scooped up fluffball number three and clutched it to her breast. "Another *bambino* for us, Rae.

I picked up fluffball number four, the last kitten in the basket. "I guess Ishigo and Janet have absolutely earned this one if they want it."

Gabriella and I had a meeting in the conference room. Bailey, Connor and the junior investigators sat next to Kibe and Jesus. Zinni and Josh also sat close together, matching tattoo sleeves touching. Fluffball number four sat on Ishigo's lap and stared at Janet. Gabriella filled our glasses with Uncle Timo's estate wine as Phil, Marina, and Phil, Jr. came into the room via Skype. Phil and Marina raised their glasses with ours. Retrieval Inc., by unanimous vote, became Retrieval International.

A Heist Made in Heaven

Zinni stopped me on the way back to my office. "There's a Joya Linsky on three for you, Rae."

"Who?"

"Joya Linsky, she said you know James."

"The playwright?"

"I don't know. Do you want me to put her through?"

"Yes." I picked up the phone as my mind did a quick walk down memory lane connecting James Linsky and my cousin, Myra Talley. Myra had been James' personal assistant and sometimes muse.

"Hello Ms. Linsky. Of course, I remember James. I haven't seen him since I had dinner with him and my cousin Myra in Manhattan ages ago."

"Hello, Rae. Actually, James is gone."

"What? Oh, no," I said, shocked. "Did he pass away?"

"I didn't say that. I said he is gone. *I* used to be James Linsky, Rae. Now I'm Joya Linsky. Myra says hello, by the way. She said you might be able to help me. I'll explain when I see you."

"In New York?"

"No, I live in San Francisco now. By the way, I finally persuaded Myra to move to San Francisco."

"That's wonderful news, James, I'll give her a call."

"I knew you'd be happy to have her closer. But, please, Rae, do call me Joya. Listen, I'm staying with friends in West Hollywood. Are you free for lunch today? I really do need to talk to you."

"I'm sorry, Joya, I have back-to-back appointments, but I'm meeting my partner, Gabriella, at the Polo Lounge at four. Can you join us then?"

"That's even better. It'll be great to see you again."

"Joya, wave when you see me. I'll be looking for James."

Gabriella was out with Ishigo looking at office buildings. Ishigo had come into an inheritance sizable enough for her to invest in real estate, and Gabriella suggested we consider buying an office building to house Retrieval International. I texted her that an acquaintance from New York, a potential client, will be meeting us at the Polo Lounge.

There was a text from Bailey. She said she was studying with Connor and having dinner at his house. They use the same excuse with Connor's mom. That gives them twice a week to make out in the privacy of her room or his. Why do kids think we're so stupid once we become parents?

Gabriella and I sat near the bar watching for Joya. She was already fifteen minutes late. Gabriella was irritated and I tried distracting her with amusing conversation. She kept her eyes glued to the entrance as celebrities wandered in and out. Renzi Barcelona made a grand entrance on Leni Roth's arm. They waved and Renzi blew us a kiss.

"*Madonna mia*, I think your Joya Linsky is here."

I turned and looked in the direction of Gabriella's eyes. Joya Linsky, all six-foot two inches of her, was in a fashionable black silk habit, a silver veil over a soft plum-colored wimple, with a large silver cross on her chest.

Joya spotted me and waved as she glided to our side. "I'm so sorry I'm late."

I saw what Joya meant when she said that James didn't exist anymore. Her eyebrows were a perfect thin arch and her subtle makeup on smooth skin looked professionally applied. She could have been a runway model for designer habits.

Joya seemed completely unaware that people were staring at her. She took a quick look around the room, smiled, and grabbed me out of my seat into a big hug.

"Rae, darling, it's so good to see you. You look lovely. And who is this breathtaking creature?"

I paused, feeling a little tongue-tied. "This is Gabriella—the love of my life, Joya, the woman who lovingly shares her daughter, Bailey, with me, and she's my talented business partner."

Joya held out her hand to Gabriella. "Ah, I can see what keeps Rae looking so ravishing."

"Pleased to meet you, uh...." Gabriella blushed.

"And *so* Italian." Joya's eyes twinkled right into hers. I have rarely seen Gabriella blush.

"Gabriella, I'm Joya to you and Rae, but formally, I am Mother Superior Joya of The Order of Sisters of the Lost Lambs."

I was bursting with curiosity to find out why Joya needed us, but, quite frankly, I was even more curious how James Linsky, one of America's most successful playwrights, had become Joya Linsky, the Mother Superior of the obviously not Catholic Sisters of the Lost Lambs.

Now that we had Joya, Gabriella led the way to our client table at the back of the Polo Lounge. Our martinis arrived. Joya lifted her glass and took a deep, satisfying swallow. I ignored mine.

"Joya, How? When...?"

Joya interrupted me and laughed. "Here's the quick version of my story. I was born in St. Louis. My childhood was traditional Catholic. My older brother was scripted to work in my father's family clothing store that became Charles Linsky and Son. My oldest sister was trained to serve God and became a nun. My next sister and her husband moved into the house bought by Mom and Dad, for Sis to take care of them in their old age. They had *already* given their daughter to the church, but they wanted the greater glory of having a priest in the family. Since they were not having any more children, I was it, no questions asked."

"How did you...?"

"I'm coming to that, Rae. I was twelve. My sister, Sister Anne, was home for a visit. She was taking a bath and her habit was on the bed. I snuck into her room, slipped on the habit, and looked at myself in the mirror. I didn't want to be a boy—I wanted to be a girl. I didn't want to be a priest—I wanted to be a nun. I knelt on my knees, made the sign of the cross on my chest, kissed Sister Anne's cross and committed myself to the church."

Joya waved to the waiter and held up three fingers. Gabriella and I attended to our forgotten martinis and got caught up.

"Ten years later I graduated with a degree in English and taught at a private prep school for three years while writing my play. Despite the incredible success I've had on Broadway with *Nuns on the Run*, I was still a man, I hadn't become a nun, and I'm ashamed to say, I actually thought about doing away with myself."

Joya left us with that dreadful thought and headed for the ladies' room. She ignored every head in the room turning to look at her as she swept past.

"*Che diavolo*, Rae, what the hell! What could the Mother Superior of the Lost Lambs want us to do?"

"I don't know, Gabriella. I'm as blown away as you are. I haven't seen James Linsky in five years. Myra didn't tell me James had become Joya."

"Or a nun! Didn't she mention anything about the Sisters of the Lost Lambs or Joya's move to San Francisco?"

"Not a word!"

"We better find out what this is all about, Rae."

Joya came back to the table and I blurted out, not as gently as I had intended. "I spoke to Myra last month.

She didn't mention anything about you, not as James and not as Joya, and certainly not as a nun in San Francisco. What's going on and what does it have to do with us?"

"Rae!" Gabriella pressed her hand on my shoulder. "I'm sorry, Joya."

Joya bowed her head. "I need your help, I really do."

Gabriella sat down and put her hand on Joya's. "Can you come to our office tomorrow morning?"

"Rae, I...."

"I'm sorry, Joya, Gabriella's right, of course. Can you come at eleven?"

We said goodbye. So much for my happy reunion with James Linsky—excuse me—Mother Superior Joya of the Sisters of the Lost Lambs.

The next morning Joya showed up twenty minutes late in a beautifully structured black silk suit, plum colored shirt, sheer black stockings, black leather heels, a black and silver scarf on her head, the silver cross in place, and designer sunglasses. Right behind her was Kibe in one of her jaw-dropping outfits, and bringing up the rear was Zinni, also in something outrageous. It was an image that could not be ignored.

"Wait! Don't move!" I grabbed my phone and captured the three of them in my lens. Gabriella came out of her office and stared at Joya. Kibe and Zinni we were used to.

"*Mucca sacra!*"

That's *holy cow* in Italian, one of Gabriella's favorite expressions. Not the most tactful choice of words on this occasion, and I didn't translate.

"Joya, is this your daytime, more casual habit?" Gabriella asked, giving Joya a tentative hug.

"No, this is my *it's serious business* look, but I do have some fun casual outfits." Joya pulled Gabriella in, letting her know she was worthy of a real hug. I caught the image.

"And who are these two? Do you get your staff from a badass modelling agency?"

I introduced Kibe and Zinni. Kibe did a little runway pose, and I handed her my phone.

"Take a picture of the three of us," I said.

Joya, Gabriella, and I grabbed one another around the waist and said *cheese*.

"Rae, I'm sorry about yesterday, about laying all this on you and Gabriella so suddenly."

"Let's go into the conference room and sort it out."

Gabriella went to the kitchen and came back with three cappuccinos and a plateful of almond biscotti.

"This is probably where I should have started yesterday. Three years ago, I secretly sought therapy for gender dysphoria and the following year I started my transition from James Linsky to Joya Linsky. I was supposed to have gone to a retreat in France to write my new play. In actuality, I was hiding out in my friend Jack's house on Twin Peaks and continuing the process toward gender reassignment surgery at UCSF Medical Center. I swore Myra to secrecy, even to you, Rae. I wanted as few people as possible to know what I was doing."

"Okay, Myra's off the hook. What I want to know is how you became Mother Superior Joya of The Order of the Sisters of the Lost Lambs? It's obvious that you are not a Catholic nun."

"They wouldn't have me, not even if I looked like Audrey Hepburn."

"So, you started your own order? What's the religion? Where's the church?" Gabriella looked confused.

I grabbed another biscotti and wondered when we were ever going to hear if James' problem has anything to do with something that's been lost, hidden, or stolen.

"I'm getting hungry. Let's have lunch here," I said. "Are corned beef sandwiches all right for you two? Zinni, text Nate 'n Al for delivery. You want one? Ask Kibe, and don't forget the potato salad and lots of pickles. Now, Mother Superior, let's hear it."

"It all started this past year with an auction. There was a notice in the San Francisco Chronicle for the sale of St. Matthew's, a deconsecrated church on Fillmore Street, and I went to the auction and bought it.

"You bought a Catholic church, just like that?" Gabriella asked.

James snapped his fingers. "Just like that. The archdiocese closed St. Matthew's because of dwindling attendance and mounting maintenance costs. I bought the church with the rectory and a small school building to establish a spiritual home for The Order of the Sisters of the Lost Lambs, and to renovate the church as a permanent non-profit theater for *Nuns on the Run*. The school building will become a separate center for gender dysphoria—like the one that saved my life."

"Wait a minute, don't say another word until I come back. Anyone want more coffee?"

I passed Zinni on my way to the kitchen. She reminded me that Gabriella and I were meeting a realtor with Ishigo and Janet at three to look at another office building.

"Joya, Zinni just reminded me that Gabriella and I have to get to another meeting by three," I said, pouring out more coffee. "Before our lunch arrives, tell us how you think we can help you."

"My friend Jack, the man I stayed with in San Francisco, had a group I attended for men in transition. One day I talked about my longing to become a nun in the Catholic Church when I was a young boy. Three men in the group said they had wanted to become nuns and I said, half-joking, let's start our own order. Soon we were ten men discussing it seriously. Then I went to that auction and ended up buying St. Matthew's. The mission of The Order of the Lost Lambs is to serve the transgender community with free support services and to help clients with the cost of gender reassignment surgery.

Creedy, our delivery guy/sometimes actor from Nate 'n Al's arrived with our lunch. He didn't look at all surprised by Joya's outfit.

Between bites of corned beef, Joya finally told us her problem. "The contractor had started the renovation on the church. He asked me what I wanted to do with the statues and boxes in the locked room behind the sanctuary while his crew worked in that area. The sisters and I hadn't moved into the convent yet. We moved everything into a secure storage area in the building.

There were three beautiful statues of Mary, a rack of religious-themed paintings and boxes of relics."

"You mean, like bones and stuff of saints?" I asked.

"Yes, and there were other things in the room. Several small stained-glass windows, a box of antiquarian prayer books and antique-looking rosary beads."

"*Oh, Dio,* Joya, don't tell me they're stolen objects from other churches."

"Right on the money, Gabriella, they *were* stolen."

"I found an account book, the kind bookkeepers used before computers. Listed were all the objects in the room, numbered, and the value of each item. There were letters in the book. Father Paul was having religious objects stolen to sell on the black market to try to save St. Matthew's. He must have been desperate to think that the means justified the end. Why else would he do it? When Father Paul died suddenly, St. Matthews was closed and deconsecrated and then I bought the property."

"And you want us to trace the objects and find the churches they belong to? I don't know. That may be difficult with not much to go on except inventory numbers in an account book."

"I do want to find the churches and return the objects, but that's not why I've come to you."

I all but rolled my eyes. "Joya, why have you come to us, then?"

"The sisters and I moved into the convent two weeks ago. Every last object was gone from the storage room. Only the sisters and I knew where we had hidden the stolen objects. That's why I'm so upset. I do not want to believe that we have a wolf among the sheep."

At last Gabriella and I understood. Joya was already living with the terrible knowledge that Father Paul and maybe others in the church had engaged in criminal activities. Now she was questioning whether there were thieves in the newly established Order of the Sisters of the Lost Lambs.

"Joya, I don't know if we can take the case yet. Gabriella and I want to discuss it with our partners, Ishigo and Janet. They've had experience recovering stolen religious objects."

Gabriella nodded in agreement. Joya gave us the account book and the letters to examine and we said our goodbyes.

At three o'clock we met Ishigo and Janet at Zelda's. Victoria, the realtor, called to say she was running late and would meet us at three-thirty. That gave Gabriella and me enough time to tell Ishigo and Janet the story Joya told us.

The attractive mixed-use building Victoria showed us on Robertson Boulevard had just come on the market. It had two retail shops facing the street and plenty of space for Retrieval International on the second floor. The top floor had two spacious apartments with a private entrance.

We were excited when we left Victoria. Ishigo and Gabriella had visited five buildings with Victoria, and she knew what we were looking for. After our long search, this could very well be the one.

We headed back to the office to look at the financials regarding the property. Ishigo called Victoria and made an appointment for a closer inspection of the building.

Joya came to the office for another meeting before she flew back to San Francisco. She was dressed in black jeans, a plum-colored tee shirt, a black hoodie, a small silver cross around her neck, and black and silver tennis shoes. Without the wimple, Joya's hair was pulled back in a loose bun and her make-up was minimal.

I met Joya in the reception room. "You sure have some beautiful nun clothes, Mother Superior." Joya did a whirl around and folded me into her arms.

"That's because Frederico designed our wardrobe."

"Frederico, from Universal Studios?"

"Not anymore. He's one of our nuns now and he's designing the costumes and the sets for *Nuns on the Run.* By the way, I ran into your delivery man, Creedy, and offered him a full-time job as assistant stage manager and understudy. He's on his way to San Francisco as we speak."

I introduced Ishigo and Jesus to Joya. Gabriella was out of the office, so I pulled out my secret stash of white chocolate macadamia cookies to have with mochas.

"Not a word to you-know-who!" I said to Ishigo and Jesus. They shook their heads and I asked Ishigo for an update.

"Rae, nothing has turned up so far matching the objects in the account book. I'm having Jesus follow up on several leads to see if we can uncover anything linking the objects to churches here in California. There are no real descriptions in the account book and it just may be a dead end now that the physical evidence is gone."

Disappointed, Joya went back to San Francisco to start rehearsals for *Nuns on the Run* and the grand opening of The St. Matthew Theater.

While Ishigo, Janet, Gabriella and I were busy buying the building on Robertson, Jesus sort of solved the mystery that had never actually become a real case. He read an article in the San Francisco Chronicle about a *miracle* at St. Andrew's church in Daly City. A statue of the Virgin Mary that had disappeared and was presumed stolen had been returned to the church. There was a typewritten note that said *We have sinned. Pray for our forgiveness.* Father Leonard said the congregation was grateful that the thieves had returned their beloved statue and did pray for their forgiveness.

I called Joya and faxed her the story. She met with Father Leonard at St. Andrew's and identified number sixteen, a statue of the Virgin Mary listed in Father Paul's account book.

The next story about the missing objects hit the media and went viral on the internet. Every stolen religious object in Father Paul's account book had been returned to churches from Oakland to San Jose in the same way. Mother Superior Joya, the former playwright James Linsky, was interviewed on CNN, *Good Morning America*, and all the local radio and TV stations.

Gabriella and I took everyone from Retrieval International to San Francisco for the opening of *Nuns on the Run*. It was a sensation. Joya, the Sisters of the

Lost Lambs, the cast, and the crew got a standing ovation that night and glowing reviews.

Maybe it was a miracle after all.

Kibe for Hire

Kibe was in the bathroom when a man walked into our reception room and pulled a gun on Gabriella and me. Kibe came out of the bathroom, saw the gun, grabbed a magic marker and pushed it into the gunman's back.

"Dude, you make one move and I'll shoot a bullet through your butt and it'll come out your dick. Drop it—now—and don't move until I tell you to."

Much to our surprise—even more surprised that some bozo had pulled a gun on us—he dropped it and put his hands up.

I looked down at the gun. *Oh, my God,* I thought, *someone sent a hit man to kill us.*

The shooter had a pipe in his hand and stuck it in his mouth. "Can I have my lighter back?"

He pointed to the gun on the floor.

"It's a freakin' lighter, Gabriella, not a gun," I said.

"I don't care what it is." Gabriella picked up the lighter. "You can't smoke in here, you *stupido pazzo*. Where the hell have you been since two thousand three?"

The bozo looked at Gabriella. "Hey, I speak Italian. I don't think you should call me a stupid fool. I came here to talk business. It's not my fault you thought my lighter was a gun."

Oh, my God, I thought. *Is this the theater of the absurd, or what? That pazzo had a damn lighter to shoot us with and Kibe had a damn magic marker to shoot him with. This better never get around."*

"Whoever you are, nobody's a client until we accept the case—and you don't have an appointment." Gabriella handed our would-be assassin his lighter.

"I'm Dimitri Volkoff, and I want her," he said, pointing to Kibe. "Little lady, you're exactly what I'm looking for."

Strange that he should call Kibe *little lady*. He was a squat five-foot-six inches, if that, and Kibe was more than six feet in her black leather platform boots.

Mr. Volkoff held out his hand to Kibe. She turned away, looked at us with a scowl, and headed for the door. "I need a triple espresso," she said, but I heard her mumble under her breath, k*iss my ass, Mr. Volkoff,* before she slammed the door.

"I recognize you two from the article in *L.A. Magazine*, the one about you being lesbo detectives who find things. That's where I saw her picture. She's magnificent! What's her name, Kathleen, Katherine? I want to hire her."

"Mr. Volkoff, first of all, we are not an employment agency. We don't rent out our operatives. They are assigned to specific cases. Second, unless you have something that's been stolen or is lost or is missing, you don't have a reason to be here." I saw Gabriella's neck start to pulsate. Not a good sign.

"Mr. Volkoff, you can't just barge in here and scare us half to death with your lighter," I interjected, placing my hand on Gabriella's arm. "We only work by appointment."

"I don't know why we can't meet right now. I'm here and you're here, but since you insist, I'll have my secretary make an appointment." He took a card out of an ornate gold case and handed it to me. *Fantasy Studios, Hollywood Boudoir Photography, Dimitri Volkoff, President.*

"I have something that's been, whatever, and I only want that Katharine, or Kathleen, to handle it." He stuck his pipe in his mouth, took his gun lighter out of his pocket, and left the office.

I handed the card to Gabriella. "I know where this is. It's a cheesy photography studio on Sunset Boulevard, not far from Tiki Ti's. The sign in the window says *Every woman becomes a star at Fantasy Studios.* Yuk!"

The next couple of weeks were insane. Kibe and Jesus moved from the guest house into one of the apartments in our building and they were supervising the office move. The villa had become Retrieval International. We had forgotten all about Dimitri Volkoff.

Gabriella was in the kitchen soaking ladyfingers in espresso. She was making tiramisu for our case conference meeting and potluck dinner. I stuck my finger in the sweet mascarpone and licked it quickly before Gabriella caught me.

Zinni stuck her head in the kitchen. "There's a woman on the phone who wants to make an appointment for Dimitri Volkoff of Fantasy Studios. Isn't he the guy who pulled a lighter on you? Do you want me to make an appointment?"

"Get her name, Zinni, and tell her I'll call her back."

Gabriella handed me the bowl and a spatula after she layered the custard on the ladyfingers. "We should just meet him so we get that *bastardo* off our backs."

Bailey came into the kitchen and wailed when she saw me stuffing the spatula into my mouth. "Hey, that was supposed to be for me."

Gabriella produced another bowl. "Get a spoon, Bailey. I saved one for you."

"Thanks. Listen, can Connor and I come to the case conference meeting? We may have a case."

"Sure," I said, as I wiped my mouth and put the bowl and spatula in the dishwasher.

"Gabriella, I don't think we want that scumbag in our office again and he's not anyone I want to meet at the Polo Lounge. What do you think about meeting him at Tiki Ti's? We can listen to his bullshit, have one Mai Tai One On, and be out the door in thirty minutes."

"Perfect! Now, both of you get out of the kitchen," she said.

Trista London had a throaty film noir voice. She identified herself as Dimitri Volkoff's assistant, not his secretary. I wondered if Trista London was her real name, probably not, and pictured her as a hundred-pound, thirty-something aspiring actress who had not yet given up her Hollywood dream.

I told Ms. London that Gabriella and I could meet Mr. Volkoff at Tiki Ti's on Thursday at four. I heard her nails clicking away on the keyboard. She said Mr. Volkoff was only free on Wednesday at five. I clicked my nails on the keyboard for effect, and the appointment was set.

Everyone came to the villa for the meeting and potluck. Janet and Ishigo started us off with *Bruchetta di Pomodori*. Zinni and Josh brought an antipasto salad. Kibe and Jesus surprised us with warm loaves of *Pane di Olive*, which they made from the Italian cookbook we had given them at Christmas. Gabriella served her homemade spinach ricotta ravioli with a special sauce that is to die for. My contribution was a couple of bottles of very nice Prosecco. Bailey and Connor put cans of soda in the cooler and we proceeded with the meeting.

Kibe and Jesus brought us up to date on two cases, an antique Aston Martin spirited out of a garage on a Beverly Hills estate, and a guest at The Beverly Hills Hotel whose wallet and Rolex were stolen by a hooker named Glow. Ishigo was on several assignments from the Los Angeles Art Theft Division and Janet was working undercover with Detective Emilia Gonzales on an industrial theft.

After dinner Bailey and Connor served the *tiramisu* and coffee. We finally got around to discussing what to do about Dimitri Volkoff.

"No, absolutely not!" Kibe levelled a challenging stare at Gabriella and me. "I am not having anything to do with that sleazebucket, Dimitri whatever his name is. He doesn't have a real case and you know it."

"Kibe, just hear us out, please. Volkoff's assistant said he has something missing, maybe stolen, and wants an appointment. Rae and I are meeting him at Tiki Ti's on Wednesday so we can get rid of him as fast as possible."

"Tiki Ti's, you two are meeting that man at Tiki Ti's, together?" Bailey asked. "Seriously?

"Yes, seriously, Bailey. Volkoff has his photography studio on Sunset Boulevard. Rae and I agreed that we don't want to meet him in the office or at the Polo Lounge. Don't worry, Kibe, nothing is going to come of this—nothing. Bailey, Connor, let's talk about your potential case."

"Wait a minute, I have something to say, okay?" Jesus said. "Whatever Kibe decides, I agree with her, okay? If she doesn't want to work a case, she should be respected for that." Jesus looked around the table for approval. "Don't you think?"

"Jesus, nothing is going to come of this with Dimitri Volkoff and, of course, any assignment can be discussed for any reason." I responded calmly. "Now, let's see what Bailey and Connor have come up with."

"One of our classmates, Kirsche Stanhope, has a missing dog. She's worried that it's been stolen and asked if we'll try to find it." Bailey passed around a copy of a large, white, standard poodle sitting next to a pretty young woman, presumably Kirsche.

"This is not a freebee," Connor interjected. "Kirsche is pretty upset that Lola has disappeared and said her mother will pay us to find her."

"Kibe, you're the animal retrieval expert. Would you be willing to interview Kirsche and her mother? If it's a viable case, you can assign Bailey and Connor to assist you."

"Works for me, Rae. Zinni, plug me in anywhere I have an extra couple of hours. Make it after school so Kirsche will be home, and Bailey and Connor can come with me."

"All right!" Bailey and Connor did a little dance and clinked their sodas.

Parking on Sunset Boulevard is impossible any time of the day or night. Gabriella called Uber and we were Volvo-ed to Tiki Ti's by one of the many comics who perform in clubs scattered in the City of Angels. She was actually funny, and we wished her well in her bid for stardom.

In how many cities would we get an Uber driver in a Volvo entertaining us all the way to a Tiki bar on wacky Sunset Boulevard to meet a sleazy boudoir fantasy photographer? Only in Los Angeles.

Most of the action at Tiki Ti's takes place around the bar. There are a few tables pushed up against the wall, and we were lucky to get one just a few minutes before Dimitri Volkoff showed up. To his credit, he was right on time.

"Hey, I love this place. It's not far from my studio. Do you gals like Mai Tais?" He sprinted away to the bar without waiting for an answer.

I hadn't been to Tiki Ti's in a long time. A bartender I didn't recognize looked at us, and he and the dickhead started laughing as the bartender hit the gong and everyone yelled, *It's Tiki Time.* Obviously, Dimitri Volkoff wasn't offended by our choice. Chalk one up for him.

"Hey, I want to apologize for last week," he said, putting our drinks carefully down in front of us. "I'm sorry we got off on the wrong foot, but it's pretty funny if you think about it." He went back to the bar for his drink and a bowl of pretzels.

Gabriella's voice was measured. "Mr. Volkoff, you asked for an appointment and we're here. Please tell us what is stolen, lost, or missing, and why you need our services."

"All business, are you? I like that in a professional. That's how I run my business. Here's why I need you. My dog is missing. I bought it for my niece, and I want that Kathleen to find it. That's what you do, find things that are missing, right? Well, I have something missing. Good Mai Tais, huh? They're special here. I love this place."

"Unfortunately, Ms. Jackson-Smith is not available to take your case. I can assign another operative to find your dog."

I waited for the response Gabriella and I had counted on. He'd say no, he only wanted Kibe. We'd say sorry, drain our Tiki cups, and be out the door in the thirty minutes we had allocated for the meeting.

It worked!

But two days later Dimitri Volkoff was back in our lives. Kibe called an emergency meeting.

"You won't believe this! Bailey, Connor, and I were sitting on the patio talking to Kirsche and Monica Stanhope, and in walked Dimitri Volkoff. I almost fell off my chair. He looked at me and said, 'Hey, your bosses said you weren't available to find Lola. I got the impression they didn't want me as a client. I'm glad they changed their minds.'"

I was stunned.

"Moms, Mr. Volkoff is actually Kirsche's uncle. She introduced us. It was so weird. You should have seen Kibe's face when Mr. Volkoff came in."

"It was too funny." Bailey shot Connor a warning look to shut up. "Well, not really funny, just uncomfortable. Mr. Volkoff grinned and thanked us in a sort of slimy way. Then he looked at Connor and me and said, 'nice meeting you, kids' and left."

"What's Monica Stanhope's relationship to Dimitri Volkoff?" Gabriella asked Kibe.

"She's his late wife's sister, so that makes her his sister-in-law. She told me she works full-time in the studio as a photographer. Volkoff trained her because he said women feel more comfortable having boudoir pictures taken by a woman. She and Kirsche live in his guest house. I didn't get the impression that she's happy with the arrangement."

"Kibe, will you take Ms. Stanhope as our client? It won't be Dimitri Volkoff."

"Sure, Rae, I'll take the case. I really want to help Kirsche and Monica."

"Good. Let's now consider Volkoff a suspect in the theft. Let me know if he becomes a nuisance."

"Kibe, don't you want some surveillance on Volkoff if he's your suspect?" Jesus asked. "I can work that in with the car theft case, no problem."

"Can I work with you, Jesus? It's time I learned surveillance techniques." Connor's eyes were begging Jesus to say *yes*.

"Sure, I can use you, but not on surveillance. Volkoff has already seen you. Kibe, is that all right with you?"

"Please say *yes,* Kibe. I want to help nail that...."

"Connor!"

"All right, Connor, you work with Jesus, but no skipping school, okay?"

"Yes, ma'am."

"Bailey, you try to get some more information about Volkoff from Kirsche. And both of you, stay away from Dimitri Volkoff. That's an order," Kibe said sternly. "I don't trust that weasel."

Gabriella and I needed to get away from Beverly Hills, the villa, the office, and Dimitri Volkoff. We agreed it was time to visit Margarite of the magic hands at Sappho Spa. It had been a while since we had been to Ojai.

I booked us in for a long weekend. We stayed in bed all day Friday, had a full day of head-to-toe massage orgy on Saturday, and took a slow drive back on the Pacific coast highway on Sunday.

We met Jesus and Kibe in our beautiful nearly finished offices on Monday morning. Jesus was anxious to give us his report.

"Since Kibe was spending the weekend with her mom and sisters, I decided to shadow Mr. Volkoff just to see what he does on the weekends."

"And, what did he do?" I asked.

"On Saturday morning, around ten, he drove to Crannock Kennels out in Alta Dena. I found the kennel online. The owner, Allen Crannock breeds poodles and boards dogs. Volkoff came out with a cage full of puppies that were not poodles. I followed him to the back entrances of pet stores in Glendale, Burbank, and Pasadena."

"Jesus, show Rae and Gabriella the pictures you took. It's illegal, you know, for pet stores to get animals from breeders in California. They can only sell rescue animals."

"So, Kibe, tell me what this has to do with finding Lola?" Gabriella asked. "You're not investigating Volkoff in connection with an illegal puppy mill. Your assignment is to find Kirsche's poodle."

"I'm investigating him as a suspect, Gabriella, to see if he snatched Lola. The surveillance led Jesus straight to the kennel. Puppy mill or not, it is possible that Mr. Sleazy may have stashed Lola at Crannock's kennel."

The next day there were two new clients in the reception room, one for Gabriella and one for Janet. Josh was waiting to take Zinni to lunch. The blinds had finally arrived for the conference room windows and the two installers were pushing boxes on wheeled carts through the reception area.

Kibe came into my office.

"How was your commute this morning?" I asked.

Kibe laughed. "A minor slowdown on the second-floor landing, but no complaints. Oh, Rae, Jesus and I are so happy with our new home. We can't thank you enough. I know Phil and Marina are going to love the villa."

"They should be here in a couple of months. That gives us plenty of time to renovate the guest house. So, what do you have?"

"I looked up Volkoff's businesses. It turns out that Volkoff is Allen Crannock's partner and half-owner of Crannock Kennels. You know, I wouldn't have made that connection without Jesus' weekend surveillance. Volkoff has owned Fantasy Studios in the same location in Hollywood for six years. The Better Business Bureau has had three minor complaints, nothing significant. Prior to his boudoir photography business, Volkoff owned a dry-cleaner, which he sold after his wife died."

"Kibe, just for shits and grins, go ahead and research puppy mills in California to see if Crannock's or Volkoff's names come up anywhere. This is on our time and our dime, not Ms. Stanhope's. Let's see if we can get Volkoff and Crannock shut down if they are operating a puppy mill."

It was family dinner and movie night. I picked up salad and pizza loaded with mushrooms, sausage, and pepperoni from Upper Crust, then stopped at Amorino for a large tub of spumoni gelato. We usually eat and watch the movie on our bed and Gabriella and Bailey were already sprawled out, waiting.

"You must be telepathic. I was hoping for pizza tonight. Did you get it from Upper Crust?" I nodded. "Perfect!" Gabriella's lips brushed mine.

"Yeah, perfect, Mom." Bailey pressed play on the remote and *Benji* popped up on the screen.

I brought in bowls of spumoni gelato and a plate of amaretti cookies when the movie ended. "Bailey, did you ask Kirsche how she got Lola and where she came from?"

"Kirsche said her Uncle Dimitri got Lola for her when they moved here after her aunt died, about five years ago. He told her mother he got the puppy from a friend who breeds poodles."

Gabriella piled some gelato on top of her cookie. "I have an idea. Let's ask Zinni and Josh to go to Crannock's and look for a poodle puppy to celebrate their engagement. Zinni wasn't in the office when Volkoff showed up so he won't make the connection if he happens to be there."

"That'll work, Gabriella. We need to get someone inside the kennel quickly to look around."

"Hey, Moms, let's watch another dog movie!" She hit the play button on *1001 Dalmatians*.

Kibe, Jesus, and Zinni were admiring the new blinds in the conference room when I got to the office. Gabriella came in with a multi-colored ceramic bowl filled with exquisite yellow chrysanthemums. She placed them on the new teak conference table.

The phone rang and Zinni hit the speaker. "Retrieval International."

"This is Dimitri Volkoff. I'd like to speak to Ms. Jackson-Smith."

"I'll see if she's available." Zinni pressed hold. "Kibe, do you want to take it?"

Kibe frowned and nodded.

"Mr. Volkoff, what can I do for you?"

"I'm calling to see if you have any leads on the dog. My niece is very distraught."

"We're doing everything we can to locate Lola, Mr. Volkoff."

"Mrs. Stanhope and I may have some new information. Can you come to the studio tomorrow afternoon at five?"

"I'll see you and Ms. Stanhope then." She hung up.

"Listen, Zinni, you and Josh have to get into Crannock's to look around before I meet with Volkoff and Monica. Can you back them up tomorrow afternoon, Jesus?" Kibe asked.

"I can be there. How about Josh?"

"I know he can make it."

Zinni called Crannock on her cell phone and made an appointment for one o'clock the next day.

Kibe instructed Zinni and Josh to go crazy about a puppy and tell Crannock they would come back with Zinni's mother that afternoon to buy the dog.

Zinni and Josh got back to the office around three. Kibe, Gabriella and I joined them in the conference room.

"Lola's there! I got a picture on my cell phone when I called to tell 'Mom' we had found our puppy." Zinni grinned. "Josh and I did our first undercover job. Oh, my God, it was such a high, Wasn't it, Josh?"

"Yeah, we saw Lola as we walked through the kennel. Zinni recognized her from the picture and she poked me in the ribs."

"What a beautiful dog, I told Crannock." Zinni's eyes were sparkling. "I hope ours grows up to be that beautiful, I told him. We want a puppy, but my mother may be interested in this one. Is he or she for sale?"

"Crannock told us he was boarding the dog for a friend who was on a cruise. Zinni was making such a fuss with Lola." Josh put his arm around Zinni's shoulder. "She was great! Maybe she'll be an actress as well as a rocker."

"I was talking to Lola in a baby voice, like, 'you are such an adorable doggie and what's your name?' Then Crannock said it was Lorna or Lola, or something like that."

Jesus came into the conference room.

"You helped find Lola, Jesus, thanks to your surveillance." Kibe hugged Jesus and gave him the type of kiss you wouldn't give a colleague. "Sayonara, Mr. Volkoff and good riddance."

"Not yet. We still have to get Lola out of Crannock's. What's your game plan, Kibe?" I asked.

"I'll have Zinni call Crannock and ask him if she and her mother can pick up the puppy at five. That's when I'm meeting Monica and Volkoff at the studio, so I'll know where he is. Then Jesus, you take Kirsche to Crannock's to get Lola. Josh, will you be backup this time?"

"How about you take Bailey and Connor with you, Jesus."

I looked at Gabriella. She smiled and nodded without hesitation. "Is that all right, Kibe? I think reuniting Kirsche and Lola belongs to Bailey and Connor."

"Absolutely! Jesus, bring the kids and Lola here. Text me when you're out of Crannock's so I can tell that shithead I solved the case."

Gabriella and I went to the Polo Lounge to wait for the call. Gabriella ordered a vodka martini and I ordered a flan and coffee. Kibe's call came at six. She said they were all at the office, including Monica.

I ordered dinner for nine people and a steak for Lola to be delivered from the Polo Lounge restaurant. Gabriella and I cabbed back to the office, relieved that Kirsche had gotten Lola back and the case was solved.

Not quite!

I noticed that Kibe and Monica were unusually quiet as everyone hugged one another and made a fuss about Lola. Kibe caught my eye.

"Rae, come help me with the coffee."

"What's going on?" I asked in the kitchen.

"Rae, can Kirsche and Lola stay with Bailey tonight? Monica is going to stay upstairs with us. I don't want them going home, not after getting Lola back from Crannock's, and after what happened at the studio today."

I had a feeling what Kibe and Monica had to tell us was bad news.

"Let's have Jesus drive Connor home. I don't want Jesus to meet with us. Just you, me, Gabriella, and Monica. Zinni and Josh can take Bailey, Kirsche, and Lola to the villa."

After everyone left, Kibe and Monica told us what had happened. "When I arrived at five o'clock Volkoff told me Monica was still out on an errand and would be back in a few minutes."

"That was a lie," interjected Monica. "Dimitri asked me to leave a little early to pick up some supplies. I didn't even know Kibe was coming to the studio."

"Volkoff offered me a drink and I refused. He told me he knew where Lola was and not to bother anymore, the case was through. Remember, by that time, I already knew that Zinni and Josh had found Lola. Then he offered to do boudoir pictures of me for free, as a bonus for taking the case. I said, 'Up yours, Mr. Volkoff', and headed for the door. That's when he grabbed me from behind and tried to force me to the bed in the boudoir setting. I broke out of his hold...."

"Just as I came back into the studio. I had forgotten my purse," Monica said.

"And I landed my boot as hard as I could right on the goal post," added Kibe.

"Dimitri yelped and passed out on the floor," Monica finished.

Kibe and Monica hi-fived, and collapsed, giggling, into one another's arms.

"He sexually assaulted you, Kibe?" Gabriella and I looked at one another in shock.

"He tried, but he was no match for me or my boots. Now I have Monica as a witness. I'm gonna press charges—and win."

Monica, Kirsche, and Lola stayed in our guest house for a few weeks. As soon as it was ready, they moved into the other apartment in our building, and Monica leased the retail space as a photography studio.

Thanks to Retrieval International, the puppy mill was closed down, a very prominent lawyer took Kibe's sexual assault case, and Dimitri Volkoff was also investigated and indicted for money laundering and tax evasion.

There's a moral to this story. Pretending your dog has been snatched is probably not the best way to try to seduce a woman when Kathleen Isobel Barbara Elaine Jackson-Smith is on the case.

Finding The Turquoise Sun

My cell phone rang. It was Ishigo.

"You'll never guess who called me."

"Ellen DeGeneres? Does she want Retrieval International to do surveillance on someone? I hope you told her we don't do that sort of thing."

"It was Charles V. Cooper," said Ishigo, totally ignoring my repartee.

"I'd rather work for Ellen."

"Do you know who Charles V. Cooper is?" Ishigo asked, with enough sarcasm in her voice to make me stop joking.

"No."

"The Museum of Forgotten Art?"

"No."

"Takashi Kubuto?"

"No."

"*The Turquoise Sun?*"

"No."

Ishigo hung up and I heard Gabriella's cell phone ring. I didn't hear the conversation from Gabriella's end because she went into the bathroom and closed the door. Ten minutes later my cell phone rang again. It was Gabriella calling from the bathroom.

"What did you say to upset Ishigo?"

"Nothing. She told me I'd never guess who called her. I said Ellen DeGeneres. I thought that was a pretty good guess. She asked me a whole bunch of questions and I answered her. Boy, Ishigo can get really touchy."

"She doesn't strike me as touchy, Rae." Gabriella hung up and came out of the bathroom.

"Gabriella, there are several definitions of touchy in English. One is to take offense on slight provocation. Jeez, I was just having a bit of fun."

"Ishigo wants to discuss a call she got from a wealthy art collector who knows her by reputation. He had a famous painting stolen from his private museum in Los Angeles a few months ago."

"You mean Charles V. Cooper?"

"Yes."

"The Museum of Forgotten Art?"

"Yes."

"Takashi Kubuto?"

"Yes."

"*The Turquoise Sun?*"

"Yes."

"I'd still rather it was Ellen DeGeneres."

Gabriella rolled her eyes. "Ishigo wants you to call her in the morning. Don't forget we're leaving for the airport in a few hours. Phil's plane gets in at six. I hope this rain doesn't get any worse."

Bailey came home and found me eating a peanut butter and strawberry jam sandwich in the kitchen. She got one for herself and we watched The Weather Channel with interest. The meteorologist pointed to lines with arrows on a digital screen of the Los Angeles area.

"A storm system over the Pacific has reached Southern California due to a massive trough of low pressure loaded with energy from the Gulf of Alaska."

"Mom, what does that mean?"

"It means the wind is blowing the rain around." Not wanting to scare Bailey with her father, stepmother, and baby brother in the air, I turned off the television."

Gabriella came into the kitchen. "I got a text from Phil. The had a good flight from Monte Carlo. The plane left New York right on time."

"Will they be able to land all right in this blowing rain?" Bailey looked worried. Gabriella put her arm around her.

"Sure. Marina and Phil, Jr. will be just fine. I don't know about your dad, Bailey. He's always been a barf-bag kind of guy."

By the time we left, not even the weight of the vehicle could stop it from lurching in the ever-strengthening torrents of rain and wind. Just as the chauffeur eased the limousine into a space meant for two cars, Gabriella's phone rang, and she hit speaker.

"Hello, everyone. We're here. Quite an exciting welcome home Los Angeles is giving us two ex-pats."

"Hi Dad. How's my brother?" Bailey asked. "I'm so glad you and Marina are home."

"Phil Jr. slept through the entire rock-and-roll landing. By the way, we were on the last plane allowed to land at LAX."

"Phil, we're right outside baggage in a white stretch limousine."

"That's great. Marina's gonna feel like a movie star."

The chauffeur drove us back to Beverly Hills in the unrelenting storm. Phil, Jr. slept in Bailey's arms. Marina looked exhausted and closed her eyes. Phil tried to keep up a conversation. He was gray and I wondered if there were any barf-bags in the limousine. Gabriella and I held hands and grew quiet to let Phil and Marina rest. This was not how we had planned to welcome them back to America. Only Bailey looked happy. She had what she wanted—her father sitting next to her and her baby brother in her arms.

Gabriella stayed home the next day to help Phil and Marina get settled in the guest house. Bailey's school was closed, and she took charge of Phil, Jr. The storm was not my only worry. I still had Ishigo to contend with, so I called Janet.

"Ishigo's mad at me. I was just having a bit of fun. She didn't have to get all nutted up and call Gabriella."

"She's not mad at you, Rae. She was just excited when she got a call from *the* Charles V. Cooper, puffed up, really, between you and me, and you didn't take her seriously."

"Gabriella wants me to call her and I don't want to get on her wrong side again. So, what does she want me to do?"

"She wants a meeting with you and Phil Reagan. She said she needs him right away on this case."

"He just got here last night from Monte Carlo in a torrential storm. Last time I saw him he was in the bathroom puking his brains out while Gabriella and Marina were discussing plantation shutters."

"Go ahead and call Ishigo. Just don't mention Ellen again."

The sun was shining by Tuesday morning. Gabriella took Marina to lunch and shopping at the Beverly Center. Phil and I went to the office to meet with Ishigo.

Zinni, Janet, Kibe, and Jesus welcomed Phil to the new office. He nervously arranged things on his desk while I answered a few phone calls. Ishigo brought a homemade apple coffee cake to celebrate Phil's arrival. I grabbed the coffee pot and followed her into the conference room.

"Welcome to Retrieval International, Phil. I'm glad you're here. You and I now are the art and cultural property theft team. I'm sorry I had to call you in so soon, but this request from Charles V. Cooper can't wait."

Phil's eyes widened. "Are you talking about the owner of The Museum of Forgotten Art? Is he your client?"

We're off to a good start, I thought. "So, you know Mr. Cooper?"

"I know of him and his museum, and I knew that *The Turquoise Sun* had been stolen."

Ishigo shot me a withering look. "Rae doesn't know who Takashi Kubuto is or the story behind The Turquoise Sun."

"Really, Rae? Everyone knows that story."

I smiled. "I don't." I casually sliced a second piece of coffee cake and poured another cup of coffee.

Phil's face had taken on a reverential look. I recalled the same look on my high school history teacher's face when she talked about Thomas Jefferson.

"The artist, Takashi Kubuto, is a Living National Treasure in Japan."

"What's a Living National Treasure?"

The look faded from Phil's face and I realized I shouldn't have asked a question so soon. I recalled the C I got in history because I couldn't keep my mouth shut.

"Just what it implies, Rae." Ishigo wasn't smiling. "In Japan it's an honor for special people with great talent under the Law for the Protection of Cultural Properties. Mr. Kubuto is so honored."

Phil continued. "Takashi Kubuto was a young art student in Taos, New Mexico in the nineteen-fifties. He painted six scenes of contemporary Pueblo Indian life. Apparently, he needed money to return home to Japan and sold the paintings to a gallery in Taos."

"It was the Minna Alpert Fine Art Gallery. Ms. Alpert died in two thousand five. Her niece put five of the paintings up for auction with Christies in two thousand six. They were purchased by the Miho Museum in Shiga and hung in the Takashi Kubuto room with other paintings by their Living National Treasure."

Ishigo gave Phil a smile and continued to ignore me, so I asked another question just to irritate her. I hadn't yet forgiven her for calling Gabriella. "What happened to the sixth painting?"

Phil and Ishigo looked at one another and both answered. "It disappeared."

I was relieved to see Gabriella burst into the office with Marina, Bailey, and Phil, Jr. in tow. I needed a break from Retrieval International's new art theft team—the former FBI art theft Pitbull and Europe's slipperiest illegal art dealer. Aren't we lucky? *Yes, we are,* I grudgingly admitted. I slipped the last piece of coffee cake onto my plate as everyone took turns holding Phil, Jr.

Ishigo handed Phil, Jr. back to Marina and eyed the empty plate. I knew she knew I took the last piece of coffee cake. She continued with the history lesson.

"Cooper converted his forty-room family home on Wilshire Boulevard into a museum, displaying only early or forgotten works by well-known and important artists. He was at an estate sale in Santa Barbara and recognized *The Turquoise Sun.* The owner had inherited it with his late uncle's property and had no interest in keeping the painting. With it was a sales slip for the two hundred dollars the uncle had paid Minna Alpert for the first sale of the six paintings. It hung in The Museum of Forgotten Art from the day Cooper bought it for fifteen hundred dollars until someone lifted it right off the wall and walked away with it."

"You're putting me on. Nobody just walks into a museum and walks out with a painting. What about guards...alarms...security?" I was thinking of Jay Cusak and the time he asked me to steal his painting off the wall of the Getty.

"Museums, especially small museums like The Museum of Forgotten Art, are not as heavily secure as the larger museums. Phil, remember the heist at the Isabella Stewart Gardner museum in Boston in nineteen ninety?"

I all but raised my hand to get their attention. "I remember that one."

Ishigo ignored me.

"It was pretty much the same thing only a bigger heist, thirteen works of art valued at five hundred million."

"Never recovered, right?" I asked, satisfied that I was finally in the loop.

Phil looked at me sideways. "It was two men posing as police officers. They walked in, subdued two college students working as night security, and walked out with thirteen paintings. There's still a ten million reward just for information leading to the recovery of the artwork, which includes a Rembrandt."

"Maybe...." I was going to say, maybe we could find those paintings and become truly famous, then thought better of it. Ishigo would go batshit again thinking I wasn't being serious. I shut my mouth.

"Maybe, what?

"Oh, nothing. So, how did the thieves get Cooper's painting?"

Ishigo's eyes were glowing and I could tell she was totally turned on by the heist. "It was so simple. The museum had two security guards at night from an agency. One guard worked an eight-hour shift from six p.m. to one a.m. The second guard worked from one in the morning until the day guards employed by the museum came on duty at eight. The guard on duty sat at a bank of monitors in a small, locked room. He controlled the alarms and the doors and made periodic rounds."

"How did the thieves get in?" I discreetly checked my watch. I wanted to go home with the family.

"It really was simple," Phil said, echoing Ishigo.

"There were two thieves, one the size of the second shift guard. They snatched him into a van. The thief put on the guard's uniform and presented himself as a temporary guard from the agency. Once inside and alone, he took *The Turquoise Sun* off the wall and just walked out. The thieves let the guard get dressed, put him out on the street, and drove away. Just like the Gardiner heist, it was that easy. The thieves have not been identified in the LAPD or the FBI files."

Ishigo and Phil started to talk FBI talk and I escaped to the kitchen. Gabriella cornered me and asked how Ishigo and Phil were getting along. "Great! When can I come home? I'd rather be changing Phil Jr.'s diapers."

"I just want to make sure they'll work well together. This is a big case for Ishigo. If she finds *The Turquoise Sun* with Phil's help, it will establish us as top-level private art theft investigators."

"Just for finding a small painting. How much can the guy's little school project be worth? This whole Ishigo drama with Cooper seems way over the top."

"*Cara mia*, Ishigo says the Miho Museum had offered Cooper a million dollars for the painting before the theft, which he didn't accept because the painting was not for sale."

A call from Cooper came on Wednesday morning. Zinni was in the bathroom so I answered the phone. "Retrieval International."

"Charles V. Cooper calling Ishigo Tanaka."

"Hold, please. I'll see if she's available."

Holy Shit. Charles V. Cooper. I'm glad I didn't reveal my name. I wouldn't have wanted *the* Charles V. Cooper to know I had answered the phone. Then I'd really be in deep doo doo with Ishigo.

I buzzed Ishigo. "Mr. Charles V. Cooper on two for you." I watched her and Phil jump up as if they had been hit with cattle prods. Ishigo took a deep breath and Phil stood at attention. Zinni came back to the reception desk. I headed for the kitchen and a donut. I had generously bought a dozen donuts to try to ease the tension between Ishigo and me. So far, she had eaten none. I was on number three and feeling no stress whatsoever.

Ishigo was waiting for me at Zinni's desk, Phil right behind her, eyeing my donut.

"Phil, there's more in the kitchen. Grab yourself a donut and a cup of coffee. Ishigo, I assume you have news. Let's go into the conference room." I felt wonderfully in charge. "You want a donut and coffee, Ishigo? Phil grab a tray and bring in a plate of donuts."

"Black for me, Phil, and I like glazed."

I smiled at Ishigo. "I'm assuming this is good news for us. You know, we're damn lucky to have you."

"We have an eleven o'clock meeting tomorrow with Mr. Cooper at the museum." Praise God, Ishigo smiled back.

Gabriella had her finger on the down button in the elevator when Ishigo came tearing out of the office looking wild.

"Charles Cooper just received a two hundred fifty-thousand-dollar ransom note for *The Turquoise Sun*."

Phil, Gabriella, and I followed Ishigo back into the office.

Now Phil's eyes were glowing as bright as Ishigo's. I once heard that only a small percentage of stolen art is ever recovered, maybe up to ten percent. I wondered how much of the remaining ninety percent Phil may have had his hands on in his long art-theft-middleman career. It's ironic that Phil's first case for Retrieval International with Ishigo turns out to be art napping. I have no doubt that his reformed-criminal skills will be a definite asset to Ishigo's legendary work on the art crime team.

The meeting took place in Charles V. Cooper's private wing, sixteen rooms that housed Mr. Cooper's eight-room apartment on the second floor and the museum's administrative offices on the first floor.

The administrative assistant, a twenty-something understated beauty with an attractive French accent, led us into an astonishingly beautiful conference room. Mr. Cooper sat at the table with a nice-looking Asian woman, around forty, I surmised. Was she Cooper's wife or, maybe, president of the museum board of directors? I was wrong on both guesses.

Mr. Cooper shook Ishigo's hand warmly and murmured how happy he was to meet her. He shook our hands, noting that I was Rae and Phil was Phil. He led Ishigo to a chair next to his and across from the woman, who stood to face us.

"May I present Haruko Saito. She is the acquisitions director at the Miho Museum in Shiga. She flew in for our meeting at my request. Ms. Saito has renewed the Miho's offer of one million dollars and has agreed to pay the two hundred and fifty thousand-dollar ransom if I get *The Turquoise Sun* back in reasonable condition. I have accepted her offer.

Haruko Saito and Ishigo bowed to one another at exactly the same level and for exactly the same length of time.

Ms. Saito said in perfect English. "Ms. Tanaka and I know one another, Mr. Cooper. It is a pleasure to see you again, Ms. Tanaka."

"Yes, I'm honored to, perhaps, work with you, Ms. Saito." Ishigo voice sounded strained.

Oh, oh, I thought. *These two know one another. They know one another very well.*

Phil and I bobbed our heads and shoulders downward. Ms. Saito bowed to each of us with a measured greeting. She shifted her gaze momentarily to Ishigo and we all sat down. The understated beauty appeared with bowls of coffee and perfect croissants that looked like they had just arrived from Paris.

"*Merci.*" Cooper smiled at her, his eyes lingering on her face. He was about fifty, a youthful-looking attractive man with salt-and pepper hair pulled back in a small ponytail. I understood how he could attract a beauty like her.

"This is my daughter, Giselle Dubois-Cooper. She graduated last year from the Sorbonne with a degree in art history. She wants to follow her old man into the biz and I'm starting her off as my assistant."

Giselle sat down next to me and placed a laptop on the table.

I may have called it wrong with Charles and Giselle, but I knew I was spot-on with Ishigo and Haruko. How I was going to squeeze the story out of Ishigo, I didn't know.

The Los Angeles Times interviewed Cooper the next day and ran a story about artnapping and a picture of *The Turquoise Sun.* Cooper said he was optimistic that *The Turquoise Sun* would be returned to him.

Gabriella and I met Ishigo and Phil at the Polo Lounge for a working lunch. Gabriella and I were totally fascinated by the former FBI art theft agent and the criminal art dealer. They were like one person—thinking alike, gesturing alike, laughing together, and hatching a negotiation plan at the same time.

"They're amateurs. Look at how they did it, hardly more than a snatch and grab. They can't do anything else except a ransom because they don't know how or where to unload it now that they have it." Ishigo looked like she was sucking on a lemon.

"By now they found out how difficult it is to traffic a well-known painting in the art world. Without a buyer, all they have is a piece of canvas in a frame." Phil's voice held just a touch of swagger, as though he knew he could have found a private buyer in his former life.

"So, do those fools really think they have the power in this deal because they have the painting?" Gabriella asked.

"Yes, but they're in for a rude awakening. First, we'll negotiate them down to less than half their demand, just to play with them a bit. When the exchange goes down, the FBI will grab them, and Charles V. Cooper will have his painting back."

"You're sure?" I asked.

"We're sure." Ishigo and Phil's voices blended together. We clinked our glasses in a triumphant toast and went back to the office.

At four o'clock, Ishigo took a call and bolted out of her office.

"Rae, Phil. We have to meet Mr. Cooper and Haruko at the museum."

"What happened?" I asked.

"I'm not quite sure. A police detective brought a woman into Cooper's office with a painting that may or may not be *The Turquoise Sun.* That's all I know. Hurry! He's going ballistic!" Ishigo ran for the elevator. "Come on."

The conference room was full of people, all talking at once. Ishigo and Phil dove right into the conversation with FBI art theft agents, LAPD detectives, an art authenticator that Haruko called in, and Charles V. Cooper, looking less put together than the last time I saw him. They all stood around a small, framed painting on the conference table.

Giselle sat next to a nervous-looking woman. I introduced myself and sat down next to her. Giselle poured coffee for me and a refill for the woman.

Everyone sat down. Cooper introduced Nella Wyburn and asked her to tell us how she acquired the painting.

"I work in housekeeping at the Bonaventure Hotel, been there for about two years. Before that I worked for an agency cleaning private homes, mostly in Beverly Hills. This job was in Brentwood. Their name was Stoltz and they were moving to New York. He was in television something, like a news show. I helped Mrs. Stoltz with the packing and the cleaning. At the end of the day, she asked me if I wanted anything from a pile of stuff she was donating to Goodwill. I took a stepstool, an iron—mine wasn't working too good—and a small picture in a frame. I didn't care for the picture, like a southwest theme with Indians, but I liked the frame. I put the picture in my closet. I forgot about it and never did change the picture.

"What made you think of your picture in the closet and why did you contact the police?" asked one of the detectives.

"I was cleaning a room at the Bonaventure and I saw the picture of *The Turquoise Sun* in the Times. I took the paper home and compared it to mine. It was the same picture. I thought to myself, that original must have been the one stolen from the museum and mine was just a copy. Then I noticed it was signed by Takashi Kubuto, the same artist. I figured it could have been a fraud copy, so I called the police station. They came to my house and brought me here with my painting."

"Ms. Wyburn, did you notice that your frame was different than the one in the paper?" Ishigo asked.

"No. I was only looking at the picture."

"The frame on Ms. Wyburn's picture is the same as the frames on the five paintings in the Miho. However, it could still be a copy. We won't know until it's tested and authenticated." Haruko's eyes met Ishigo's and lingered there.

"Has anyone contacted Mrs. Stoltz to find out when and how she got the picture?" Phil asked.

"That's in the works with the FBI in New York," Haruko said.

Nella Wyburn looked upset. "I don't think Mrs. Stoltz did anything wrong. She was a very nice woman. Don't you think Mrs. Stoltz would have kept the picture if she knew it was valuable? She was giving it to Goodwill."

Giselle came around with more coffee and I noticed that Ms. Wyburn didn't get her question answered.

Haruko gave Mrs. Wyburn a receipt. The authenticators wrapped the painting and took it away. The FBI agents and the LAPD detectives left in a group and we gave Mrs. Wyburn a ride home.

Technically, Ishigo and Phil did not find *The Turquoise Sun*. They were credited with helping the FBI capture the thieves and return the stolen painting to Charles V. Cooper, which turned out to be the copy.

The legal owner of *The Turquoise Sun*, Nella Wyburn, sold the painting to the Miho Museum for one million dollars, quit her job at the Bonaventure Hotel, and appeared on the cover of People Magazine.

Charles V. Cooper hung the copy back on the wall of The Museum of Forgotten Art along with the Los Angeles Times articles about artnapping and the recovery of the real painting that belonged to Nella Wyburn.

The artist who painted the copy of *The Turquoise Sun* and how the original ended up with the Stoltzes still remains a mystery. I have yet to work up enough courage to ask Ishigo about her and Haruko. All in good time.

Channeling Dorothy Azner

I woke up suddenly with the fear of a horrible nightmare misty in my brain. I had sold my family home in Studio City, finally able to accept that Gabriella and I were a committed couple, even though we weren't married. I remember leaving the house with a check and driving back to Beverly Hills. All of a sudden, I couldn't find my way back to the villa. I kept driving around looking for it. I stopped at a 7-Eleven and bought two peanut butter cups and stuffed them in my mouth, then I called Gabriella. She said if I loved her, I would find my own way home, it was no good if she helped me. I pleaded with her. She hung up. I called her back and told her I had a check from the sale of my house. She told me to look at the check. It was blank.

I was horrified by the nightmare and drenched in sweat. I took a shower in a guest bathroom so I wouldn't wake Gabriella. Then I sat in a chair in my old terrycloth robe staring at her. She was snoring, mouth open, nose tilted upward to the ceiling. I snore, too. I wondered if Gabriella ever gets afraid in the night and stares at me while I sleep. I must have fallen asleep in the chair, but I woke up in bed. Gabriella's leg was thrown across mine, and in the soft morning light all was right again in my world.

At eleven o'clock that morning, Gabriella was meeting with the contractor for a final walk-through of Betty's newly built cottage on the estate. She had sold her house and was moving to the villa in a few weeks. Marina and Phil had invited her to become a part-time nanny for Phil, Jr. and she happily accepted.

I was on my way to help Betty finish packing when the phone rang. I knew it was her. She always has last minute instructions for me.

"Hi, Betty, I'm in my car."

"Jim and Len, you know, the guys who bought my house, want to stop by to measure something or other. I invited them to lunch. I called Crazy Jane and Mackenzie. They're coming, too. I made plenty of chicken salad, coleslaw, and potato salad. Just stop at Nate 'n Al's for rolls and pickles and get eight bear claws—two extra for me for later. Okay?"

"I'm on my way."

James Kilmer, a freelance screenwriter, and Leonard Dean, a documentary filmmaker, are friends of Crazy Jane Guss and Mackenzie Macklin, the couple who rent my house. I don't know exactly what Crazy Jane does in the film industry, it's whatever an assistant art director does. Mackenzie has written a book about feminist film theory, something to do with male gazing in the movies.

Jim and Len bought Betty's house the first week it was on the market. A bidding war netted her thirty thousand more than the listing price. Crazy Jane and Mackenzie want to buy my house, but the best I can do right now is to give them first refusal. I panic every time I think about selling. It's my security blanket to know I still have my home if Gabriella dumps me. I'm sure Gabriella loves me and I'm just being an insecure dope, but I'm not ready to sell. Not yet.

Betty had the table set in the dining room. She had not yet packed her dishes with the small pink tea rose pattern or the sterling silverware Jim had given her on their first anniversary. I had eaten lunch on those dishes with Betty and my mother since I was five. There were yellow roses in the Murano glass vase we bought for Betty in Italy. It all sat on a cream-colored Irish linen tablecloth with matching monogrammed napkins, my gift to Betty and Jim for their anniversary, the last they had together.

Betty had on one of her old aprons strewn with purple cornflowers. It made me smile and brought tears to my eyes. She bustled around, not letting any of us do anything. After lunch, she served us her beloved coffee and perfectly warmed bear claws in the living room. I sat on the dusty rose damask sofa. Today my feet touch the floor. Back then I would swing my feet and sit quietly between my mother and Betty, listening to them gossip about the neighbor who ran away with the insurance man.

I helped clear as the others said their goodbyes.

"They're nice kids, Rae. If you ever finally decide to sell, I hope it will be to Crazy Jane and Mackenzie. I hope, too, that Jim and Len have a good long, happy marriage like James and I did. You know, it wasn't the extra money from the bidding war that made me sell to Jim and Len. It was because Jim's name is James. Silly, aren't I?"

At that I teared up again and sniffled. "C'mon, let's get to work, Betty, I need to meet Gabriella and Bailey at six."

Betty had boxes and bubble wrap littering the floor of her bedroom. These were things that she didn't trust the movers to pack. One was the collection of James' model airplanes and they filled her bed.

"Remember when that bitch, whatever her name was, stole these, then returned them in pieces? Bailey and the kids did such a good job of putting them back together. I can't wait to hang them in the cottage. I hope you don't mind, Rae, I'm leaving most of the collection to Bailey, but I'm giving James' favorites to you."

"Mind? I think it's wonderful. Hey, any more coffee in the pot?" And I ran to the kitchen before I blubbered for the third time that day.

Gabriella and I had a surprise for Betty. Although the cottage was five hundred square feet smaller than her house, we had the architect design the exact floor plan as her house in Studio City, with upgrades, of course.

On the day she moved in, Betty kissed us and slipped into the cottage. The movers delivered her furniture. The only other activity was the Von's market home delivery van. We did not see her for five days. Just to make sure we understood, there was a sign on the front door. *Not yet—and no peeking in the windows.* We didn't.

The next time we saw Betty she was sitting on Marina's patio rocking Phil, Jr. She and Marina were deep in conversation and clammed up when Gabriella and I walked in to say hello. The next week invitations arrived for a housewarming party at Danzig Cottage.

A flower van rolled up the driveway at nine o'clock in the morning on party day. At ten a wine shop made their delivery. Two hours before the party a white catering van parked in back of the cottage. Four people carried padded bags and boxes into the house. A truck arrived and two men in uniform set up a good-sized tent by the patio and pool. At four two young guys buzzed in and said they were the parking crew. Where did we want them to park cars? This was not the small family housewarming we thought she was having.

Right on, Betty, I thought.

At five o'clock, the parking guys got busy. Betty had invited everyone from Retrieval International and their families, including the junior investigators, lots of friends and neighbors from the San Fernando Valley, Detectives Emilia Sanchez and Joel Katz, and their families, Kirsche and Monica Stanhope with Lola, Jim and Len, and Crazy Jane and Mackenzie.

Gabriella and I walked into the cottage for the first time since Betty had moved in. Bailey was carrying Phil, Jr. right behind us. Phil and Marina were already there helping with the party. Betty had everything in place, exactly as it had been in Studio City all the years I was growing up. James' model airplanes floated down from the ceilings in every room in the cottage.

"Welcome home, Rae," Betty said softly with outstretched arms. I fell into them, then ran to the bathroom and closed the door.

I found Gabriella on the patio with Jim, Len, Crazy Jane, and Mackenzie.

"Do you think the rumor is true?" Gabriella asked, as she made room for me at the table. "Rae, have you heard of the late movie director, Dorothy Azner, from the old thirties and forties movies?"

A server stopped in front of me and I grabbed some appetizers off the tray. "Sure, I know Dorothy Azner. She directed a movie I saw on Turner Classic Movies. It was *Dance, Girl, Dance* with Lucille Ball. What's this about a rumor?"

"It's one that's been floating around Hollywood for more than sixty years. The rumor is that Dorothy Azner, her lover, Marion Morgan, and their lesbian friends, including well-known movie stars deep in the closet, made a secret studio-quality feature film that has never seen the light of day. Supposedly, everyone associated with the film, from the leading lady to the grip, was a lesbian.

Jim draped his arm on Len's shoulder. "My husband here is Dorothy Azner's cousin. Len's father was her next of kin and inherited her estate. That's how we started talking about the rumor."

I saw that Len was used to telling this story. He was narrator-voice perfect.

"Dorothy and Marion met in nineteen twenty-one while working on the same silent film. Dorothy was an editor and Marion was a dancer. They were a couple for forty years. Despite the studios' intense suppression of any hint of homosexuality, Dorothy, who became a major studio director, and Marion, who was a choreographer for musicals, were never in the closet. After Marion died in nineteen seventy-one, Dorothy moved to La Quinta and lived there until her death in nineteen seventy-nine.

"Len owns the house now," Jim added. "It's like a small museum of gay and lesbian Hollywood history, but we never found Dorothy's film in the house."

"Can it have survived all these years without disintegrating? I'd sure love to know who the cast and crew were. Do you think anyone knows?" Crazy Jane asked.

"We will—*if* the movie was really made, and *if* a print has miraculously survived, and *if* we're lucky enough to find it. It's a lot of *ifs* but I think we should try to find it."

Mackenzie looked at Gabriella and me. "Look, we've got the two top retrieval experts in Los Angeles sitting right here at this table. What do you think?"

Gabriella looked at me and smiled. "This could be fun, and a real coup for Retrieval International."

"We're in." I raised my glass and they all raised theirs.

"Let's keep this to ourselves and start quietly poking around." Len raised his glass again and I drained mine.

At nine o'clock the caterers cleaned up and left, the tent was dismantled, and the parking guys got their check. Phil and Marina carried a sleeping Phil, Jr. home. Bailey, Kirsche, and the junior investigators said goodbye and went to the house to watch a movie. Gabriella and I tucked a very tired, very happy Betty into bed and went home to make popcorn.

The next week Gabriella and I drove north to Placerville, right in the heart of California gold rush country. Friends of ours had transformed a mansion built on top of a closed gold-mine into a lesbian-only bed and breakfast. Gabriella said to forget panning for gold. She was ready for a week of *lascivia*—lust and wonton-ness—Italian-style. We did both in the Gertrude Stein suite right above the sealed-up entrance of the gold-mine.

When we got home there was a message from Jim and Len, an invitation to a barbeque at their house with Crazy Jane and Mackenzie. Were we ready to officially start our search for Dorothy's film?

Walking into Jim's and Len's back yard is like walking onto the set of *Grill World*. We didn't know that among his many talents, Len was a certified grill master. He was turning the grill marks on chunks of raw meat into art before our very eyes. It's a good thing I'm not a vegetarian. I would have passed out right on the spot!

After a glass of the fine wine that Gabriella and I brought from our wine cellar to pair with the Tuscan Florentine steaks, Len started the discussion with a startling announcement.

"I think we should make a documentary about our search for Dorothy's film. Even if we don't find it in the end, the unfolding story will be interesting. I've got it all figured out. Jim can write the script. I'll direct and hire the crew. Crazy Jane, I'll leave production development to you. Mackenzie, how about doing the research and you and Crazy Jane conduct interviews. Rae and Gabriella, we need you and the Retrieval International resources to find out if Dorothy's lesbian masterpiece really exists. What do you think?"

I grabbed a rack of baby back ribs drenched in Texas-style barbeque sauce. "I say—one, two, three...." We all shouted a resounding *Yes!*

The next day Gabriella and I had coffee with Betty. She poured cups of her favorite coffee from her old coffee maker into blue Danzig cottage mugs with an icon of one of James' model planes on it. I slipped an apple fritter onto a matching plate.

"Betty, we're going to La Quinta for a working weekend on the documentary with Jim, Len, Crazy Jane, and Mackenzie. Bailey is coming with us to stay with some tennis pals in Indian Wells. Phil, Marina, and the *bambino* have gone to San Diego. Will you take care of things here, you know, be in charge of the villa while we're away?"

Betty's eyes danced with joy. "Yes, of course, yes!" She held out the plate of donuts to Gabriella.

Good sport that she is, Gabriella extracted the smallest donut from the plate and took a sip of coffee without flinching. "Thank you, Betty, *deliziosa,*"

Nowhere in sight was our housewarming gift, the expensive grind-and-brew twelve-cup coffeemaker, the assortment of coffee beans, and the high-end grinder. This is one battle Gabriella is not going to win.

"You can top me off, Betty, and I just think I'll have another apple fritter."

Betty smiled at me. "Just like in the old days, huh, Rae?"

Three weeks flew by without seeing much of the documentary team. Jim distributed copies of the script, without the ending, of course. Crazy Jane and Mackenzie studied Dorothy's and Marion's extensive collection of letters, photographs, papers, and studio publicity memorabilia. Len's cinematographer, Gary, was already filming Mackenzie conducting interviews for background material. Len was everywhere doing everything a director does that the rest of us don't understand because we're not directors.

We got a key from Len and made another trip to La Quinta. This time, unscripted, off-camera, and alone, we took pictures and made notes. The sum total of our investigation to date consisted of two trips to Dorothy's house and a cursory review of the photographs and historical data that yielded no secrets.

Len wanted the team to see what had been filmed to date. Jim's office and the room Betty called the den had been turned into one good-sized media room. There we sat, Gabriella, Crazy Jane, Mackenzie and me, in front of a sixty-inch flat screen, in super soft, burgundy leather entertainment chairs, with plenty of space for drinks and snacks. Jim was busy getting martinis and other goodies. I felt like a Hollywood mogul ready to watch the daily rushes and I wanted to bellow out—where the hell is my martini, Jim boy, for Christ's sake? And bring me a Havana cigar.

Gabriella sank down deep in the leather and curled up. "It's just like being in the womb except it comes with movies." Her hand stretched up and Jim put a martini in it. "And martinis."

"Oh, my God!" I took a big gulp of my martini as the opening scenes at the house popped up on the screen. "Gabriella, look, it's us in our Retrieval International shirts. I felt so foolish in front of the camera, but we look so professional on the screen, like the guys in *Ghostbusters*. Wow!"

In this scene Gabriella and I had been searching the house. Ordinarily, it would take us a couple of hours to do an initial search of a house this size. It took six hours to reshoot scenes under Len's direction. At the end of the day we hadn't found the film, and Gabriella and I had come home and fallen into bed. This movie-making business was quite exhausting.

"Len, Mackenzie has a really great idea. Tell them, Mac." Crazy Jane gave Mackenzie a supportive smile.

"I think my idea will add more drama to the documentary. My friend, Sylvie Tomlik, is Madam Shawna, you know, the medium."

"Madam Shawna, the medium to the stars is your friend?" Len was all but jumping out of his seat.

"Yeah, Sylvie and I went to college together in Little Rock. I thought it might add visual depth to the film to have her do a séance with us, especially since we haven't found the film yet."

I looked at Gabriella. The artery on her neck was pulsating.

"A séance! What does a séance have to do with our search for the film? I don't go in for that hocus pocus *merda*, talking to the dead. We do serious work, right, Rae?" she said.

"Don't you think doing a séance to channel Dorothy Azner would be great fun? And it will add so much to the film. Sylvie is just as serious about her work as you are, Gabriella." Mackenzie held Gabriella's stare.

I looked around for a plate of something to shove in my mouth. A double chocolate fudge brownie did just fine. I finally swallowed and said to no one in particular. "It's true we haven't found any substantial clues yet. If it's unorthodox methods you want for the documentary, let's take a vote."

Four hands shot up and I tentatively raised mine without looking at Gabriella and took another brownie.

"That's a great idea, just what we need. Jim, add a séance to the script. Mackenzie, call Madam Shawna and get us booked." Len was all smiles. "Channeling Dorothy Azner it is!"

On the ride home Gabriella and I chatted about the successful closure of two cases before she broached the subject.

"Do you really want to go to a séance. That stuff is so stupid and fake."

"I've never been to one and I'm curious. What harm can it do?" I said.

"The way the documentary is going, we could end up an industry laughingstock. That might hurt Retrieval International."

"Gabriella, lighten up and let's have some fun. Let's just not wear our Retrieval International shirts to the séance."

"Don't you think anyone will notice them when we searched the house? Don't you think anyone will see Len introducing us, and our names in the credits?"

"It will be okay, *cara mia*. Trust me." I said a silent prayer to the make-everything-work-out-right goddess.

The séance took place at Madam Shawna's incredible home high up in the Hollywood Hills. I didn't know anyone getting live people in touch with dead people could make so much money.

The only place I had ever seen séances was on television. The rooms were always eerie in a tacky sort of way. The weird lighting always made people's skin look strangely green, and the medium always tended to voluminous caftans, big curly hair, and earrings that rested on her shoulders.

An Asian woman in a tailored white suit greeted us at the door before we knocked. She led us into a beautifully decorated room, served a blend of tea I had never tasted, and some type of too-healthy rice crackers.

Mackenzie spoke in a low voice. "Mika and Sylvie have been together for about twenty-three years and got married last year."

Twenty minutes later, Mika came back and led us into a room with nothing in it but a large teak table, twelve chairs, and crystal glasses of water. Nothing tacky or eerie about this place. The walls were a soft gray pearl. The crystal sconces on the walls created a non-intrusive glow in the room, and our skin still looked skin color—

that is, until someone set up some extra lights. Now we all looked ghastly green. Gary started filming.

Madam Shawna slipped into the room unheard from an unseen door. She looked like a taller, younger version of Bette Midler. I noticed Gabriella eyeing her black dress. She'll know the designer of that totally simple, expensive garment. No caftan for Madam Shawna. Her blond hair was pulled back in a smooth bun and she had pearl and diamond studs in her ears. I saw Gabriella visibly relax.

There was no conversation, no holding hands, or anything that looked like it would levitate off the table.

All of a sudden, Madam Shawna threw her head back with such force that I jumped and spilled my glass of water onto the teak table. Madam Shawna's head came forward and she stared straight ahead.

Mika came in with a cloth and wiped up the spilled water. Madam Shawna didn't move a muscle. How did Mika know I had knocked over a glass?

Mika slipped out as quietly as she had appeared. Madam Shawna shuddered and her head snapped back again. Her eyes closed and when they opened, she spoke in a voice not her own.

"Len, hold my hand."

Len was sitting next to Madam Shawna. He took her hand. He was trembling.

"Len, you are my blood through your father. I will trust you with my secret, the most important film I ever made. Don't be afraid. Everyone must leave the room except you and Madame Shawna."

There was the elusive Mika again. She led us back to the reception room and served more tea.

Gabriella grabbed my hand and we found the powder room. "This is total bullshit, Rae. I think Jim and Len know where the film is and have deliberately kept it hidden."

"We're being played, is that what you mean, Gabriella? Why?"

"Jim and Len can have us *find* Dorothy's film and present it, and their documentary, with lots of publicity. It's a brilliant idea."

"Do you think Crazy Jane and Mackenzie are in on it?"

"I'll bet my last dollar that Jim, Len, Crazy Jane, and Mackenzie set this up after we met them at Betty's housewarming."

We went back to the reception room. I looked at Crazy Jane and Mackenzie. They sat silent, ashen faced, holding hands. Jim looked perfectly relaxed sipping his tea. He caught me staring at him and smiled.

Len came out of the séance room. "I talked to Cousin Dorothy." He unceremoniously fainted, the camera still rolling right in front of him.

I asked Gabriella if she wanted to go for a martini and she said maybe two or three. We left the team and called a driver to take us to the Polo Lounge.

"What about Madam Shawna," I asked. "Do you think she's in on the game?"

"Oh, yes, I think Sylvie will do anything for her old college lover." Gabriella summoned the waiter and ordered two lemon-drop martinis and a seafood platter.

"Should we tell them we know what's going on?"

I caught the server's sleeve as she turned to leave. "One order of bread pudding topped with that sinful white chocolate sauce."

Gabriella's smile was *diabolica*. "Hell no, I suggest we let the executive producers make that decision—hey, that's us! I think we should let Dorothy tell Retrieval International exactly where to find her film."

"*Si!*" I was feeling pretty *diabolica* myself. "Let's write that scene ourselves as a big—what's the Italian words for big surprise?"

"*Sopresa grande.*"

"While the cameras are rolling?"

Gabriella and I did a double smooch and high-fived.

"You bet your *dolce culo.*"

"What's a *dolce culo?*" I asked with a grin.

"Your very delectable, sweet ass."

Our dining room table was completely covered with the pictures we had borrowed from Crazy Jane and Mackenzie. They had been selecting images to use as a background for their interviews. I told them we had taken pictures of every room in the La Quinta house and wanted to match as many as we could to the rooms in the old pictures to look for changes.

The first thing we did was remove all the pictures that were not taken in the house. We lined up the remaining pictures starting at the front door and ending with the door that led to the garage. Then we put every picture we took of that space under the original.

"Gabriella, look at the ceiling in the media room." I placed the old picture of Dorothy's screening room and the picture we had taken side-by-side. "Doesn't this ceiling with the newer sound-arresting tiles look lower than the original ceiling in the screening room?"

"Look at this next picture of the old screening room. That ceiling looks even lower than the original but higher than the present one."

I picked up the picture and looked at it closely. "I think you're right, Gabriella."

"Here's what I think, Rae. Len found the film when he inherited the house. Perhaps he and Jim were already planning to make a documentary about the rumored film before they met us."

"Or they could have been waiting to book the theatre at The Academy Museum of Motion Picture Arts and Sciences when it opens. Finding Dorothy's film is going to create a hellava lot of buzz in Hollywood. The documentary could even be nominated for an Oscar if it's good enough.

"Then we all came together by coincidence, Len and Jim, Crazy Jane and Mackenzie, and you and me, and with us on the team they concocted the séance to have us find the film in Dorothy's house."

"Do you think they'll privately tell us where to find the film if we don't find it on our own?"

"We'll find it on our own. Where's Jo?"

Jo is our radar scanner, our number one tool in the retrieval business. It uses radar technology to detect exactly what's behind walls, above ceilings, or under floors.

I called Len and told him Gabriella and I were heading down to La Quinta to check out a couple of new clues that looked promising.

"Do you want Gary to go along for some footage?"

"No, I'll call you if we find anything. If we do, you and Gary can zip down."

"Dorothy told me it's somewhere in the house. I believe her. I'll take the walls down to the studs if I have to."

Gabriella rolled her eyes. "You may have to, Len, if you have that much faith in Madame Shawna. Rae and I are not so sure the film is not just another urban legend. We've got to get back to other cases soon."

"Len, if Dorothy told you it's in the house, in heaven's name, why didn't she tell you where?" I made a silent *duh* sound.

"She faded away and Madame Shawna said she couldn't connect with her again. C'mon, guys, we're so close. I know if it's there you'll find it. Final shoot this weekend. We'll wrap it up with or without the film. Okay?"

Len was good. An actor at heart, he had pulled off that fainting scene at Madame Shawna's and had managed to stay in character ever since.

Gabriella and I went to the office to get Jo, then we hit the I-10 to La Quinta before the morning commute got crazy.

"*Cara mia,* did I ever tell you what I did on the I-10 shortly after I moved to Los Angeles?"

"Does it involve Karma Sutra positions with a hot yoga instructor?"

"No, I already told you all those stories."

"Okay, what did you do on the I-10 shortly after you moved to Los Angeles?"

"I bought myself a red Lamborghini, drove to the Pacific Ocean in Santa Monica, got on the I-10 and drove it east all the way to Jacksonville and the Atlantic Ocean."

"You drove from the Pacific Ocean to the Atlantic Ocean on the I-10, three thousand miles, in a red Lamborghini?"

"Yes, actually that's where I met that double-jointed gymnastics teacher. I told you about her, didn't I?"

"You did, Gabriella, you just forgot to mention that it was after you drove three thousand miles across the country in a red Lamborghini."

"And she, her name was Lorena, fit into that little car just right." Gabriella gave me a sweet smile and turned into the driveway. I think I could live with Gabriella for a hundred years and I'd never hear her final story.

Jo is so amazing! She can detect what's behind drywall, wood, concrete, tile and, even marble. This was the best seventy bucks Retrieval International ever spent. It's our secret, secret weapon.

Gabriella and I have a personal ritual. Only one of us will retrieve an object that is small enough to be removed by one person. It was Gabriella's turn to toss our lucky Kennedy half-dollar. I won.

"We were right, Rae. The ceiling has been dropped, twice. It's a good place for Jim and Len to hide the reel, and not too difficult for us to find. Let's see if it's up there between the ceiling and the acoustical tiles."

Jo did her stuff and we did not have to remove even one tile to find what we were looking for.

I got on the phone with Len and told him we had no luck finding the film. We were packing it in and heading to the hotel for the night.

"Len, we'll be back at the house tomorrow morning. We still have a few more places to check out before the final shoot this weekend. We have a feeling about the media room."

"Oh, my God," Len shrieked. I held the phone away from my ear. "I had a dream last night. Dorothy came to me and whispered something about the media room ceiling. I didn't quite hear where. I think you're onto something. You and Gabriella are brilliant."

Gabriella exaggerated a huge belly laugh and stuck out her tongue to the phone. She's such a child sometimes. Then she called Bailey who put her in touch with Hadley's father, a building contractor.

We were all there on Friday morning—the crew, Len and Jim, Crazy Jane and Mackenzie, Madame Shawna and Mika, and, of course, the two dupes from Retrieval International—Rae and Gabriella.

Len wasn't taking any chances that Gabriella and I wouldn't find where he and Jim had planted the film. Jim had written a dramatic reveal in the script that included a last-minute appearance by Dorothy through Madame Shawna, just in case.

"Action," Len yelled, then he and Jim jumped into the scene and sat next to Madame Shawna under an eerie glow. The camera panned the room, stopped briefly at Gabriella and me walking around the room checking the walls and ceiling against pictures. The camera hurried back to the table in time to see Sylvie go into a trance and whisper, "Ceiling." Right on cue she came out of the trance and slumped with fatigue.

Len gave a faint cry. "I knew it!" He looked at me. "You and Gabriella figured it out with the old pictures of the ceiling. There's a gap between it and the acoustical tiles. Dorothy hid her film there after she had the tiles installed. I think she wanted the reel to be found one day. She told Madame Shawna where it is. It's got to be there!"

The rest of the morning Gary filmed the crew up on ladders taking down sections of acoustical tile. He caught the tense looks on our greenish faces, and close-ups of Len and Jim's tightly clasped hands.

I felt Gabriella's hand press into my back. Half the tiles had been removed. Len and Jim knew they were close, and I could smell their anticipation. This was the moment we were waiting for, right out of our own devious playbook.

The moment came—and went. The rest of the tiles came down. The camera caught the shot of the completely exposed ceiling and every one of us silently staring up at it. No one knew what to do next. We all turned to Len, waiting for direction.

Gabriella sat down at the table. All of a sudden, her head snapped back just like Madame Shawna's had, and the camera whipped around as she cried out. "*Dorotea, si, il sento,* I hear you, *Dorotea.*"

The camera followed Gabriella as she sleepwalked around the room, all of us trailing behind her. She stopped at a closet and pointed up. The ceiling had the same dropped acoustical tiles. I climbed the ladder and poked a few tiles off and reached around until I felt the old metal box.

"It's here! I feel something." I was emoting in ways I never dreamed I could. I handed it down to Len. Jim caught it before it tumbled to the ground. This time it was Madame Shawna who fainted dead-away.

In the final scene, following Jim's script, Len laid the metal box on the table. He clasped his hands in the prayer position and looked up toward heaven, then straight into the camera.

"We started this project because we believed a sixty-year old rumor that refused to die, that my cousin, Dorothy Azner made an all-lesbian feature film, hidden somewhere all these years. We don't know what's in this box. You'll be seeing it with us. Right now."

Len bowed his head and his lips moved in a silent prayer. Mackenzie crossed herself and caught Crazy Jane's hand. Jim stood a little behind Len, the ever-supportive husband. Sylvie sat, still shaken.

'I'm giving the honor of opening the can to those two master magicians from Retrieval International, Rae Talley and Gabriella Sabatino."

Len's eyes cut to ours and he grinned.

"Ladies."

Six months later the restored film was ready to be viewed. Gabriella dimmed the lights. Len's voice floated through the darkness. "Ladies and Gentlemen, I give you Dorothy Asner's greatest film—*My Desire*—starring Greta Garbo and Marlene Dietrich."

A Horse Named Revenge

I sank down in the hot tub with a long sigh, letting the bubbles whip around my neck, wondering why Gabriella and I stayed in this crazy business. It had been a long, hard, unproductive week and my life felt totally out of whack.

I was thinking about our most difficult client, Gannon Paige, referred to us by our friend, Harry Boyce. They were horse-owner buddies, and Harry thought he was doing us a favor by bragging about our ability to find *anything* that had been lost, hidden, or stolen.

Gannon Paige flew Gabriella and me to Lexington, Kentucky in his private Cessna Citation X, had us picked up in his white Mercedes, and met us in the bar at The Lexington Cavendish Hotel, which he owned.

Nothing had diminished the hatred in Gannon's voice for his soon-to-be ex-wife, Phoebe Lorca-Paige.

What blasted into our eardrums was his inability, despite running through several local private investigators, to find his beloved five-million-dollar, three-year old thoroughbred, ironically named Revenge.

Phoebe, who was half-owner of the horse, had spirited it out of their stable and hidden it somewhere—just for spite.

"I own this hotel," he had bellowed, gesturing around the room. "I had your bags moved to my penthouse suite. I know you're used to good living. I had you checked out after Harry told me about his wife's jewelry fiasco."

After the length of time it took Gannon to gulp down two scotches, he had bellowed once again. "Look, I gotta get to a meeting. Here's the deal. You two come to Lexington. I'll cover expenses and your fee for up to thirty days. Stay here in my penthouse. If you find Revenge, I'll give you one percent of his worth—that's fifty thousand bucks, ladies."

I guess Gannon thought we couldn't compute one percent of five million dollars that fast.

"What do you say?" he'd asked.

Gabriella and I looked at each other. "It's a deal, Mr. Paige," I said, and we shook hands.

We spent a couple of days poking around the edges of BrightStar Farm, Gannon's and the absent Phoebe's twelve hundred acre working horse farm and thoroughbred racing stable. It turned out that Ms. Lorca-Paige is a highly respected trainer at the stable and Mr. Paige wouldn't know one of his horses if it fell on him—except for Revenge, his Kentucky Derby hopeful, and the most expensive horse in the stable.

It was January, cold and rainy in Kentucky, and I was more than ready to curl up again in the incredibly soft leather seat on the Cessna. All the way home I kept wondering if fifty thousand dollars was worth the trouble of being in the middle of that wealthy couple's nasty game. Gabriella and I were going back to Lexington to start the case in a week, so I guess I had answered my own question.

Then, something happened that entirely changed the direction of the Paige case. I was rinsing the shampoo out of my hair in the shower when my cell phone rang. One moment I was reaching for a towel, and the next moment I was flat on the floor in the type of pain I imagined I'd feel if I had a baby's head pushing through what seems like an impossibly small opening for it. I crawled to my phone and called 911.

I was sitting in the Cedar Sinai hospital emergency ward waiting for the results of the x-ray of my left foot when Gabriella and Bailey rushed right in behind Dr. Susan Lu.

"You have what's known as an acute Lisfranc fracture of your second metatarsal. This particular fracture usually requires surgery."

Dr. Lu recommended I make an appointment with Dr. Cassandra Hernandez, an orthopedic surgeon specializing in leg and foot injuries.

"You'll be in a soft splint until the swelling goes down. Meanwhile no weight whatsoever on your left foot. Any questions?" Dr. Lu looked at her watch.

I went for the most important question. "How am I supposed to walk?"

The nurse brought in crutches. I moaned, but Dr. Lu was already out the door.

Gabriella was quiet on the drive home. She turned and looked at me. "Rae, Gannon Paige called me this morning. Phoebe has gone missing, like in completely disappeared. Nobody seems to know where she is. He wants us to find her, too. Harry told him how good we are at finding missing persons."

Good at finding missing persons, I thought. The only person we ever found was Harry Boyce when he left Lauren after an argument, and Gabriella already had his telephone number in Santa Barbara. I laid my head back against the headrest and closed my eyes. I had had enough for one day.

Three days later, Gabriella wheeled me into the office of Dr. Cassandra Hernandez. The usual framed medical degree hung on the wall of the treatment room, hers from Stanford University School of Medicine. Certificates from various hospitals attested to her competence to practice orthopedic surgery. The rest of the wall was tastefully decorated with pictures of her and her celebrity Hollywood and sports patients. Tennis star, Marina Povatalona, had written, *With all my love and gratitude, Marina.* Wow! I'll have to tell Bailey that the hands that once held Martina Povatalona's legs were now fondling my left foot.

Dr. Hernandez wore black skinny jeans, a magenta tank top, and a softly draped silk version of a medical jacket. Her name was embroidered above her quite perky left breast. One of the pictures on the wall was that of young Cassandra in a bathing suit as Miss Brazil, a runner-up in the nineteen ninety-five Miss Universe contest. Gabriella stared at the picture. I could hear her silent *wow* across the room!

The next time I saw Dr. Hernandez she had good news and I was still on *wow*.

"I reviewed your CT scan and you do not need surgery. The ligaments, which usually separate from the bone in this type of fracture, are still intact. You need to stay in a non-weight bearing cast for six weeks, then you can switch to a walk boot. We should have you right back on your two feet in a couple of months."

"This was not my idea of good news. "That's great, Dr. Hernandez! Isn't that great, Gabriella?"

Gabriella didn't answer. I think she was still on *wow!*

"I'm going to Lexington with you next week to work on the Paige case," I said in a tight voice once we were in the elevator.

"No, you're not."

"You can't tell me what to do. You're not the boss of me."

"Oh, really? You can't even get yourself out of this elevator."

I shot Gabriella one of my most effective fuck-you looks, as a caregiver smiled at her and wheeled a woman wearing a sexy grandma tee shirt into the elevator.

Since Gabriella and I had met with the arrogant Gannon on his home turf, I had temporarily lost my ability to walk, and he had received a threatening letter from the soon-to-be ex-wife who had hidden Revenge. It was right to the point.

G. Get rid of those two private investigators from L.A. or you'll never see Revenge again—or me. P.

Metaphorically speaking, we were both up shit's creek without a paddle.

Now Gabriella and I were meeting Gannon again, this time on our home turf. I wheeled myself into the conference room and pasted a smile on my face. "Hello, Gannon."

I braced myself for a hate-filled tirade. Instead, Gannon slumped in his seat.

"I don't know what to do," he said in a soft, trembling voice. "Harry convinced me to come to this meeting with you and Gabriella in secret, so here I am. What happened to you? Where's Gabriella?"

"She's coming with lunch. I broke my foot."

"That's too bad. What happened?"

I stared at Gannon. Where was the I have to get to a meeting, Gannon? The fifty-thousand-bucks take it or leave it, Gannon?

Before I could answer, Gabriella burst into the room with an enormous tray of food. Behind her were Lauren and Harry Boyce followed by Kibe and Jesus.

"*Buongiorno,* Gannon. I'm so glad Harry convinced you to come. It's buffet style, everybody, serve yourself. We'll talk after lunch."

Gannon shook Harry's hand and gave Lauren a peck on the cheek. Lauren came around the table and gave me a wheelchair-style hug. I just stared at her. Gone were the wild, blond extensions and fake eyelashes. She had gained about twenty pounds and was stunning in tailored, black slacks, a yellow cashmere sweater, and an abstract patterned silk scarf.

Jesus poured coffee after lunch, one of Gabriella's special Italian blends reserved for clients, and Kibe returned from the kitchen with an enormous, warm apple pie and French vanilla ice cream.

"Harry told me how much you like apple pie, Gannon. Kibe makes the best apple pie this side of Kentucky."

I hadn't seen Gannon smile, not once, since we met him. His mouth seemed to be fixed in a perpetual scowl. He took one bite of Kibe's magic and his smile could have lit up Dodger stadium for a night game. Gabriella's a good investigator and, damn, she sure knows how to handle difficult men—and I also know from experience— cranky women.

Gannon excused himself and went to the rest room. When he returned Kibe caught him eyeing the apple pie.

"Another slice, Gannon?" she asked sweetly, and he gobbled a second piece as fast as he did the first one. I understood his need for the sugar fix in desperate times.

"What am I gonna do?" Gannon asked again. He tossed Phoebe's note on the table and sunk his head into his hands. "Phoebe is the only woman I ever truly loved, and I still love her. Please, find my wife so I can tell her it's not too late for us. I'll even *give* her Revenge, one hundred percent hers, if that's what she wants, and she can make all the decisions about his future."

Gannon didn't yet know that it was Kibe and Jesus who were replacing Gabriella and me as his secret operatives in Kentucky. As far as Gannon knew, Kibe and Jesus were in the room to help with lunch, and Harry and Lauren were just here to lend support for the latest development in his nightmare.

I sat eyeing the last piece of apple pie on the plate as Gabriella laid out the strategy for Gannon. While he was distracted with the logistics of the plan, I quietly moved the lone piece onto my plate. Gannon caught the movement and he looked at Kibe.

"Don't worry, Mr. Paige, I have another pie in the kitchen. You can take it with you."

The scowl came off his face, replaced by another bright smile for Kibe, and we got back to business.

Gabriella's plan was brilliant. The two Los Angeles investigators, Gabriella and I, were history. Harry and Lauren would arrive as guests at BrightStar Farm to invest in one of Gannon's horses. With the Boyce's will be their personal assistant, Kathleen Jackson, who would have a room adjoining the Boyce's in the main house. Jesus Smith would be hired as a live-in stable boy to take care of the horse. Gannon was sure Phoebe had a mole reporting to her so nothing in the investigation could look suspicious.

Kibe and Jesus were instructed not to make any Los Angeles contacts while they were at the farm. On their day off they were to go to Hampton Inn in Lexington to have a Facetime meeting with Gabriella and me, and I assume, spend the rest of the day making good use of Gannon's hundred-and-forty-dollar per night suite. Not unmindful of their marital inconvenience, Gannon had promised Kibe and Jesus a luxurious vacation in the penthouse at the Lexington Cavendish Hotel after the case was resolved.

I was still not able to bear any weight on my left foot. I had just about had it wheeling myself around the house and the office in the wheelchair because I still couldn't manage crutches. Gabriella had just about had it with me, and Bailey had just about had it with the both of us.

"Mom, will you stop bitching about the wheelchair. Why don't you get yourself a knee scooter?"

Gabriella, who was making a beeline for the door, turned and rolled her eyes. "That's a good idea. Get one, Rae. Maybe a new toy will distract you for a while."

"Do you mean, if I get a new toy I'll shut up for a while?"

"Mom—Gabriella, stop it, both of you! Gabriella, go do whatever you were going to do. In the meantime, I'm going to make three cheese tortellini with marinated eggplant, zucchini, and red peppers for dinner tonight. Is it okay if I invite Connor?"

Cooking was Bailey's and Connor's newest hobby. They had both enrolled in a summer course, *Cooking on Your Own*, before they left for their colleges in Boston.

"I'm going to DiPasquale's. Do you want anything?"

"Bring me back a large tin of amaretti cookies." I smiled at Gabriella.

"That won't work," she hurled back at me and left the room.

That afternoon I was the proud owner of a black foldable, steerable knee walker scooter. It had a basket in front. I wheeled it back and forth yelling *Whee!* like I did when I got my first bike. I felt old in the wheelchair, I felt like a kid on the scooter. *"Whee!"*

My cell phone rang. I lifted it out of the basket, straddling the scooter, careful to keep my left foot up.

"Hi, Zinni, what's up?"

"Kibe and Jesus need to talk to you and Gabriella. They're at the Hampton Inn. They think they have a good lead where Ms. Lorca-Paige may be hiding with Revenge. Can you Facetime with them at three?"

"You bet!" And I texted Gabriella that it was safe for her to come home.

It was one o'clock on the west coast when we connected with Kibe and Jesus at the Hampton Inn. Gabriella and I were sitting in the middle of our bed with the large red tin of amaretti between us on a tray with coffee. Gabriella loves amaretti. It's one of my peace offerings when I send her over the edge with my nonsense.

Kibe and Jesus were sitting primly on the sofa. I noticed their rumpled-up bed. "Might as well make yourself comfortable, kids. You won't be seeing that bed for another week."

Kibe grabbed the bowl of popcorn off the coffee table, Jesus took the two cans of soda, and they jumped into the middle of the bed, laughing.

Jesus looked at Kibe. "You start, Kib." He stuffed a handful of popcorn into his mouth.

"Resentment is high at the farm, and it doesn't take much to stir up the pot around loyalty. The administrative staff in the house were barely cordial to me when we first arrived and the stable crew pretty much ignored Jesus. Almost everyone just tolerates Gannon and loves Phoebe."

"Yeah, they were pretty closed-mouthed and would stop talking when I came into the room, but they were curious and asked me questions, like, where did I work last, and stuff like that. I told them I was originally from Fresno in California and had been taking care of Mr. Boyce's two horses in Santa Barbara for a couple of years. They asked why I moved to Lexington and I told them I broke up with my girlfriend and it was time to move on. They had no problem with that."

"So, the first week was a great big nothing burger. Every day I pretended to have paperwork to copy for Harry, and finally I got invited to join the women in the office for coffee."

"Yeah, at least Kibe was comfortable in the warm main house. I only got to go into the hired hands dining room for meals. The rest of the time I was in the stable mucking out the horse stall, brushing *Just Dandy*, feeding him, or walking him. All the guys and the two gals love their charges. They finally warmed up to me when they saw I was taking good care of my horse."

Gabriella stuck her hand in the tin and pulled out a couple of cookies, and I knew I was easing off the hook for my less than admirable behavior. "So, Kibe, what did you find out?"

"One of the first things I did when I got there was walk around the public areas and look at the pictures on the walls. There were lots of Ms. Lorca-Paige on horses. She's one of the country's top trainers, did you know that? She's originally from Argentina and super-rich, too, without Gannon and his money. I started gleaning information slowly, asking about the pictures, because the women still weren't talking, except to say they did not blame Phoebe for leaving, and for taking Revenge with her. But no one would tell me why. Then came a break. You tell them, Jesus."

"Wait, potty-break." I proudly pushed my scooter across the floor.

"Where did that come from?" Kibe asked, as I shouted *Whee* and closed the bathroom door.

Gabriella said something in a low voice, and I heard them laughing. I didn't care. I was out of the damn wheelchair.

Jesus continued with the story. "One day the guys and I were sitting around knocking back a few brews after work. The stash was getting low and no one wanted to go to the store. I said I would, and one of the guys tossed me the keys to his pick-up truck. When I came back, I could hear snatches of conversation about Revenge, then, more distinctly, something about Tennessee walking horses. When I came into the room, they changed the conversation."

"Jesus mentioned the walking horse conversation to me because the guys had ended it so abruptly when he came into the room."

"What's the difference between a thoroughbred racehorse and a Tennessee walking horse?" I asked, and Kibe answered my question.

"I found out that both are elegant breeds and look similar. The Tennessee walking horse is known for its unique running-walk in competitive shows. I went in search of the picture I remembered of Phoebe on a beautiful horse in front of a sign, Crosswinds Walking Horse Farm. I learned that it's a small stable in Laurel, Mississippi owned by two sisters, Carmen and Camilla Perez, who, co-incidentally, are originally from Argentina."

"So, Phoebe just might know the Perez sisters and be hiding Revenge there with the Tennessee walking horses. Isn't that a longshot, Kibe?" I asked

"It's the only lead we have so far, and Kibe's got good vibrations about it." Jesus took the last handful of popcorn from the bowl and finished off his soda. "What do you want us to do?"

Gabriella and I smiled at one another. Kibe's vibrations were good enough for us, and it was also time for Kibe and Jesus to get back to their conjugal visit. Gabriella pulled a few more amaretti out of the tin between us, and I knew we were, thank God, headed in that direction, too.

"Kibe, I want you to find the best shops in Lexington," Gabriella said. "You and Jesus get yourself some upscale outfits, just enough to look like you can afford to buy a horse. Jesus, call the Perez sisters and get an appointment to visit the stable. Have Harry get you out of the stable for a couple of days. Kibe, once the appointment is set, book two suites at the Hattiesburg Hilton—it's the best they've got—one for you and Jesus and one for me and Lauren Boyce.

What! I thought. Why would it be Gabriella and Lauren in a suite at the Hattiesburg Hilton when it should be Gabriella and me? I stuffed an amaretti in my mouth. This was a conversation for later.

Gabriella continued without looking at me or missing a beat. "Let Zinni know when you're meeting with the Perez sisters. She'll make plane reservations for you, Lauren, and me, and rent us a Mercedes. It's about an hour drive from Hattiesburg to Laurel. You know what to do. Good luck!"

As soon as we were alone, I put the cover on the amaretti tin. "Gabriella, Kibe and Jesus can find Phoebe and Revenge all by themselves. That's what we pay them to do. Why are you going to Mississippi on a flimsy lead? What are you going to do, and why do you need to do it with Lauren?

"If Phoebe is at Crosswind Farms, Lauren and I need to talk to her before we tell Gannon that we found Revenge—and Phoebe."

"Why?" We're in the retrieval business, not marriage counselors. If Kibe and Jesus find Phoebe and Revenge, that's all we contracted to do for the fifty thousand, nothing more."

"Trust me, Rae. It's not enough."

"Why not?"

"Because Lauren told me that Gannon and Phoebe still love one another, deeply, and it's owning Revenge that has ruined their marriage."

"Why can't I go, too?"

"Don't start!" Gabriella warned, and when she took the cover back off the amaretti tin I shut my mouth.

A couple of weeks after we closed the Paige case, the fifty-thousand-dollar check arrived. A week after that the fiberglass cast was cut off my leg and Dr. Hernandez put me in a walk boot. Those two occasions called for a celebration in one of the private rooms at the Polo Lounge for Gannon and Phoebe, Harry and Lauren, Jesus and Kibe, and our entire Retrieval International family.

Kibe and Jesus told us the story. "As we walked around the stable, Kibe and I got a look at a horse in a stall that looked like Revenge, and there was a woman in with the horse. Although we didn't see her face, the woman was the same height and build as Phoebe. The Perez sisters were busy talking and didn't notice that Kibe got a phone picture of the horse and the back of the woman."

"I asked if the horse being groomed by the woman was available to be shown. It wasn't. Jesus and I were told that the horse belonged to the woman in the stall and she was boarding it at the farm. As we walked around the stables, we noticed a small cottage way back in the trees. The garage door was open and when no one was looking Jesus used his binoculars and memorized the license plate. I managed to get a picture of the cottage with my phone. The vintage Alfa Romeo was registered to Phoebe and the horse matched our picture of Revenge. That's when Jesus and I knew we had found them at Crosswinds Farm.

Gannon stood up, glass of champagne in hand. "Phoebe and I have accepted an offer for BrightStar Farms, which includes Revenge. I nearly lost Phoebe, the great love of my life, because of my obsession with Revenge. I was just pretending to be a bigtime racehorse owner. Phoebe's the real expert. I just got in the way and resented it—and her."

Phoebe smiled and laid her hand on Gannon's. "The Perez sisters want to go back to Argentina to retire. We're buying Crosswinds Farm to breed Tennessee Walking Horses together, thanks to you.

Kibe stood up, looking rather shy. "And thanks to you, Gannon, and the Hampton Inn, we're in the breeding business, too. Jesus and I are expecting twins—girls.

"Twins?" I shouted. "Twin girls?"

"Si, Rae, *gemelli identica*," Gabriella said. "Oh, Kibe."

We closed the Gannon case with hugs all around and we raised our glasses to the next generation of horses—and twins.

The Ladies of Peele House Square

Zinni and I were at Tiki Ti's waiting for Josh. Now her manager as well as her boyfriend, he had gotten her a spot opening for The Crybabies at Xenophobe on Sunset Boulevard.

Josh had graduated from Yale with a degree in business, paid for by the father who thought Josh would run the Pearlman Electronics empire. Instead, Josh hung out in Big Sur meditating at a Zen Buddhist retreat before starting JaxPax Entertainment in Los Angeles. Xenophobe is the hottest club on Sunset Boulevard. I have absolutely no doubt that Josh and Zinni are on their way to the big time.

I sat like a proud parent watching Zinni and Josh fold into one another, their blended tattoos looking like an abstract painting. Of course, I still hate her mother for sleeping with the love of my life, even if it was only once, and before my time. I haven't crossed paths with Judy and Hank Inkman since the damn Steinway fiasco, although we are still neighbors in Beverly Hills.

I got a text from Bailey.

Mom, I have a case. I mean the junior investigators, those of us who are here in Cambridge, have a freakin' real case. Call me. Love, Bailey.

"I just got a text from Bailey."

"Oh," said Zinni grabbing her phone. "I'm texting her right now to tell her my good news about Xenophobe."

Josh used the distraction to head to the men's room, his thumbs flying across his phone as he moved away from the table.

Zinni held up her phone, waving it around madly. "Bailey is going to fly home for my opening."

Josh came back barking into his phone, "Look, I can get you Tacoma Trash, but not at what you're offering. They're gold right now. Well, think about it and get back to me."

What had just happened? A minute earlier it was the three of us talking about JaxPax representing Zinni, and the next moment we were all off in different directions.

I got another Mai Tai One On and texted Bailey.

What's up?

Mom, I said call me. I want to discuss it with you and Gabriella, she answered.

I said goodbye to my future stars and had a half-hour drive from Sunset Boulevard to Robertson Boulevard to try and solve my immediate problem. Gabriella and I were sort-of not talking to one another. We had an argument on the subject of getting married. Then it segued to money, hers not mine, an ongoing problem since the first day we met at the Polo Lounge instead of Tiki Ti's. We had retreated into silence, neither issue resolved.

Gabriella was getting coffee and didn't respond to my wave when I came in. *So, she still wants to play that game,* I thought. I went into my office and dialed her extension.

"Gabriella, Bailey sent me a text. She wants us to call her to discuss a potential problem. Is this a good time?"

I knew nothing would keep us apart where Bailey was concerned, and problem seemed a better word choice than case. Gabriella and I met in the middle of the reception room, hugged and walked hand-in-hand to the conference area. Marriage and money were tucked away for another day.

Bailey, then Connor, popped up on the screen.

"Hey, Moms. It's April and it's still snowing. Good weather to study for finals. I love it here in Cambridge."

Gabriella and I looked at one another. I felt a lump in my throat. It was Bailey's first year at Harvard and Gabriella and I were still in the early stages of empty nesting.

"Here's Connor. Connor, say hello to my moms." Bailey pulled him close to her on the sofa.

"Hey, Ms. Sabatino, Ms. Talley." Connor moved a little away from Bailey. She smiled into the camera and quickly pulled him back to her.

"So, what's your problem, Bailey?" Gabriella asked, watching Connor give up and stay thigh-to-thigh with Bailey.

"We don't have a problem, Gabriella. I told you, Mom, we have a case. It's Allison's grandmother, Shirley, who has the problem and we want to help her. Don't forget Brooke, Connor, and I are still junior investigators."

Before Gabriella and I could say anything, Connor interjected, "I know we haven't solved a case since we graduated from high school but, Ms. Sabatino, Ms. Talley, this is a real case with a real client, actually with four real clients.

You mean, Allison, your landlady?" Allison's parents had moved to Hilton Head and she, a student at Boston University, was renting rooms in their Cambridge home to Bailey, Connor, and Brooke.

"I think Brooke is home," Bailey said when a door banged. "Hey, Brookie, we're on the phone with the moms about Allison's grandmother. Come on in."

"God, it's twitchy cold out there. Hi Ms. Talley, Ms. Sabatino. Nice to see you looking all California healthy."

"Here's the bones of the case. Allison's grandmother, Shirley, and her three friends, Sheila, Sonia, Millie, live at Peele House Square in Manchester-by-the-Sea, about thirty miles north of Boston. They're in their eighties and nineties, but they look and act much younger. Sonia still skis every winter with her family at their chalet in Switzerland."

"We really like them a lot, we really do." Connor looked like he felt the need to put his stamp of approval on the ladies of Peele House Square as potential clients.

"They have this book club, which they call The First Edition Book Club," Bailey continued. "They go to estate sales, garage sales, and bookstores like Manchester By The Book, searching for first editions."

"Then they each read the book in a week," chimed in Brooke. "And they discuss it at their monthly meeting. They meet at one another's homes for lunch. I think Sonia, who is Austrian, you know, serves vodka when it's her turn to hostess."

"Sounds wonderful—so how is that a problem?" I asked.

"It has something to do with a valuable map that may have been stolen. Would you be willing to Skype with us and the ladies? Oh, and we've made Allison an honorary junior investigator, so it will be four of us on the case."

"The map has been stolen from one of them?" I asked.

"No, that's the problem. The only information we have is in a note the ladies found in a book they bought at an estate sale in town."

"OK, we'll have Zinni set up the meeting."

We said goodbye, and Gabriella left for her weekly private hair appointment and gossip fest with Adolfo on Rodeo Drive. He charges her three hundred dollars and sends her back looking exactly like she did when she left. She insists I have my hair cut at Adolfo's, too, but my stylist is Janelle in the regular salon. She charges me eighty bucks every six weeks and promises not to change a hair on my head. But I must admit, Gabriella's hair looks incredible coming and going. And Janelle has managed to glam me up a bit and I don't know how she does it.

I grabbed a cup of coffee and six chocolate cookies from my hidden stash and googled Manchester-by-the-Sea, which turned out to be a picture-perfect town on the Atlantic Ocean. I found Peele House Square on the map. It was right on the bay. Nice! I have never been to New England. My one trip east was to Fort Lauderdale for spring break many years ago. Somehow, I managed to lose two hundred and sixty dollars and sprain my ankle falling off a sidewalk at two in the morning. I finished my coffee and ate three more of the banned cookies. I always know I'm safe when Gabriella is at Adolfo's.

A week later, Shirley, Millie, Sheila, and Sonia, sat around Sonia's antique dining table with Bailey, Connor, Brooke, and Allison. Bailey introduced us and we sat silent, waiting for someone to begin.

Shirley cleared her throat. "Sonia, Millie, Sheila and I have been friends for years here in Peele House Square. About five years ago we started our First Edition Book Club. We are very good at finding first editions, some rare, some signed, and we own quite a valuable collection. A few months back we went to an estate sale at the summer home of the late J. Addison Crowley. He was a highly reputable antiquarian map and book dealer in Manhattan and spent most summers working from his home here. His adopted daughter, Patricia, who inherited his estate, was summer friends with Allison's older sister, Susan."

"He was a young widower, about fifty, but he never dated any women here. All he seemed to do was work and go fishing with Patricia when she visited." Millie was satisfied that she had cleared up an important point.

Gabriella shot me a look. "Tell us about the book you found." She did not want to get off-track with a conversation about the dating life of a middle-age widower in a small Massachusetts town.

"We were shocked when we heard that Mr. Crowley had a heart attack and dropped dead in his New York City condo. I don't think it would have happened if he'd found himself a good wife, don't you agree?" Sheila asked.

The ladies nodded.

Sonia poured tea and centered a large plate of muffins on the table. "Patricia is planning to open a bed and breakfast with the house. She had weeded out the books she wanted to sell at the estate sale. There were no first editions we wanted, but we each bought a box of books to donate to our library."

Sheila unwrapped a package. "When I got home, I dropped my box and the carton split open. It exposed a false bottom, and this is what fell out."

It was a small book with a worn yellowed leather cover. The title on the book was *Two Years Before the Mast* and the author was Richard Henry Dana. I had read it in school. Richard Henry Dana sailed from Boston to California on a merchant ship for two years and then wrote about it. My class had taken a field trip to Dana Point to see the tall ships.

I stared at the screen. "Is that a first edition? Is it valuable?"

"Yes. It's a first edition all right and we learned it's worth about thirty-five hundred dollars." Sheila held the book up so Gabriella and I could see it.

"Good for you, ladies," Gabriella peered at the screen. "Great find, but what does the book have to do with a stolen map?"

Sheila opened the book and slipped out a white envelope. She rummaged around in her purse. "Oh, darn, I forgot my glasses. You read the letter, Shirley."

Shirley held the typewritten note up to the screen, then read aloud.

Addison,

Thanks for letting me know you have the map. Ready to buy. Name the date, time, and place. Agree to five thousand if it is in good condition. Wish I could get the book, too. Prepared to go higher for both. Any ideas?

T. L.

Gabriella looked confused. "What makes you think this is about a stolen map?"

"Intuition. It sounds like a shady deal, doesn't it, Gabriella?"

Gabriella shrugged. "I don't know, Bailey."

"But I found the book and the note hidden in a false bottom of my box. Why was it there?" Sheila asked. "We went to the police with the book and the note, and we explained how we got them."

"And the police said there is absolutely no evidence that the note is about a stolen map or that any crime has been committed. They congratulated us on our find," Millie offered.

"We are convinced that Addison and T. L., whoever he is, were up to no good, and the map Addison was going to sell had been stolen by him or someone else," Millie said firmly. "That's why Bailey suggested we let the junior investigators take the case on a volunteer basis."

We told the ladies and the junior investigators that we would discuss their proposed case and arrange another meeting.

Gabriella and Zinni were in the conference room when I arrived for the eleven o'clock meeting with the ladies. It was two o'clock in the afternoon in Manchester-by-the-Sea. The junior investigators were in their respective classes and we wanted to have a private talk with the ladies.

Zinni's eyes were red and swollen.

"What's going on?" I asked.

Gabriella rolled her eyes. "It's Judy, she's on the warpath."

Zinni lowered her head. "She wants me to quit. She says you and Gabriella are a bad influence, encouraging me to sign with Josh and sing in clubs. He hasn't done anything wrong and I love him—and he's even Jewish. I told Mom my good news about Xenophobe and she went off the rails. She made it sound like I was stripping or hooking. I have to start my career somewhere. Why can't she understand that I don't want to be a concert pianist? Why can't she accept it? Dad does."

"Zinni, your mother has her dreams for you, and she holds on to them. Your dad just wants you to be happy." I sounded lame.

"And I'm *not* quitting my job here either. She's the failure, not me. I didn't ask her to get pregnant and give up concertizing, did I?

"Zinni, you're welcome to stay with us until you get this sorted out."

Zinni looked up. "Mom will have a fit."

"This is about you, Zinni, not about her." And as Zinni left the room, the image of Judy Inkman mercifully faded as Shirley, Sheila, Millie, and Sonia appeared on the screen.

"Hi, everyone. Today we're celebrating with Captain Dusty's gourmet ice cream sundaes." When it warms up *everyone* in town hits Captain Dusty's. It's a yearly ritual. We all got salted caramel with homemade strawberry topping made by Mrs. Captain Dusty." said Shirley.

"They look delicious. Listen, ladies, Gabriella and I want to talk to you seriously without the kids. I don't think we would have taken your case on such flimsy information. We might have agreed to let Kibe, one of our researchers, spend a very little time for a very small fee to see if she could come up with any additional information linking the note to a stolen antique map."

"But," Sheila interrupted.

"Before you get to the buts, Sheila, let me tell you what we have decided," Gabriella said gently. "Rae and I have no objection to the junior investigators working with you if they want to pursue it on their own after the semester is through."

"So, *you* still don't believe us?" Sonia asked.

"It's not a matter of not believing you, Sonia. We project the probability of a successful outcome before we accept a case at Retrieval International. Our track record of actual finds is what keeps us in business. If we were wrong too many times, who would hire us? Rae and I will help in any way we can. We hope you and the junior investigators prove us wrong."

"I think we *will* prove you wrong," Millie exclaimed. We signed off while all of them were talking at once.

Bailey hadn't called after our meeting with the ladies and we felt the anger and disappointment in her silence. A few weeks later we got an email.

Moms,

Aced my finals and I think I'll end the year with a 3.8 GPA. The ladies are all right with your decision. The junior investigators not so much. We're staying in Manchester-by-the-Sea to help the ladies find the stolen map (even though you don't believe them, we do!) Patricia Crowley has hired us to work at the B&B during the renovation. We'll be home in time for Zinni's opening.

Oh, damn, I can't be as mad at you as I would like to be. Love you and miss you. Bailey

P.S.: Here's a picture of The Ladies of Peele House Square, the junior investigators, and Patricia Crowley in front of the future Old Corner Inn. Nice, huh?

P.P.S.: Can we, just the junior investigators, have a meeting with you? We really, really need your advice.

Needing advice was an understatement. They were clearly in trouble, having taken on the case against our better judgement. The problem turned out to be Patricia. No one wanted to tell her that her father may be outed as a thief. To complicate matters, the junior investigators will be working for her at the B&B. The ladies are upset. They want to let sleeping dogs lie to protect Patricia. As Bailey put it, the case that may not be a case at all got stuck before it even got started.

Gabriella and I went to the Polo Lounge. We both needed a couple of martinis and a few small plates after spending an hour with Bailey, Connor, Brooke, and Allison. Privately we thought all along that Bailey should spend her time more productively at home. We supported her desire to help the ladies but still thought there was nothing to it. At the same time, Gabriella and I didn't like the idea that the junior investigators were willing to fold so quickly. We finally decided that as much as we wanted Bailey home this summer, we would lend our support and encourage them to stay. Buzzed from the martinis, I wondered if Gabriella and I should have our heads examined.

Our next meeting with the junior investigators and their clients included Patricia Crowley. We were surprised when she told us she suspected her father may have been buying and selling stolen maps and books, but she didn't believe that he had been stealing them himself. She thought it was possible that the illegal business may have been taking place in Essex during the summer season but the rest of the year, his legal business was in Manhattan.

Based on the information from Patricia, we took the case. Bailey, Connor, Brooke, and Allison were officially assigned as associates under my direction as lead investigator. The fee was set at expenses only. Zinni faxed the contract to the ladies. They signed it and we left them hugging one another.

Jesus was working on a research project for Gabriella and wanted to finish it before he and Kibe took the twins, Roza and Loray, on vacation to Catalina Island. Kibe took on the Crowley research herself. Before she left, she got a print-out of the current FBI and Interpol databases of stolen cultural property.

Bailey texted.

Moms, What's up on your end? Patricia is back from New York. She cleaned out her father's condo and the shop on 4th Street. She UPSed her dad's laptop, phone and some personal paper files and address book to Kibe. We hope it will be helpful. The ladies have searched every piece of furniture for hidden clues and we're going into every nook and cranny in the house. Nothing yet! Patricia's interior decorators, Lisa and Paul, start tomorrow. This week we're boxing up the books in the library. Tomorrow Connor, Brooke, Allison and I are having a lunch meeting with our clients at Seven Central, just like you do at the Polo Lounge with yours. Lots of love, Bailey

Gabriella and I decided to take a few days off and drive down to Cove Beach in La Jolla while Kibe and Jesus were in Catalina. We closed the office and left Betty to handle the phones from the home office. She loves it when we leave her in charge. We came home happy and ready to get back to work.

Just as I walked into the office, Kibe yelled *bingo,* and jumped up from a pile of papers. There was a client in the reception room who almost fell off his chair when she streaked by in a leopard print leotard and a skintight tee shirt that said *Researchers know where to look.*

"I found something, Rae! Look at this!" Kibe dropped a printout of stolen maps on my desk and herself into my client chair.

"I've got to see that client out there who almost had a heart attack. Gabriella will be back at three. Let's meet in the conference room. Please, Kibe, walk sedately past Mr. Jamison. I'd like him to live long enough to pay our fee."

Gabriella returned with a box of homemade almond biscotti she gets from a secret source, an Italian woman who bakes only for celebrity caterers. Gabriella will not let me, or anyone, know who the baker is. Of course, she doesn't know about my hidden stash of chocolate mint cookies, and that I've already eaten six today. I always appreciate her small gesture of reward for thinking I actually keep my sugar addiction under control. That's my business, not hers. I made three perfect cappuccinos and met her and Kibe in the conference room.

At our next Manchester-by-the-Sea meeting, everyone looked worn-out. Gone was the bubbly enthusiasm. Despite the exhaustive search of the large old house, they had found nothing linking Crowley with stolen maps. Also, Lisa and Paul had a very tight schedule for the renovation and needed the hired hands to work full-time. There was little time left for the junior investigators to continue their search before they returned to school. The ladies looked like they were ready to throw in the towel.

Patricia started the conversation this time, as everyone's shoulders drooped. "I feel so guilty for ever thinking my father was a thief. I don't know why I had that feeling from a conversation I overheard. It may have been entirely innocent, just like the ladies thinking it about him from the note in the book."

Bailey looked straight into the camera, stress etched on her lovely young face. "We should have listened to you right from the start. You're the successful retrieval experts and you *said* you didn't think we had a case."

Gabriella looked like she was going to cry. She put out her arms as if she could reach through the screen and comfort our daughter, then put them down again. "I know you all have been working so hard on this case, and it *is* a case. It isn't finished yet."

"Gabriella is right. Sometimes we have no place else to go, but we stay with the case to its conclusion no matter how bad we feel. So, no apologizing. We're convinced there are maps hidden somewhere, at least the one in the note—and we have developments."

Everyone looked at one another in confusion.

"Developments?" Connor croaked and hugged Bailey.

Allison kissed her grandmother.

"OK, enough. We have work to do. Kibe, you're on!"

Kibe stood up and I noticed she had put a more modest long black shirt over the tee shirt and gathered it together with a silver belt. I guess for the ladies.

"The first thing I did was research the FBI and Interpol databases of stolen cultural property." Kibe pressed a few keys on her laptop and held the FBI database up to the camera. This is a list of all the missing maps not yet recovered, names and details of the maps, where they were stolen, and the date the theft had been discovered."

"What good does that do when we don't know what map T.L. was going to buy from my dad, and we don't even know who T.L is?" Patricia asked.

"I checked everything you sent to me, Patricia, that was on the computer, phone, and in the files. I cross-checked your father's calendar for appointments and travel before and after a map had been reported stolen. I've narrowed it down to four maps I know had been stolen before the travel dates. One is from Yale University Sterling Memorial Library and Map Collection, one from the Yale University Beinecke Rare Book and Manuscript Library and two are from the Boston Public Library Norman B. Leventhal Map Center." Kibe grinned. "That's a good start. There may be more."

"That was really smart." Connor looked at Kibe with admiration.

"Yeah, but we still don't know who T.L. is to link him to the specific map in the note."

"Patience, Brooke, this is a process. You don't think Rae and I find what's missing because we're psychic," Gabriella said.

"I found a Theodore Lepke, Jr. in the contacts, and an on-line file." Kibe continued. "He was Crowley's only legitimate customer with those initials. All the maps he purchased during the years were from the shop in Manhattan, and there were copies of paid invoices. Mr. Lepke is a wealthy department store owner in Chicago and may or may not be the T.L. in the note. Patricia, you found a map on hold for Mr. Lepke in the shop. Your dad was going to meet Mr. Lepke in Chicago before he returned to New York. The information is promising, but probably not enough for the FBI yet. We haven't found the *body*, so to speak, to prove that a *murder* has been committed."

"What do they want?" asked Millie. "We know who T.L. is now. Isn't that enough, Rae?"

"No, we don't have enough evidence linking Addison Crowley and Theodore Lepke to a stolen map. We have pieces of the puzzle, but we need to know more. Keep searching the house. I still think whatever you're going to find is there."

And, eventually, they did.

The call came the next Sunday while we were bouncing Phil, Jr. around in the pool. Betty had gone to visit a friend in Santa Maria for the weekend. Phil and Marina needed a babysitter and we happily volunteered.

"Hallo, Bailey." Gabriella put the phone on speaker. "Hallo, where are you? Bailey?" All we could hear was a cacophony of noise and lots of laughter. Gabriella shrugged and yelled into the phone. "What's going on? Somebody, say something."

The noise stopped. In unison, as if on cue, the group chanted. "We found it! We found it!" Then Bailey yelled out. "Get to your computer and Skype us. We found a freakin' vault."

We lifted Phil, Jr. out of the pool and took him to his first meeting of Retrieval International. He fell asleep on the sofa.

The walls of the library were now a beautiful buttery yellow and the dark floor-to-ceiling built-in bookcases holding the Crowley collection had been painted a soft cream. The patina of the hand-hewn wood floor glowed. The library looked completely different. It was warm and inviting, a place to read a book and enjoy a glass of wine.

I looked around the mostly empty room, waiting. Patricia looked wistful and sad.

"We would like to reenact the scene," Sonia said quietly. "Exactly as it happened."

"Yes, please do." *They deserve their moment,* I thought. They were about to give Retrieval International an important success on the national stage.

"We were helping Patricia get ready for the grand opening of Old Corner Inn in a few weeks. Lisa and her installer were in the library hanging the new drapes. Aren't they gorgeous? Sheila, Sonia, Shirley, and Millie were sitting at this table drinking coffee and dusting books," Brooke said.

"Bailey pulled the ladder in front of one of the bookcases. We were following Lisa's schematic and placing books back on the shelves using this ladder on a mechanized ceiling track to get to the upper bookshelves. Allison was here on the ladder placing books on one of the top shelves. Allison, show them," Sonia said.

Allison climbed to the top of the ladder. "I lost my balance and grabbed onto the shelf right here to steady myself."

As Allison grabbed the shelf, hitting a sensor below, the entire wall holding the bookcase to her left moved forward and locked in behind the ceiling track. There was just enough room behind the wall for one person to squeeze in.

Patricia's voice shook. "The lock code is M-A-R-Y, my mother's name, oh five oh eight, the date of their marriage, and oh seven oh two, the date they adopted me."

It turned out that the four maps Kibe found on the FBI list before Crowley's travel dates were in the hidden vault. One of them by Lewis Evans, a seventeen fifty-five general map of the middle British colonies in America taken from the Boston Public Library, was the one stolen for Theodore Lepke. There were ten other maps, some still intact in books, that had been reported stolen. Patricia found her father's inventory lists and bank records. He had stolen and sold antique maps and books for more than twenty-five years while maintaining his reputable business in New York.

The ladies of Peele House Square and the junior investigators appeared on Good Morning America in

New York. Then, they and Allison came home with Bailey, Connor, and Brooke for Zinni's singing debut.

Thanks to Gabriella pulling some strings, we got a table in the VIP section at Xenophobe. Judy and Hank were there. Hank looked so proud of his daughter. Judy gave me the *if looks could kill* stare and pretended we were not there before the room went dark.

The spotlight followed Zinni as she strode onto the stage in a black lace dress hardly bigger than a scarf and thigh-high red leather boots to match her long flaming red wig. The ladies of Peele House Square clapped enthusiastically. Sonia yelled, above the applause. "Oh, my! I think we all need a couple of vodkatinis."

Gabriella's Double Trouble

"Who?"

"Lynnie Ledgewood, Rae. I told you about her. I was in love with her for two-and-a-half weeks." Gabriella stretched and her hand grazed my breast.

"In love? You never mentioned a Lynnie Ledgewood." I didn't move and neither did her hand.

"I'm sure I did, Rae. I didn't leave anyone out during our true confession." There was a slight movement of her fingers.

"Lynnie Ledgewood? She sounds like one of your debutantes. What was she, a tennis partner, a riding buddy?"

Gabriella removed her hand and sat up.

"Now I remember why you don't remember her. I only gave you her stage name. Remember Busty?"

"Busty? Lynnie Ledgewood is the Busty who could balance two glasses full of something on her natural double D's, not silicone, breasts, and not spill a drop. That's Lynnie Ledgewood?"

"That's her." Gabriella smiled and rested her hand back on my breast. "I knew I had told you about her."

I moved, and Gabriella's hand landed on my belly.

"What does she want?"

"She's lost something, or it's been stolen. I'm not sure. We're going to meet her for lunch at the Polo Lounge on Monday. I haven't seen Lynnie in ten years."

Gabriella moved her hand south. I looked down at Gabriella's hand and put mine on hers. "Well, as long as you're down there you might as well keep going."

Gabriella had an early Monday morning manicure and was gone before I left for the office.

Zinni jumped up and met me at the door. "Rae, there's a Markie Passini here to see you," she whispered, looking toward the conference room.

"Does she have an appointment?"

"No, but she insisted on waiting for you."

"Did you ask her why she wants to see me?"

"I did. She wouldn't tell me. She plunked herself down in the conference room and asked for coffee. I gave her some. Is that all right?"

"Thanks, Zinni, you did the right thing. Where's Kibe and Jesus?"

"Kibe's out meeting a client and Jesus went for donuts."

"Tell Ms. Passini I'll be right with her. Buzz me when Jesus comes in. Tell him to bring a plate of donuts into the conference room." I got myself a cup of coffee and slipped into my office.

Zinni buzzed and I went into the conference room to meet the insistent Markie Passini. She stood up and extended her hand. I did a mental jaw drop. Jesus came in with the plate of donuts. I looked at him and knew he, too, was doing a mental jaw drop. Gabriella and Kibe are beautiful women, but Markie Passini was the most beautiful woman I had ever seen this close.

I extended my hand to meet hers. "Ms. Passini, I'm Rae Talley and this is my associate, Jesus Smith."

Jesus put the donuts on the table. He shook Markie Passini's hand and we all sat down.

"I don't usually see anyone without an appointment. What can I do for you, Ms. Passini?"

"I'm Lynnie Ledgewood's sister—her twin sister."

I felt my jaw do a physical jaw drop. "Her twin sister?"

"Yeah. We're identical twins. We were Lynnie and Markie Passini before Lynnie got married and changed her name to Ledgewood."

"Are you a dancer, too, Ms. Passini?"

"No, I'm a stunt actor at Universal Studios. Please, call me Markie." She reached for a donut. "Oh, banana cream, my favorite."

I shot Jesus a look. "Jesus, is there another banana cream in the kitchen?"

Jesus shook his head and I took a raspberry-filled with a sigh I hoped Markie Passini didn't hear.

"I'd just as soon talk to you in private, if that's okay."

"Jesus, grab some petty cash and go get a half-dozen banana cream doughnuts." I just knew something was going on that was going to require more than a raspberry-filled donut, and Markie Passini was already one up on me.

"Thanks, Rae," Markie whispered as Jesus left the room. "I'll get right to the point. Lynnie had never been with a woman when she met Gabriella, about ten years ago. Neither had I, for that matter. Gabriella didn't know Lynnie had an identical twin or that we both were with her for the couple of weeks that the lust-filled romance lasted."

"I don't think that would have bothered Gabriella. Why didn't you tell her?" I asked. "She probably would have thought it great fun."

Because, while one of us was with her, the other was secretly making a video. It was just for us, you understand. We were straight women. Lynnie was already divorced from Ledgewood. I was just playing the field, with no hurry to curtail my increasing stunt work. Look, Gabriella was just one of those impulsive larks."

I felt an angry knot in the middle of my stomach. "I wouldn't call that just an impulsive lark, Markie. Deceiving Gabriella and making a secret sex video was a reprehensible thing to do."

"I know, but only Lynnie and I had the video. We never showed it to anyone. It was like a memento of the occasion for us, like visiting an exotic land that we will never go back to."

I was facing the door and saw Gabriella come in, stop at Zinni's desk, and head for the conference room.

Gabriella walked in and stopped. "Lynnie, what are you doing here? I thought we were meeting you for lunch at the Polo Lounge."

There was an awkward silence, then Markie stood up and extended her hand once again. "Gabriella, I'm Markie Passini, Lynnie's twin sister."

"What? You're who?" Gabriella looked confused.

"Go get a cup of coffee, Gabriella. It's important that you hear what Markie has to tell you before we meet with Lynnie."

"Do you have a birthmark on your right hip, like Lynnie?" Gabriella asked when she got back.

"I do."

"Show it to me."

"Listen, I have some phone calls to make. Let's leave at noon to meet Lynnie."

I grabbed a couple of banana cream donuts and went back to my office. Every now and then there were squeals of laughter coming from the conference room.

"What's going on in there? Is she a client?" Zinni asked.

"Don't know yet. It's up to Gabriella."

The gorgeous Markie and my beautiful Gabriella had become instant buddies. I must admit that I was feeling a little jealous. I did a mental head slap to get over it as I entered the conference room.

"Did you say something, Rae?"

"No, just thinking out loud. Boy, I'm starving."

Lynnie jumped off her seat at the bar as soon as she saw us. She hugged Gabriella. She hugged Markie. She would have hugged me if I hadn't deliberately dropped my purse and came up with a handshake. Gabriella gave me a quizzical look as we headed to our client table at the back of the room. I wasn't feeling too kindly toward Lynnie Ledgewood or Markie Passini.

I sat quietly sipping a Bloody Mary, listening to the three of them reminisce about the infamous two-and-a-half weeks. Gabriella seemed pleased to be hearing the real story.

"Oh, you bad girls," she said playfully.

I broke into their collective turn-on. "So, this is all very interesting, but what exactly is missing?"

Lynnie looked at me like I hadn't completed third grade. "I thought we made that clear. It's the video that's missing."

Markie smiled at me. "And we want you and Gabriella to find it."

"Has it been stolen?" Gabriella looked concerned.

The twins answered together. "We don't know."

"I thought Markie had it. You know, I just moved back to Los Angeles and I'm staying with her until I find an apartment."

"I thought Lynnie had the video and I asked her about it. Thought it might be fun to watch it again after all these years."

That night I tossed and turned and woke up every hour in a cold sweat. Gabriella slept like a baby with a smile on her face. How could she take this catastrophe so lightly? I finally dropped into sleep without picturing Gabriella in bed with Lynnie. Or was it Markie?

Gabriella, Lynnie, and Markie were laughing when Janet came into the conference room. I looked at her and could tell she was doing more than a mental jaw drop. I had already briefed her on the twins and what was missing.

"Gabriella, it's illegal in California to videotape sexual encounters with someone without her or his consent. The criminal code defines the act of doing so as voyeurism."

That was Janet, the former FBI agent. All business, right to the point.

"It was just a bit of fun. I don't know why everyone is so uptight. If I had known about it, I would have consented, and I certainly would have told Rae about it when we became a couple."

"You don't seem to understand, Gabriella. You are the victim here. It's like bank robbers coming back with the loot to deposit in the bank. Do you really want me to find the video?"

Gabriella's face lit up. "Yes, of course I do. I'd like to see it."

She left the room and came back with a pot of coffee and freshly baked cinnamon raisin rolls. She sweetly offered me one first and I abruptly waved her away.

Janet took the case with one stipulation. Gabriella and I were not to interfere in any way with her case or her clients. We agreed.

Lynnie and Markie faded out of our lives as quickly as they had come into them. Gabriella and I got busy with other cases. Janet reported that she had yet to find a reason for the lost video beyond what seemed like Lynnie's and Markie's carelessness. She had ruled out that the video had been stolen for blackmail purposes.

Bailey and Connor had invited Zinni and Josh for our pizza and movie night. We joined them for pizza then decided against seeing *Star Wars—The Empire Strikes Back* again and we went out for a walk. Gabriella had been unusually quiet during dinner. She kept looking at me and then at Bailey. I wondered if it had anything to do with the video.

"*Cara mia,* I'm sorry." Gabriella all but sobbed as soon as we were out of the house.

"Sorry? For what?"

"I feel ashamed. I'm not the same woman I was ten years ago, certainly not since I met you. I was thinking about Bailey. I would not want her to see that video."

"To be fair, no parent wants their children in their sex life."

"I wish Lynnie and Markie hadn't told us about the video. I wish we hadn't taken the case. I wish...."

"Janet will do her best. That's all we can wish for."

We walked along hand in hand for a long time and came back just in time to hear Darth Vader confess to Luke Skywalker, who thinks Darth Vader killed his father. *No, I am your father.*

The next day was my lunch and shopping day with Betty. She called and said she caught a head cold and not to come.

"Betty, do you have everything you need? I can come and take care of you."

"And catch my cold! Don't you dare! I've taken cold caps and I'm wrapped up in bed. Marina dropped off some chicken soup. Call me tomorrow."

With nothing much to do, I called Janet and asked her to meet me at Nate n Al's for lunch. I figured I'd pick up some fresh bear claws for Betty. That would do more for her cold than Marina's chicken soup.

"Janet, bring me up to date. This case doesn't seem to be going anywhere."

"You're right, Rae. I've got nothing. I've ruled out theft for blackmail purposes or someone stealing the video to flood the internet to embarrass Gabriella or the twins for revenge. Lynnie and Markie weren't very helpful with information. Now they've gone on a cruise through the Panama Canal or somewhere. Honestly, at this point I'm not even sure there is a video. Maybe they just wanted to see Gabriella again. I don't know."

"It's got Gabriella so rattled and unhappy. I can't stand seeing her that way."

"Rae, the twins will be back next week. I want to talk to them again before I close the case. Honestly, though, I don't know how you can be so supportive. I'm not sure I would be, if this had happened to Ishigo and me."

"I admit I was angry when I met the twins and found out what happened, and kinda jealous, too. Then I remembered how honest Gabriella had been with me. She would have told me about the video if she had known. You know, Janet, Gabriella's past belongs to her. It has nothing to do with me or our relationship."

Our enormous Nate n Al's Reubens arrived with coleslaw drenched in mayonnaise and half-sour pickles. I didn't tell Janet that *kinda jealous* wasn't exactly the truth. I was, for the first time in our relationship, utterly consumed by it. To be honest, I didn't want Janet to find the video.

We polished off our Reubens pretty much in silence. There's something about Nate n Al's that makes everything painful go away, and a large piece of six-layer lemon cake would just about do it for me.

Betty's cold wasn't a cold at all. It was walking pneumonia. Gabriella, Bailey, Marina, and I took turns nursing her until she was out of danger. She told us we had made a big deal out of nothing, but I was scared, really scared. Betty's in reasonably good health for her age, but she is eighty-two years old. I put that thought out of my mind.

Janet called Gabriella and me into her office.

There was a small box on her desk, unopened, addressed to her from Lynnie Ledgewood.

"Is that the video? Who found it?"

"I don't know. I spoke to Lynnie and Markie a few days ago, and this turned up today. Do you want me to open it or do you want to take it?"

Gabriella reached for the package. "I'll take it," she said and walked out of the office.

When I got home, Gabriella was sitting in the family room drinking tea and eating amaretti out of the tin. On the coffee table was the unopened package.

"I was waiting for you."

My mouth was dry. I poured myself a cup of tea. Gabriella held out the tin to me.

Bailey came into the den. She took one look at us drinking tea and eating amaretti cookies and she quickly slipped out.

"Do you want to see it, Rae?"

"Do you?"

"Don't answer a question with a question."

We drank some more tea and stared at the package.

"I don't," I whispered.

"Perhaps there's a note inside with an explanation." Gabriella picked up the package.

"I don't care, do you?" I waited for her answer.

Gabriella hesitated for just a nanosecond. "No."

We finished our tea and cookies. Then we got a metal bucket from the shed and watched the package burn.

"Should we get married, Gabriella?"

"Yes," Gabriella answered, and we walked back into the house.

Lost, Hidden, or Stolen

Lost, Hidden, or Stolen on Sunset Boulevard

I love flying to San Francisco, love catching sight of that spectacular city in the distance and watching the plane skim San Francisco Bay just before hitting the runway. It's very scary and always feels a little dangerous.

It's been a year since Gabriella and I burned the twins' sex video in a bucket, and told Bailey, Betty, and our Retrieval International family that we had decided to get married. It still feels a little weird. I may have grown comfortable with the getting married side of our relationship but, in the ten years we've been together, I've never quite resolved the money side. It's true that Gabriella and I are both private investigators, but she's still a super-rich heiress and I still work for a living.

Gabriella nudged me out of my thoughts. "Lean back, I want to watch us fly in just above the bay before we land." She crossed herself. "*Madre di Dio*, I always wonder if the pilot will *sbagliare*, you know, miscalculate, and we'll end up in the drink."

I grabbed Gabriella's hand. We stared out the window until the Boeing 737 hit the runway hard and bounced a few times before heading for the gate.

Gabriella always insists we sit in the first row in first class on commercial flights so we can be the first ones out of the plane. Our friend, Joya, Mother Superior of The Order of the Lost Lambs, wasn't hard to spot. She was wearing a black cashmere tunic-length sweater with plum-colored plaid piping and black wool pants, her casual habit for picking people up at the airport, I guess. She had on a silver veil over the soft plum-colored wimple and around her neck was the large silver cross. Joya was creating her usual sensation, and everyone was staring at her without trying to stare as we went through our hugging and kissing ritual.

Joya had become quite the celebrity with The Order of Sisters of the Lost Lambs. Her play, *Nuns on the Run*, and The St. Matthew Theater had already become a San Francisco institution to rival *Beach Blanket Babylon.*

Not long after Gabriella and I decided to get married, our friends, Renee and Elise Dean-Spector, turned their gorgeous seventeen-room Victorian in upper Castro into the Rainbow Bed & Breakfast and wedding venue. We had reserved the inn for a week and started planning our destination wedding.

Joya drove us to the San Francisco Office of the County Clerk. I started shaking as soon as we walked into the office. It wasn't doubt I was feeling. It was the sheer joy of actually being able to legally marry the woman I love. We left the building with Gabriella clutching the license in one hand and my hand in the other.

"Time to meet Ferdinanda at Neiman Marcus," Joya said in a serious voice as she parked in Neiman's secret parking lot for VIP customers. "She works in the bridal department and she is a fabulous stylist. I completely trust her."

"I don't want a stylist," I whined. "We don't need to go to the bridal department. I'm *not* wearing one of those poufy wedding gowns."

"Rae, I didn't say we were going to shop in the bridal department, did I? I only said Ferdinanda works in the bridal department," Joya countered.

Gabriella sat silent, still clutching the marriage license in her hand. "Oh, for God's sake," she muttered, as she let go of my hand and swept out of the car and into Neiman Marcus.

Joya and Ferdinanda did some exaggerated air kissing, aware that everyone within eyesight was gawking at them, even Gabriella and me. Ferdinanda was at least six four, a couple of inches taller than Joya. In a short silver-gray patterned jersey dress, Ferdinanda's body looked perfect and her legs in black suede platform heels looked endless. Her deep auburn hair tinged with silver was an asymmetric bob, and she wore diamond hoop earrings.

Joya whispered to us. "Work clothes, you know, you should see her in real clothes—to die for."

Ferdinanda grabbed Gabriella's arm and headed in one direction. Joya pushed me in another, despite my protests.

Hours later we reunited in the sanctuary of the VIP lounge. Gabriella seemed right at home, drinking a latte and taking it all for granted. There were silver tea pots, fragile bone china cups and plates, and an elaborate espresso machine. The tables were laden with fruit, fancy sandwiches, scones with a variety of jams, lemon curd, and clotted cream, and elaborately decorated petit fours. And, attendants to serve! And, free! It seems ironic to me that rich people get so many goodies for free.

I had told Joya that I wanted to wear pants. She hadn't protested, much to my surprise. Without much effort, she found the most beautiful pair of off-white pants and paired them with silver leather pumps. I glanced at the price tag before Joya yanked it out of my hands. Eight hundred dollars!

Eight hundred dollars for a pair of pants. I'm glad I was only getting married once.

"These pants are silk shantung, the same fabric used in wedding gowns. The irregular threads are called slubs, Rae, and give the pants that rich texture. Now, let's find you a fabulous top."

"They're beautiful, Joya." Oh, jeez, I hope I wasn't going to get a fabric lesson with everything I tried on.

True to her word, Joya did find me a gorgeous top, a soft transparent off-white organza blouse with long, incredible sleeves. Under it she put a delicately beaded jade green tank top. From somewhere Joya produced a little thingie to pin on my hair. Perfect! I mean, really perfect. I never could have found this outfit on my own. I stared at myself in the mirror and saw, for the first time, the woman Gabriella had fallen in love with.

Ferdinanda dressed Gabriella in one dressing room and Joya dressed me in the other. We had insisted that we wanted to see ourselves in the outfits before the wedding. Joya led me onto a platform in front of a large full-length mirror.

Gabriella swept out of the dressing room and stepped on the platform like it was a stage. "Somewhere Over the Rainbow" played softly in the background. She had on a pair of beautiful beige pants.

"They're crepe", Ferdinanda had whispered.

The pants and the jade green silk shirt were the color of the outfit she had worn the day I saw her in front of my building, the day thirteen-year-old Bailey showed up at my office and asked me to find her missing Buddha. My beaded top was the exact color of Gabriella's shirt. How did Joya and Ferdinanda do that?

I started to cry.

"Stop, or you'll have me blubbering, too," Gabriella whispered.

Then she did.

Our next stop was at Renee's and Elise's so we could finalize our plans for the wedding and the reception, which was now only seventy days away. Joya and Ferdinanda had agreed to create the wedding theme, and Joya would be performing the ceremony.

"You're gonna love it," Joya said as she headed for the Castro.

A week after we got back from San Francisco, Betty invited Gabriella and me for coffee and bear claws. We assumed she wanted to show us her matron of honor dress.

"I have a case for you, girls," she said.

Gabriella always cringed when Betty called us girls. Today Gabriella just smiled. "I'll get us some coffee, Betty. I hope it's fresh. Have you ever noticed that your brand of coffee smells mildly like old socks when it gets old?"

"Gabriella, has Rae ever told you that sometimes you're full of shit? When have you ever had old coffee in my home?"

"You're right, Betty, never. So, where's your dress?"

"I have to go back for a final fitting. It needed to be tailored here and there. Bailey and I are picking up our dresses tomorrow. They are so beautiful. I love the dusty rose brocade, it's my favorite color."

Gabriella came back and served the coffee and bear claws. Betty pulled a sealed envelope from behind the cushion and handed it to me.

"Don't open this, promise me, until I am safely in heaven with my James. Do you promise?"

My promise hit a hard lump in my throat, but Gabriella croaked out a promise for us both.

"So, now, let's finish our bear claws and play Monopoly."

Betty is a fierce Monopoly entrepreneur and she takes great delight in getting Boardwalk, the most expensive property on the board, and the utilities and railroads before Gabriella and me. I told her that if she had been a businesswoman she'd be as rich as Gabriella.

"Richer," she retorted, and blew on the dice before she threw them on the board.

Betty died in her sleep a week before the wedding. Instead of limousines taking us from the airport to the wedding venue, we sat in hushed shock as limousines took us to the funeral chapel in Sherman Oaks. We buried her in the dusty rose brocade matron-of-honor dress next to her beloved James in the Oakwood Memorial Park Cemetery in Chatsworth.

Jim and Len invited all of us back to their house, which had been Betty and Jim's home for more than fifty years. I stood staring at my house next door. *Yes*, I thought, *it's time to sell my house to Crazy Jane and Mackenzie. I'm never coming back here.*

Still grieving, Gabriella and I applied for a new marriage license in Beverly Hills. We were married in a quiet civil ceremony in the county clerk's marriage ceremony room the following Friday with Bailey and Connor as our witnesses. Phil and Marina had a lovely dinner for the six of us, and Gabriella and I slept in one another's arms all night.

The next day I got a message from Betty's attorney.

Ms. Talley, I'm Mary Sabanu, the late Elizabeth Danzig's attorney. She has named you executor of her estate. I've emailed you information regarding the legal responsibilities of an executor. Please call me to discuss your duties.

Of course, Mary Sabanu. She was the attorney Betty told Gabriella and me to contact after we read the contents of the envelope she had given us. I had put the envelope in my desk drawer and forgotten about it. We had been busy with the wedding plans and everything had happened so suddenly.

Gabriella and Bailey came into the kitchen looking refreshed and happy. "Hi, Mom. I love swim time with Phil, Jr. Don't you, Gabriella?"

It was good to see the grief on Bailey's face replaced by a smile. I gave her a hug and said to Gabriella, "Betty's attorney left a message. She wants me to call her about the will."

"Oh, *madre mio,* the envelope Betty gave us—her *case!*"

"What case?" The smile had left Bailey's face. "What case?"

"Bailey, how about making some lattes? I'll go find the envelope."

When I came back Gabriella and Bailey were sitting at the kitchen island. I grabbed some biscotti out of the majolica bowl on the table and put them on a plate in front of us. No one moved to take one.

I propped the envelope up on the plate.

"Moms, what's this all about?" Bailey reached around the envelope and took a biscotti.

"Betty had invited us for coffee after we got back from San Francisco. We thought she wanted to talk about the wedding and have our usual game of Monopoly."

I slit the envelope open and handed it to Gabriella.

"Betty told us she had a *case* for us and she made us promise not to open the envelope until after she had joined James in heaven." Gabriella took a single folded paper out of the envelope and laid it on the table.

"I just stuck the envelope in my desk drawer and forgot about it. I didn't expect Betty to die." I sobbed. "I—I didn't expect her to die."

Gabriella put her arms around me. "Neither did I," she cried into my shoulder.

Bailey sat there with tears running down her face, then reached and picked up the paper. "I miss Aunt Betty so much. I can't believe she's gone."

She held the paper out to me. "Here, Mom, you read it."

It was a typed letter. I remember Betty had an old portable Remington typewriter. She said she didn't want to go to the trouble of learning the computer just to type a few letters now and then.

Dear Rae, Gabriella, and Bailey,

Jim and I couldn't have children. It was difficult for us because we made the decision not to adopt, but we adjusted in time. Then, you and your mom came into our lives, Rae. Years later, through you, Gabriella and Bailey came into my life. Even though I'm not overly religious I feel truly blessed. Every day of my life I thank God for the three of you, and for my wonderful extended family. I love you all. I do miss my Jim terribly and I am ready to be with him whenever God takes me.

Now, I'll get to my case—the problem I'm giving you to solve after I'm gone. I have hidden a copy of my will for you to find. There are absolutely no clues except that it is hidden somewhere in my house and does not require any destruction to Jim's model planes, the furniture, or the structure. Of course, Mary Sabanu, my attorney, has the original will and has explained everything to me. So, Rae, I have named you executor of my estate. I am giving the three of you forty-five days to find the hidden copy of my will before you, Rae, begin the probate process. That should be enough time, right? All three of you nod up and down. I can see you! Have fun!

All my love,

Betty

"Forty-five days? Why does Aunt Betty want us to find a copy of her will when her attorney already has the original? Is it a game?" Bailey looked confused.

I didn't have an answer. I was as confused as Bailey. "Let's just do as she asks. What do you think, Gabriella?"

"Our *client* cannot answer any of our questions and we don't have any clues. So, the *why* in this case may cause us to overthink it."

"Yeah, right, Gabriella, but we *do* know what Betty hid and the general location. I say we do what we always do at Retrieval International when we consider a new case. How many in favor of us taking the Elizabeth Danzig case?"

Three hands shot up in the air.

This time it was Gabriella and me waiting for Joya and Ferdinanda to come off the plane in Los Angeles. In a city used to celebrity, it was amusing to see how much attention the two women were attracting in the Alaska Airlines terminal. Ferdinanda was in white skinny jeans, a white tee shirt with a single light bulb stitched on the front, and a diamond encrusted baseball cap. Joya had on what looked like her formal habit, but it ended well above her black leggings, and her four-inch pumps matched the plum-colored wimple around her head.

Joya had never been to the villa. She shot me a questioning look when the white limousine hit the villa and slipped between the gates. Ferdinanda just stared out the window, speechless.

"This, this is your home?"

"Yuh, Ferdinanda. I think it will be adequate for our small reception, don't you think?"

Joya laughed. "I've never seen Ferdinanda tongue-tied."

That evening Joya and Ferdinanda joined us for dinner and movie night. Bailey and Connor had chosen *Victor/Victoria*. Nobody had time to cook so Bailey ordered a bunch of stuff from Wolfgang Puck's, which we ate *al fresco* on the patio while enjoying the movie.

The next day Gabriella met with Ferdinanda to arrange for the reception. I met with Joya to discuss our marriage ceremony and the celebration of life service for Betty. By four o'clock they were on the plane for San Francisco and Gabriella and I were asleep by eight o'clock.

The next few weeks were difficult. We had decided to each spend time alone in Betty's house looking for the will. One of us was sure to find it. None of us did. We changed our strategy and all three of us searched the house together, but we still found nothing.

"We've looked everywhere, Moms. It's only three weeks until the reception. Maybe we should just wait until the attorney reads the will?"

"Betty gave us this case for a reason, Bailey. We still have twenty-four days left. I think we should keep looking," Gabriella said.

"Where?" I asked Gabriella, and I heard the frustration in my voice. "We've searched every inch of the house."

We gave it one more week, meticulously looking in, under, and around everything in the house. Then we stopped looking and turned our attention to the celebration of life service for Betty and our marriage ceremony and reception.

Joya and Ferdinanda had turned our living room into a chapel. Dusty rose shears hung behind a canopy strewn with imported purple lilacs and small white roses. On the altar were Betty's favorite candles in her silver candle holders. In an eleven by fourteen silver filigree frame was the picture Gabriella took of Betty modeling her dusty rose matron-of-honor dress. In a matching frame was a picture of Betty and Jim taken at their wedding.

Joya stood in front of the altar wearing a simple long white dress, a stole of intricately woven colors of the rainbow, and the silver cross around her neck.

"We have gathered here today to celebrate the life gloriously lived by one who was so dear to us all, Elizabeth Danzig. Mrs. Danzig has had her final wish, that she be reunited with her husband in heaven. Betty and James Danzig's life was exemplary, loving each other and all the creatures on Earth.

Joya called upon us to share stories about Betty and, in a wavering voice, Marina talked about Betty's loving care of Phil Jr. I caught a glimpse of Bailey in front of the large coffee urn. Next to it stood Betty's battered coffeemaker, a few tins of her beloved coffee, and plates of mini bear claws. I turned my attention to Marina, then back to Bailey as she removed folded paper from the tin she had just opened and slipped it into her pocket. I knew what she had found. After everyone finished their coffee and bear claws Joya stood, once again under the canopy.

Bailey and Connor stood to Joya's side as our best woman and best man. Gabriella and I walked down the aisle holding hands. The pianist played "Oh, Promise Me" and I thought of the last two lines of that song that united my mother and father,

no love less perfect than a life with thee
Oh, promise me, oh promise me.

"We are gathered here today to witness and celebrate the marriage of Rae Talley and Gabriella Sabatino. Although you are already legally married, Rae and Gabriella, you expressed a desire to have another ceremony honoring Mrs. Danzig as matron of honor. This is not the beginning of a new relationship but an acknowledgement of the next chapter of your lives together. Do you, Gabriella, take Rae to be your lawfully wedded partner?"

She did, and so did I—for the second time.

After the ceremony, everybody headed outside to the changing room tents set up by the pool and sports area. We had the pool filled with balls for water basketball, and beyond the pool were the tennis, volleyball, and badminton courts. On the other side of the pool was bocce ball. Another tent was filled with foosball, air hockey, and some old-fashioned pin ball machines. The DJ had brought a portable dance floor. Caterers had set up an enormous barbeque, a bar, and tables and chairs.

"Get Bailey and come to our bedroom," I whispered to Gabriella as we waved from the patio and shouted for everyone to have a good time.

"Moms, I found it, whatever Aunt Betty wants us to see. I found it in Aunt Betty's can of coffee."

"I checked the opened can and the three cans on the shelf. I just shook them and thought they were all unopened," I said.

"I did, too, Rae. That Betty is—was—pretty sneaky!"

"Here it is." Bailey pulled two sheets of folded paper from her pocket and waved it around before laying it on my bureau.

"Let's change first," I suggested.

Bailey went to her room to change into her bathing suit and Gabriella and I changed from our wedding clothes into tank tops and shorts.

The three of us headed for the kitchen and I laid the paper in front of me on the island.

"Read it, Rae," Gabriella said.

My dearest Rae, Gabriella, and Bailey,

Here is the original handwritten will I wrote when I moved to the villa. Since then I've had a fancy-schmancy last will and testament prepared by Mary Sabanu, my attorney. She will formally read the will to my beneficiaries and you Rae, as my executor will enter it in probate court.

Bailey, my sweet one, you know I am leaving you Jim's model plane collection. To me it is the most valuable of my possessions. I am also leaving you my house on the villa property, and everything in it. I hope you and Connor will be as happy as Jim and I were. Oops! Have you told the moms, yet? I think it's wonderful that you and Connor will be setting up a law practice to help disadvantaged people after you're married.

Gabriella, darling, I am leaving you my coffeemaker and a large supply of my favorite coffee. I want to make sure you have a good cup of coffee once in a while instead of that stuff they charge you so much for at that Dean and Deluca.

Believe it or not, girls, I was the shrewd investor of our family, and Jim and I were always pretty comfortable financially. I am leaving the two or so million in my current portfolio to my extended family, your wonderful employees at Retrieval International. Mary is also setting up substantial college trust funds for Phil, Jr., Roza, and Loray. You can close your mouths, you three. You don't have to look rich, or live rich, to be rich. And you can quote me on that.

That leaves you, Rae, dearest. Except for what I have bequeathed above, I leave everything else to you. I never talked much about Jim's gizmo after that French bitch tried to steal it. I sold it to Northrop Grumman for twelve million dollars. My financial consultant at Edward Jones will be in touch with you.

One thing makes me very happy, Rae and Gabriella. That you finally decided to get married, and you did so before you learned about my will, Rae.

All my love to you, precious ones,

Betty Danzig

I folded the papers and stuck them in a drawer. "Let's go swimming and play some basketball."

Later that year, we sold our half of Retrieval International, with Janet and Ishigo's approval, to Phil and Marina and Kibe and Jesus.

To celebrate, Gabriella and I took the entire Retrieval International family to Tiki Ti's for a private party. Mike came over to say hello. He told us he was selling Tiki Ti's, and he and his wife were retiring to the Bahamas. The building included the restaurant next door and offices upstairs.

So, Gabriella and I bought it.

We kept Tiki Ti's exactly as it was in tribute to its original owner, Pete Scanlon. Josh and Zinni turned the restaurant into a rock club called *Zinni*.

Upstairs, painted in modest letters on the door of one of the small offices.

Rae Talley and Gabriella Sabatino
Private Investigators
"We find anything lost, hidden, or stolen."

COMING NEXT FROM LIANA MILLS

LICENSED TO STEAL

A Retrieval International Novel

The inspiration for *Lost, Hidden, or Stolen* came suddenly while I was driving home from Los Angeles. PBS was doing a small segment on the closing of Los Angeles's oldest tiki bar on Sunset Boulevard, one that had become an institution during the past fifty years. I still had nearly a hundred miles to drive. By the time I got to Palm Springs I had amused myself with the story of Bailey's missing Buddha and how Rae and Gabriella met. That's how inspiration works for me. It comes from anywhere at any time.

Ironically, I was in my car again when the inspiration came for the second Retrieval International novel. This time I was on my way to Trader Joe's to pick up some espresso bean ice cream and the segment on PBS was about houseboats. All of a sudden, Rae and Gabriella popped into my head. They weren't living in the villa in Beverly Hills, running Tiki Ti's on Sunset Boulevard, and doing a little quiet retrieval work on the side. I pictured them living on a houseboat in Marina del Rey and owning a specialty shop on the waterfront. Through a series of unexpected events, the two super sleuths get back into the retrieval business with the Retrieval International family, this time as covert operatives with a team of unusual characters who are licensed to steal.

Acknowledgements

First on my list of people to thank is Catherine Parker, my loving partner of 38 years. Rae and Gabriella became our friends during the time I spent writing this book. Catherine and I sat in our little Japanese sanctuary, drank tea and helped our two private investigators, also a couple, solve their cases.

Gene Rowley wears many hats in my life. He is, first and foremost, my multi-talented son. He is my creative listening post, tech guru, print and eBook designer, and future audiobook producer through his publishing company, Jumpmaster Press™. I couldn't have done it without him.

I met Nat Burns at the Sapphire Writers Conference in Palm Springs when *Lost, Hidden, or Stolen* was more than a dream but not quite a reality. I was looking for a good editor and I was impressed with her workshop. Nat gave me her card and said to send her a draft. A year later I did. In her quiet, no-nonsense, professional way Nat seamlessly made my book shine.

I also met Sallyanne Monti at the same conference in Palm Springs. Sallyanne is one of those special, fun, talented people you appreciate just for being. She very graciously agreed to be my beta reader and her thoughtful suggestions were invaluable.

As always, a heartfelt thank you to my family and friends for their ongoing support. They, and Catherine, are the foundation of my life.

About the Author

Liana Mills lives and writes in Palm Springs, California. She is currently working on *Licensed to Steal*, Retrieval International Book Two.

Made in the USA
Columbia, SC
09 September 2020